THE EXTRAORDINARY VOYAGE OF Katy Willacott

For Nova and Jago, little stars in their own sky.

STRIPES PUBLISHING LIMITED
An imprint of the Little Tiger Group
1 Coda Studios, 189 Munster Road,
London SW6 6AW

Imported into the EEA by Penguin Random House Ireland,
Morrison Chambers, 32 Nassau Street, Dublin D02 YH68

A paperback original
First published in Great Britain in 2022

ISBN: 978-1-78895-418-1

Text copyright © Sharon Gosling, 2022
Cover and ship illustrations © Kristina Kister, 2022
Author photograph © Phil Rigby

A CIP catalogue record for this book is available from the British Library.

Printed and bound in the UK.

MIX
Paper from
responsible sources
FSC® C171272

The Forest Stewardship Council® (FSC®) is a global, not-for-profit organization dedicated to
the promotion of responsible forest management worldwide. FSC defines standards based on
agreed principles for responsible forest stewardship that are supported by environmental, social,
and economic stakeholders. To learn more, visit www.fsc.org

10 9 8 7 6 5 4 3 2 1

SHARON GOSLING

THE EXTRAORDINARY VOYAGE OF

Katy Willacott

LITTLE TIGER

LONDON

Mizzen
Sail

Tiller

Mizzen
Mast

Dog
House

(Captain's
Cabin)

Cleats

Deck

The
SS Alerte

Main Mast

Main Sail

Jib Sail

Hull

Grab Rail

(Derby's Cabin)

Chapter One

The storm blew up without warning as they rounded the cape, a jagged seam of dark sky splitting the heavens above them as thunder rolled over the horizon. A vicious wind cut down upon the mainsail, tugging back and forth at the rigging with a *snap-snap-crack-snap-snap-snap*. A cold rain angled from the clouds, a thousand icy pinpricks stabbing at Katy's face as she fought the rudder.

"Come about! *Come about!*"

The storm was a writhing, living thing all around them, tearing at her cheeks until they were raw, stealing her breath so that her lungs ached. Between the rain lashing at her face and her eyes watering, Katy could barely see. Still, she held on fast to the wheel. If they lost the *Falcon* now—

"Hard-a-starboard, lass!" the captain bellowed over the sound of the black waves crashing and splitting against the hull. "Run along the wind! We've got to get clear!"

"We'll have to bend the foresail," Katy yelled back as she battled to keep the yacht's nose from turning with the wind. They were too close to the land's hidden shoal of jagged rocks, far too close.

"Aye!"

"We've got to unbend the storm sail too!"

"Aye, lass, aye!"

If they couldn't get their mainsail down, it would either rip from the force of the storm or the wind would catch it and smash them against the rocks. The storm sail would withstand heavy wind but they'd left it bent away because just an hour ago the glass had been set fair. It was half the size of the mainsail – it'd give them control without leaving a huge target for the whipping wind. But they were short-handed, and doing anything in the middle of a gale, with the sun almost below the horizon already, with the boat rocking from side to side and the sails overhead still fully deployed, was—

"Katy, your mama is coming…"

Katy blinked. The roaring storm dissipated into the warm evening air, leaving only the see-saw melody of the birds singing the world to sleep, the calm waters of Kew Gardens' pond, and her grandfather, wading after the wooden model of the yacht *Falcon* that was his most prized possession. She turned to see her friend Edie behind her on the grassy bank, still sitting on the wool blanket that

2

Grandma Peg had given her to keep Edie's skirts out of the dirt.

Katy lifted one hand to shield her eyes from the last gleaming rays of summer sun and saw her mother approaching across the lawn from the direction of the herbarium.

"What are you all still doing out here?" Mary Willacott called as she got closer, her voice full of laughter. "Have you forgotten the time *again*? Grandma Peg will have dinner ready, you know!"

"Storm lesson," Katy said as she scrambled back up the muddy bank while her grandfather scooped the *Falcon* from the water. "Granddad wants me to know how to handle the yacht in bad weather. Ugh –" Katy wrinkled her nose as she tried to squeeze water from her sodden skirt – "this would be so much easier if I were wearing trousers, Mama! Won't you talk to Papa again for me? I could have one of Stefan's old pairs, he'd never even miss them!"

"Katy!" Edie said, shocked. "You can't wear *trousers*."

"Why not?"

"You're a *lady*."

Katy's mother laughed. "You should listen to Edie, Katy. She makes a very sensible point."

"Pfft," said Katy, flopping down on the blanket beside her oldest friend.

Ned Dixon dripped bits of waterweed as he climbed out of the pond, hefting the model ship under one arm. His fingers were as gnarled as the bark of a tree in the Palm House and deeply tanned after a life spent at sea beneath the sun.

"And you, Grandpa Ned," Mary Willacott scolded gently. "You do nothing to discourage this wild streak of Katy's, do you? You know her father does not approve."

"Ach," Ned said dismissively. "I want Katy here to know just how important it is to practise these things in port, in good weather, that's all." He looked down at his granddaughter. "Now, the storm sail. What do you think of that?"

Katy considered. "It should have been sent flying rather than left bent. Then all we would have had to do is lash it down, rather than get it out of its mooring."

"Pre-*cisely*!" Grandpa Ned clapped her on the shoulder, grinning proudly. "She's a natural, Mary! A natural!"

Katy's mother laughed again, looking down at Edie. "Poor Edie, have you been sitting here all this time, just watching? You must be bored stiff!"

"It's all right, Mrs Willacott," Edie said. "It was only supposed to be an hour but I think Katy got carried away."

"Sorry," Katy said. "I did tell you to bring something with you to read if you didn't want to get into the water with us, didn't I? And I offered you my copy of Fran Brocklehurst's latest article but you didn't want it."

"What's the point in me reading it?" Edie retorted. "You're going to spend all evening talking at me about it

4

anyway. You'll go on and on about it, same as always, until my brains are so bored they'll try escaping through my ears!"

"Bored?" Katy said, outraged.

"Yes, bored," Edie told her. "Francesca Brocklehurst is *boring*. There, I said it. I'm sorry, Katy, but that's how I feel."

Katy looked up at her mother and raised her eyebrows as high on her forehead as they would go. She and Edie had known each other since they were babies and they always used to like the same things. That seemed to be changing more and more recently, and Katy could make no sense of it at all.

"Not everyone likes the same things you do, my dear," Mary Willacott reminded her daughter.

"But Fran Brocklehurst is the bee's knees," Katy declared. "That's a fact."

To Katy it just wasn't possible that someone wouldn't be fascinated by Fran Brocklehurst and her adventures. Brocklehurst's articles, which appeared in one of the daily London newspapers, were full of important topics such as what to do if one had been bitten by a deadly snake (ever since she'd read that one, Katy had been trying to convince her parents she needed to carry a penknife with her at all times, so she would be properly equipped for this eventuality, but for some reason they didn't think this was a good idea) and better things to do with a lady's bonnet than wearing it on one's head (for example, using it to catch

5

fish in the event of one being shipwrecked and washed up on a desert island). Who *wouldn't* want to read about those things? How could *anyone* find them *boring*?

"Well, then, here's something that'll make you smile, Katy," said Mary Willacott. "Miss Brocklehurst will actually be coming here tomorrow, to talk to your old mama. How about that?"

Katy gaped at her mother for a moment, astonished, and then scrambled to her feet. "No!"

Mary Willacott laughed. "Yes! She's coming to interview me for an article she's writing about women in the sciences."

"Can I come and meet her, Mama? Can I?" Katy begged, fizzing with excitement. "Please say yes. Please!"

"Of course you can," said her mother. "I'm sure she'd like to talk to the next generation of women botanists for her article. You can show her how you've already begun your training."

This wasn't quite what Katy had in mind. What she wanted to do was talk to the journalist about all the places she'd been and all the wonderful things she'd seen. It might help Katy work out how she was going to do the same herself.

Chapter Two

The four of them walked back to Rose Cottage together beneath the setting sun. Katy's home stood at the very edge of Kew Gardens, separated from the park's lush landscape by a sturdy hedge of copper beech that had a gate set into it. The house was too small, really, to be comfortable for the family. Grandma Peg and Grandpa Ned, Katy, Katy's father Josiah, her mother Mary and her older brother Stefan all lived within its faintly ramshackle walls. But the cottage came without a rent, because both Mary Willacott and Grandpa Ned worked in the botanical gardens. Ned was one of Kew's private constables and Mary Willacott was a botanical taxonomist, which meant that she worked in the herbarium, preserving and identifying the many specimens of plants that were sent back by naturalists from expeditions that travelled all over the globe.

Josiah Willacott, meanwhile, was an assistant archaeologist for the British Museum. Every day he took the long train journey from Kew village into Bloomsbury, where the great building of the museum was located. Once there, he would make his way to the basement laboratory rooms. Katy had been to the museum many times but had never been allowed into those secret spaces behind the public galleries. She imagined them to be full of gleaming, wonderful artefacts shipped back from all over the world. There must be bones and fossils, spears and masks, stone carvings that would tower over Katy's head. She imagined the many colours of precious stones gleaming in shafts of light, the huge, bright feathers of incredible birds, the paper-thin skins shed by immense, diamond-scaled snakes.

"There you are!" called Grandma Peg from the cottage's back step, as they all trooped through the gate. "Dinner's ready to go on the table. I thought you'd run off with the fairy folk or summat. Come ye in and scrub those paws of yourn before it spoils!"

Grandma Peg was a small, sturdy whirlwind of a woman, barely taller than Katy, with rosy cheeks and wild grey hair. She disappeared back into the house before any of them could answer. By the time they had toed off their boots and washed their hands, she was hefting a large, steaming pot of something that smelled delicious on to the big oak table in the middle of the kitchen, at which Josiah and Stefan already sat.

Mealtimes were always a little raucous at Rose Cottage because everyone was always eager to tell everyone else about their day, and so they all ended up talking at once. Katy's favourite thing to hear about, though, was what her father had been doing at the museum. Josiah Willacott was a tall man with curly brown hair and warm brown eyes to match. It was her father who had given Katy her first notebook and watercolours, and ever since Katy had been old enough to walk, had encouraged her to make sketches and notes of the treasures she found around Kew, as if she were a proper naturalist, going out to explore the wide and wonderful world.

"What have you been working on today, Papa?" she asked, as they all began to eat.

"A farmer in Lowestoft turned up a hoard of Roman coins and they have been shipped to me," he said. "They need cleaning before we can identify what time period they came from. But tell me about your day, Katy. How is the training at the herbarium going?"

"It's going well, Papa," Katy said. "Yesterday I practised with a rose that one of the gardeners let me cut. It's in the drying press now. I didn't go with Mama today though."

Her father was surprised. "Oh? Why not? Wasn't there a half day at school? I thought the Schminke expedition specimens had arrived from their trip to the Himalayas? With no school this afternoon, surely it would have been the perfect time to join your mother?"

9

"Edie is here for the night, Papa, for the Perseid meteor shower," Katy said. "And it was a sunny day! We wanted to be outside."

Her father smiled. "Fair enough. But really," he said to Mary Willacott as much as their daughter, "I would have thought the Schminke expedition too good a training opportunity to pass up."

"I know, my dear," Mary Willacott said mildly. "I'll make sure Katy gets plenty of time with the expedition specimens. She has made a very good start. She already knows how to make sure a specimen is properly dried and fastened to the specimen sheets. Her notes are also excellent."

"I was wondering, Papa," Katy ventured. "If I could come with you for some training too? At the museum? I could help you to clean the coins you just mentioned. I've been practising with the brush you gave me, and—"

"I'm sorry, Katy," said her father. "But you know that's out of the question. I've told you before – The British Museum is a serious scientific institution. One can't just wander in and out of it."

Katy frowned. "The herbarium is a serious scientific institution too."

"Of course it is," said Josiah Willacott, with a sigh. "I didn't mean to suggest it wasn't. But really, you must stop asking me about this. It would not be appropriate for me to take you into work with me – and that's the long and short of it."

"You take Stefan," Katy said sulkily.

"He's older," her father said, something Katy was often reminded of but to her made no difference at all.

"And he's a boy," Katy pointed out.

"Katy," said her father, in his warning voice. "Now that's enough, please."

"Did you hear, Peg?" Grandpa Ned asked, changing the subject. "Our Mary is to have a visit from a journalist about her work tomorrow!"

Peg's bushy eyebrows rose almost to her silver-grey hair. "A journalist, is it? Well, Mary, I hope you're not shy in coming forward with what that place owes to you. Work your fingers to the bone over those specimens sent back from all over, you do, and what thanks do you get for it? There's no one naming a flower after our Mary, is there?"

"I don't mind, Mother," Mary Willacott said. "I'm happy as I am."

"She'd have to go out and find something entirely new herself before they would do that, anyway, Grandma," Katy said, stuffing the last of slice of her bread into her mouth, eager to be done with dinner. She thought of all the specimen sheets she and her mother would be checking over from the Schminke expedition. There was Professor Schminke and his assistants, traipsing all over the world having fun and back here at home were Mary and Katy Willacott, looking after what they'd found, never going further than the village. She sighed gustily.

"And we won't find a new genus in the rose garden at Kew, that's for sure."

"You shouldn't speak with your mouth full," Stefan told her from across the table, while doing exactly that. At sixteen he was only Katy's elder by two years but he – the same as everyone else, it seemed to Katy – liked to pretend that made a big difference. "It's not ladylike."

Katy stuck her tongue out at him.

"Katy," her father admonished.

"Sorry, Papa," Katy said, and then promptly stuck her tongue out again.

Stefan shook his head. "No one will ever want to marry you."

"Good," Katy declared. "For there will never be anyone I want to marry." She finished her stew and leaned over to peer into Edie's bowl, which was also empty. "Come on," she said, to her friend, who had been as quiet as a mouse ever since they sat down. "Let's go upstairs."

"Er – I think not," said her father sternly. "There are dishes to do. Peg shouldn't have to do them all herself!"

"It's all right," said Mary Willacott. "The girls can run along. I'll help Mother in the kitchen."

"Or Stefan could," Katy pointed out, earning herself a black look from her brother.

"One day, Katy," said her father, with a long-suffering sigh. "That lip of yours will get you into trouble and I won't be around to get you out of it."

12

"Sorry, Papa." Katy grabbed Edie's hand and pulled her friend out of the room before they found themselves stuck at the sink.

Chapter Three

Katy's bedroom was in the attic, under the eaves of Rose Cottage's roof. To get to it, she and Edie had to climb a ladder propped in the hallway of the upstairs landing.

"I'll never understand why your bedroom is all the way up here," Edie said as she pulled herself into the space and then dusted off her hands.

"What do you mean?" Katy asked, looking around. "This is the best room in the house!"

Katy loved her bedroom precisely because it was so odd. You could only really stand up straight right in the middle because the room was an 'A' shape and the ceiling sloped all the way down to the floor on either side. But it was a great deal bigger than even her parents' own bedroom, which meant there was plenty of space for Katy's desk at the far end, against one of the two flat walls that formed either

14

end of Rose Cottage. Piled on the desk were all the items Katy had found for her collection – feathers, animal skulls, interesting stones, a coin from the riverbank she thought might actually be Viking – that were now patiently waiting to be properly catalogued with sketches and observational notes in her beloved field notebook. Her bed was at the opposite end of the room, on the other side of the hatch that she and Edie had just climbed through, against the other flat wall.

Best of all, though, was the big glass skylight that was set into one side of the sloping roof. Katy went to it now, cranking the lever and pushing it open. Beyond, in the festival of shadows that were gathering as twilight fell, spread the whole of Kew Gardens. *There* was the magnificent glass structure of the Palm House, gleaming in the last glance of sunlight. *There* was the elegant brickwork of Hunter House, the herbarium where her mother worked, standing proudly amid the lawns and plant beds. From up here, Katy almost felt as if she were a bird, soaring above the world – as if all she had to do was spread her wings and she'd be able to fly anywhere she wanted, anywhere at all.

Edie came to stand beside her. "It's a good view," her friend admitted.

"It's going to get even better," Katy told her.

A breeze brushed past them and Edie shivered a little. "It's getting chilly, though. Are you sure you want to go out there?"

Katy was shocked. "But it's the Perseids," she said. "We do this every year!"

"I know, Katy, but—"

"We'll take blankets," Katy promised. "Come on – you've got to let me show you this Fran Brocklehurst story first. I just don't believe you can possibly find her boring."

She led the way to her desk. On the wall above it, Katy had used some of Grandma Peg's dressmaking pins to fasten her favourite of Fran Brocklehurst's adventures where she could see them, always.

"I think it might be her best one yet," she said, pointing to a new page she'd pinned up. It had an illustration of a small figure in a big hat sitting astride a large black horse. "She rode the whole of the pilgrim trail from Saint-Jean-Pied-de-Port in France to Santiago de Compostela in Portugal all on her own. Nearly five hundred miles! On a horse! On her *own*!"

Edie frowned. "Why?"

"Because she wanted to!"

Edie wrinkled her nose. "Where did she sleep?"

"There are hostels along the way for pilgrims. And she took a tent too and camped sometimes."

"Ugh," said Edie. "That must have been horrible!"

"No! It must have been *wonderful*!" Katy said. "Just think – no one to tell you what to do or when to do it, no one making you wash up the dishes or saying that you can't do *this* or do *that*…"

"Flies, heat, dust," Edie countered. "Whatever did she eat? She must have had an awful twist in her back from all that riding too."

"She didn't ride side-saddle," Katy said. "She rode astride, like a man. Look, like in the picture!"

Edie stared at the illustration and shook her head. "She always sounds so strange."

"She's not," Katy insisted. "She's brilliant, and when I meet her tomorrow I'm going to ask her how *I* can do all the things that she's done." She lit the oil lamp beside her bed and then picked up two big woollen blankets. "Come on. Let's get out there. I don't want to miss anything."

They scrambled out of the skylight and on to the old tiles of Rose Cottage's roof. The night was clear and quiet. Overhead, a million jewels of ancient light glittered and winked. The stars were spread out forever, as if time had unspooled itself, opened itself entirely for anyone who cared enough to look up and see.

"My mother and father would have a fit if they knew we did this, you know," Edie said, lying on her back and looking up at the universe above them. "They still think we just lean out of your window and look up. They'd never let me do half the things Mr and Mrs Willacott let you do."

"What do you mean?" Katy asked, staring up at the sky. "I don't get to do anything. If I'm not at school I'm either in the herbarium with Mama or helping Grandma Peg with something around the house. I'm not like Stefan, who gets to take the cart into the village to meet his friends whenever he wants, and goes into London with Papa to see his work."

Suddenly, a pinpoint of speeding light pierced the night sky, an ice-white streak almost too fast for the eye to catch. Katy nudged Edie and pointed. "Look!"

"Oh, I missed it! I'll catch the next one."

Sure enough, a moment later there came another streak of light, and then another, and another. The sky was full of shooting stars.

"It really is a shower," Edie breathed. "What happens to the people standing underneath them when they land?" She shuddered. "I've always wondered that. What if one falls through the roof and on to me while I'm asleep?"

"That will never happen," Katy said with a laugh. "Meteorites – that's what meteoroids are called when they make it through the Earth's atmosphere – are very rare. Even if they *could* reach Earth, we probably wouldn't notice. These ones are just tiny particles of debris, like dust, that's all, left by the Swift-Tuttle comet as it passed through the edge of our solar system. It's only because they look so bright as they burn up against Earth's atmosphere that we can see them."

Edie sighed. "You've got so many things floating around in that head of yours, Katy, it's amazing." Her friend was quiet for a moment and then said, "You didn't mean what you said earlier, did you? About not wanting to get married?"

Katy frowned. "I don't know. It's definitely not the *only* thing I want to do."

"But you know already that it won't be the only thing you do," Edie said. "You're going to be like your mother, aren't you? You'll become a botanist and work with her in the herbarium. We might end up with houses next to each other in the village! Wouldn't that be fun?"

Katy said nothing to that. She didn't tell her friend what she was thinking: that no matter how hard she tried, Katy couldn't imagine herself spending every day in the herbarium, cataloguing specimens of exotic plants that someone else had harvested. Instead, she imagined herself on a great black horse, riding across the plains of a distant, unknown country, gloriously alone and free under a sky full of stars.

Chapter Four

Next morning, Katy, Mary, Grandpa Ned and Edie left Rose Cottage while the dew was still pooling on the blades of grass beneath their feet. Together, they set off across the lawns of Kew.

"Thank you for letting me stay, Mrs Willacott," Edie said with a yawn.

"You're welcome, my dear." Mary Willacott smiled. "Although I'm not sure your mother would have approved if she'd known you were going to spend most of the night on our roof. Did the two of you get any sleep at all?"

"Oh, it was worth it," Edie said. "Watching the Perseid meteor shower with Katy is always an adventure! I can put up with no sleep for one night a year to see all those shooting stars."

"It doesn't have to just be one night a year," Katy pointed

out. "It'll be going for another few weeks. The shower isn't even at its strongest yet. That's always spectacular. You should stay another night, Edie."

Edie laughed. "Oh, I don't think so. I do need *some* sleep!"

The two girls hugged goodbye at the point where the meandering paths through Kew went in different directions. Katy waved as Grandpa Ned and Edie disappeared into the trees, heading towards the village that stood on the outskirts of the park, while she and her mother made their way to the herbarium.

"I'm so glad that you and Edie have stayed friends for so long, Katy," Mary Willacott said as they walked.

"Me too," said Katy. "Although…"

Her mother looked down at her. "Although what?"

Katy sighed. "We used to always think the same about everything. But now we don't. Edie doesn't seem to want to *do* anything with her life, Mama. She just wants to grow up, get married and have children."

Her mother lifted one arm and slipped it across Katy's shoulders, pulling her daughter to her side as they walked. "My darling, that sounds to me as if she's got something very significant indeed that she wants to do with her life."

"But it's so … *boring*," Katy protested.

"You might find you feel differently as you get older, Katy," her mother said as they walked on. "And you must try to understand that not everyone wants the same things that you do. Edie wanting to be a wife and mother doesn't make her interests any less important than yours. You're just growing up to be different people, that's all. It doesn't mean you shouldn't stay friends, just that you're becoming yourselves."

"But—"

"Mrs Mary Willacott?"

A figure had appeared on the path in front of them, a smiling young woman with a freckled face and snub nose beneath bright brown eyes. She didn't look much older than Stefan. Her auburn hair was cropped scandalously short to curl around her ears. She was dressed in a man's white shirt and a tan-coloured waistcoat, which were worn beneath a fustian jacket of nut brown and paired with trousers of coarse twill that were tucked into a pair of battered leather boots. In one hand she held a notebook and pencil, and in the other was the strap of the battered leather satchel that was slung over her left shoulder. She looked sturdy, dependable and ready for anything. Katy liked her immediately.

"You must be Miss Francesca Brocklehurst," said Mary Willacott.

"Oh, it's just Fran," Fran said with a wide smile as she reached out to shake Mary Willacott's hand. "*Francesca* always sounds as if I should be wielding a lace bobbin rather than a pen. And who wants to be a 'miss' when you could be a 'hit'?"

"It's nice to meet you, Fran," Katy's mother said warmly. "This is my daughter Katy. I thought you might like to talk to her too as she's recently begun her own training in botany. I should add that she's an avid reader of your articles."

Fran turned to Katy with an even wider smile, and Katy felt her stomach turn over in a fit of nerves. "Well!" the journalist exclaimed. "A reader, how wonderful. It's lovely to meet you, Katy."

Katy meant to say sensible things like *hello* and *it's good to meet you* and *I'm such an admirer of your work*, but instead what came out of her mouth was:

"I thought you'd be older!"

Fran laughed. "A lot of people say that."

"Come on," said Mary Willacott. "Let's head inside and Katy and I can give you the tour."

The herbarium at Kew was in Hunter House, an imposing three-storey building of red brick that had been completely given over to the storage of the gardens' specimen collection.

"The collection has grown so much in recent years that a whole new wing had to be built," Mary Willacott told Fran as they entered the building. "It opened last year."

"My goodness," Fran Brocklehurst said as they walked into the main part of the herbarium. She stopped on the threshold, looking around. "How magnificent."

The three floors of the building had been opened up – from the floor where they stood it was possible to see right up to the angular space of the roof, with wide balconies surrounding the central space.

"This is where we house the main collection," said Mary Willacott as they walked into the airy building, full of desks where the herbarium's botanists worked and cabinets that housed the collections. "The new wing is arranged like this too. We also have a wonderful library of botanical books, some really quite old and rare, to help us with our work. There would usually be more people here but as it's Saturday we've got the place to ourselves."

Fran stepped forwards, running her hands along the edge of one of the desks. "Can you explain your work to me in a way that will help my readers understand exactly what it is that you do?" she asked.

"Well," said Mary Willacott. "Why don't you come upstairs and I'll show you one of the most recent specimens I've worked on as an example?"

Katy's mother led the way to a spiral staircase that joined the herbarium's floors together and they all trooped up it, their shoes clanging on the metal steps as they went.

"At its most basic, a herbarium can be described as a library for the world's plants," Mary Willacott explained. "We have collections that were assembled over the years by gentlemen such as Mr William Hooker, who became the director of Kew Gardens in 1841, and the botanists Doctor Bromfield and Mr George Bentham. We also take in specimens sent to us from expeditions exploring the many regions of the globe, and we swap with other herbaria too, like the one at the Royal Botanic Garden in Edinburgh."

They reached the second floor and Katy's mother led them into one of the little rooms, where a desk stood with several large, flat wooden crates set atop it.

"The point of the herbarium," Mary Willacott went on, "is to assemble as complete a collection of examples of the world's plants as possible. Every time an expedition goes out, a member collects examples of plants found during the trip. When they return, they send those here to Kew so that we can preserve and store them properly."

"Why is that important?" Fran asked. "Why do we need such a library?"

"Well," said Katy's mother. "Besides adding to humanity's scientific knowledge about the Earth, it also means we have an amazing resource for research. We have seeds here from plants that were found on the other side of the globe that we can then try to cultivate here at Kew. Many of the garden's most exotic plants have been grown in this way."

"Have you ever gone out on an expedition yourself?" Fran asked.

Mary Willacott laughed quietly. "That's not really an opportunity available to me."

Fran frowned. "But there are women in the field, aren't there? I'm sure I've come across some in my research. Amalie Dietrich, for example, whose specimens of Australian wood won prizes at the Paris International Exhibition in 1867?"

25

"That's true," Katy's mother agreed. "Ms Dietrich's work is exemplary – we have some of her specimens here at Kew, in fact. But she is still an exception. Women don't usually form part of an official expedition. They're more likely to be travelling with their husbands and helping where they can."

"Right," said Fran. She looked at Katy and made a comical face. Katy grinned. She could tell that Fran Brocklehurst wouldn't want to spend her time waiting at home to be sent specimens to look after. She would want to be out there, collecting the specimens herself, like Amalie Dietrich. Katy didn't blame her. She did love the herbarium but how wonderful it would be to actually go on an expedition!

"As a botanical taxonomist," Mary Willacott went on, "it's my job to make sure that the plants we receive are preserved and catalogued correctly. If they're looked after in the right way, a specimen can survive for hundreds of years – and that means those seeds that I mentioned earlier will too. Imagine being able to take out a sample from an expedition conducted years ago, from a plant that is long since forgotten, and grow a new one! We've got some examples of plants here that go right back to the 1700s. Part of my role is also to examine each specimen to determine whether what we have been sent belongs to a species we already have here, or whether it is a plant previously unknown in the science of botany."

She stopped in front of one of the cabinets and pulled it open, revealing a collection of large folders. Mary Willacott chose one and lifted it out, turning to place it flat on the desk. Inside was a sheet of paper with a large, dried plant with a mass of small, faded pink flowers pressed flat against it. Down one edge of the paper were several notes in very small, neat handwriting. Below the specimen was written a name, a place and a date.

"This is a specimen that—" Mary Willacott began but before she could say more, a booming voice roared angrily from below them.

"Where in the devil's name *is* everybody?"

Chapter Five

Katy went to the balcony and looked over it, her mother and Fran close behind. Standing below them was a broad-shouldered man dressed in a black top hat and matching coat tails, clutching a heavy-looking walking stick. He had a bushy beard and eyebrows, cheeks flushed red with rage, and wore a scowl that was clear to see even from where the three women stood.

"Hello, sir," said Mary Willacott, beginning to make her way back to the spiral staircase. "Can I help you?"

Katy watched as the visitor's attention snapped to her mother. If anything, his countenance darkened further.

"I doubt it," he said. "I hardly think the cleaning staff could help *me*."

Katy saw her mother pause in her step for a moment.

"What are you two gawping at?" the rude stranger asked,

looking up at Katy and Fran. "Get about your business. You're not paid to stand idle."

"Sir," said Mary Willacott, reaching the bottom step and crossing the floor towards the man. "My name is Mary Willacott. I am a botanist here at the herbarium. The reason there is no one else here is that it is a Saturday, and the staff work neither on a Saturday nor on a Sunday. Now – is there something I can help you with?"

The visitor stared at her. "*You*," he said, with utter disdain. "Are *employed* as a botanist? Here? At the Royal Botanic Gardens of Kew? I had no idea that standards had slipped so low. Well, it now seems my quest is all the more pressing. Things really must be rectified."

"I beg your pardon?" said Mary Willacott.

"I am Sir Thomas Derby. You will have heard of me, of course," he said. "I am currently overseeing construction of the new Natural History Museum. It is my intention to have this entire operation –" at this he lifted his cane and whisked it in a tight circle, indicating the herbarium as a whole – "moved into our modern laboratories and away from the grasp of amateurs." He sniffed, glancing around. "Now that I have visited for myself and seen the desperate straits in which our nation's proud heritage resides, I am even more convinced this is desirable – nay, necessary. Not working on a Saturday, indeed. Employing *women* in such delicate scientific work. Preposterous."

Katy had frozen the second that the man had announced

his name. She did indeed know the name of Sir Thomas Derby, from hearing it discussed over the dinner table at Rose Cottage. Derby was Katy's father's superior at the British Museum, and never missed an opportunity to make sure that Josiah Willacott knew how lowly his position as a mere assistant archaeologist was.

"Sir Thomas!" exclaimed Fran, her bright voice ringing out over the balcony as she hurried towards the staircase. "How fortuitous! I have been trying to contact you for some weeks!" The journalist ran lightly down the spiral steps to stand at Mary Willacott's side.

Derby looked down his nose at Fran. "*You* have been trying to contact *me*? What could you and I possibly have to discuss?"

"I'm a journalist, Sir Thomas. I'm putting together a piece about women in the sciences – that's why I'm here, to talk to Mrs Willacott. Her work in the herbarium is really quite exceptional. As someone instrumental in the arrangement of the new Natural History Museum, I wanted to hear your thoughts on the future of women in the sciences."

Sir Thomas Derby gave a dismissive snort. "There is no place for women in the sciences. If they have a need for amusement, then botany is of course a suitable *hobby* for the female mind. But the idea that they should be *employed* –" here he shot Katy's mother a disgusted look – "as scientists in any serious institution is … is simply absurd."

Katy saw that Fran had opened her notebook and was diligently writing down everything Sir Thomas said.

"And why do you say that, Sir Thomas?" enquired Fran, pencil poised against her paper.

"Do you really have to ask?" Derby said, incredulous. "Why, surely even to you it is obvious. The female brain does not contain the capacity required for proper scientific reasoning, and they are forever distracted – as is only proper – by concerns to do with the home and children and whatnot. Now since there is no one here with whom I can converse seriously about the future of this institution…"

He touched the rim of his top hat in the tiniest possible show of respect, and then turned on his heel. The door to the herbarium swung shut behind him, leaving the three of them standing in silence.

"Do you think he recognized your name, Mama?" Katy asked after a moment. "I mean, you *are* the wife of one of his archaeologists…"

Mary Willacott gave a brief laugh. "Oh, I doubt that very much."

"That opinion of his," Fran Brocklehurst said. "Is that something you've experienced a lot, Mrs Willacott?"

Katy made her way down to join them as her mother sighed and said, "From some quarters, yes."

"One would have thought your work would speak for itself," the journalist observed.

"Yes," Mary Willacott agreed. "One would."

"Does it worry you, what Sir Thomas just said?" Fran asked as Katy joined them. "About wanting to move the herbarium into the Natural History Museum when it opens?"

"It worries me very much indeed." Katy's mother slipped her arm around Katy's shoulders.

Fran made another note and then looked up with a smile. "Well. He's gone for now, so I suggest we continue with our tour. I for one have no intention of letting Sir Thomas Derby take up another minute of my time. Katy – why don't you show me what you've been working on?"

"That's a good idea," said Mary Willacott, with a genuine smile. "Katy has a knack for accurate taxonomy and how to preserve a plant specimen for the collection. Kew herbarium will be lucky to have her when she finishes school."

Katy tried to smile and followed her mother and Fran back towards the staircase. She couldn't forget the look of disgust on Sir Thomas Derby's face, though, or how adamant he was that women like them did not belong in this building at all.

Chapter Six

Later, once they had shown Fran all there was to see and the horrible encounter with Derby was almost forgotten, the journalist looked at her watch and declared that she must go.

"It's been wonderful meeting you both but I've got a train to catch," she said as she shoved her notepad and pencil back into her satchel. "Thank you, Mrs Willacott, really – you've given me so much material for my article."

"You're very welcome," said Katy's mother. "It's been a pleasant day, seeing the herbarium through someone else's eyes. Or at least," she added darkly. "It's been *mostly* pleasant."

Fran reached out and patted Mary Willacott's arm. "Don't worry about Sir Thomas. He's just an old windbag, and his words – *they're* nothing more than wasted hot air."

Katy saw her mother's slight smile and knew what she'd be thinking. That Fran was right about the first bit but as for the second – well. The two of them already knew exactly how much Sir Thomas Derby could hold back their family. He'd been keeping Katy's father in the museum's basement instead of letting him go out in the field for years.

"Katy," Fran said. "Do you fancy walking me back to the train station? I don't want to get lost."

Katy was surprised. It seemed unlikely to her that Fran Brocklehurst would get lost anywhere. She looked at her mother, who nodded.

"Of course, run along with Fran," said Mary Willacott. "I'm going to check that everything is shipshape here and go back to help Peg with lunch."

Katy and Fran left the herbarium and set off in the direction of the village. They'd only gone a few steps when Fran turned to Katy with a wicked grin.

"Well, come on, then," she said. "If you don't want to be a botanist, tell me what it is you *do* want to do."

Katy looked up at her with surprise. "How do you know I don't want to be a botanist?"

"I'm good at reading people. You didn't argue with your mother when she talked about it but you didn't agree with her, either. I bet that happens every time she brings it up, doesn't it?"

Katy sighed. "It's not that I don't want to be a botanist. I like plants. They're fascinating. It's just … that's what

34

everyone is assuming I am going to be, just because it's what my mother does and because I am here, already living at Kew. And," she added, voicing something her father had said many times, "because it's an *appropriate* science for a woman."

"What does really interest you, then?" Fran asked.

"I don't know." Katy waved vaguely at the world around them. "Everything. The stars, for example."

"The stars?"

"Yes," said Katy. "Have you ever gone to the British Museum and looked at their meteorites? They're beautiful and strange and they're from somewhere so far away that we can't even imagine the distance. What is it like there? Is there another Earth out there somewhere? If there is, how would we get there?"

"And this is what you really want to do? You want to study the cosmos?"

"Yes … no … it's not *all* I want to do." Katy tried to find a way to explain. "That was just an example. Fossils, I find those fascinating too. Animals, sea creatures, rocks. Sailing! I want to sail the seas, like my grandfather Ned. He's been teaching me how to handle a yacht. I suppose what I really want to be is … an adventuring naturalist, like Charles Darwin."

Fran laughed. "I'm not sure that's quite what he calls himself."

"Well, it's what *I'd* call myself," Katy said firmly. "I'd go everywhere and see everything for myself, instead of just reading about other people doing it."

The journalist grinned. "Excellent. Well, let's keep in touch. I'd love to be friends with an adventuring naturalist. Your mother has my address."

"Oh, I won't get to do any of that," Katy said gloomily. "I'll be just like my mother, spending all my time in the herbarium, preparing the dried specimens that other people have travelled all over the world to find."

"Would that be such a bad thing?" Fran asked. "Your mother is so accomplished. She is very much respected – it's why I wanted to talk to her for my article. It was so difficult for her, at the beginning, being the first woman in the herbarium when she started. I admire her very much, Katy."

"So do I," Katy said, with a familiar feeling of misery. "I love her, I admire her and I don't want to let her down. It's just … not for *me*."

Fran stopped and looked at Katy with a serious look on her face. "Katy. If it's not what you want to do, you need to tell your mother that."

"I have," Katy said. "But she just keeps saying that I'm the next generation, and she seems so excited about the idea of us working together, and…" She trailed off unhappily.

Fran put a hand on Katy's shoulder. "I understand."

They began to walk again.

"You could put together your own expedition," Fran said, after a moment or two. "I bet you're more than capable of being captain of your own ship. Then you could go wherever you want."

Katy laughed. "I've never heard of a lady captain."

"There's Ching Shih," Fran pointed out. "Of the China Seas. She was rather successful. She commanded a whole flotilla of ships."

"Really?"

"Absolutely. Of course, she was a pirate queen known for being particularly vicious, so perhaps not quite the example you want to follow. But it does go to show that a woman has the mettle to be capable of such feats. There's also Eleanor Creesy," Fran went on. "In 1851 she was navigator of the clipper *Flying Cloud*, which on its maiden voyage made the fastest journey ever between New York City and San Francisco. It's a record that still hasn't been broken."

"She was one of the crew?"

"She was. The *Cloud*'s captain put the journey's speed down to her expertise. A hundred years ago there was Mary Lacy too," Fran added. "She disguised herself as a man called William Chandler so she could join the navy during the Seven Years' War. Then she apprenticed as a shipwright and qualified as one too. She was so good at her job that she retired with a full pension and wrote her memoirs. How about that for a woman doing a 'man's' job?"

Katy was still taking this in as Fran went on speaking.

"The world is full of extraordinary women doing extraordinary things. Why, just this morning I was reading the dispatches of Lady Sarah Montague, who is at this very moment navigating the great waters of the Amazon river with her adopted daughter Zinnie. How I wish I was there with them to witness their adventure." Fran grinned. "This is why I am absolutely sure that you, Katy Willacott, can be captain of your own ship if you choose to be. Extraordinary women, doing extraordinary things. There are more of us than folk realize. There always have been. Your mother is one of them. And you will be too."

Katy bid goodbye to Fran at the station and walked slowly back along the village's dusty roads, thinking about what her new friend had said. Daydreaming, really. Imagining herself at the helm of a ship heading out on to an unknown ocean.

Chapter Seven

When she reached home, Rose Cottage was in uproar. There were piles of equipment on the kitchen table – everything from climbing crampons to her father's tin of watercolour paints and excavating trowels. Katy could hear footsteps rushing this way and that.

"Hello?" she called.

Peg bustled in with her arms full of clothes and added them to the free-for-all.

"Grandma? What's happening?"

"No notice, indeed!" Peg cried. "Just a letter in the second post and whoosh, off they must go! Oh, your brother's second-best breeches! I was mending them, and—"

She rushed off again, leaving Katy none the wiser. The door from the hallway opened and Stefan burst in, an old suitcase in his arms. This he also dumped on the table and began to fill with rapid and untidy abandon.

"Stefan? What's going on?" Katy asked.

Stefan glanced at her but didn't stop his frantic packing. His face was pink with excitement. "There's been a fresh rockslide at Hastings. A whole new fossil bed has been revealed. The museum wants Father to lead the excavation – and I am going with him!"

"What?"

Stefan stopped packing for a moment and stared down at his crammed-full case, a frown on his face. "I'm missing something. What is it? What—"

Katy turned to the sideboard behind her and hooked up his leather expedition belt, left there from the last time he'd used it. From it hung a series of sturdy leather pouches containing a trowel, a small garden fork and two paintbrushes. Dried mud was still stuck to the tools. Katy handed it to her brother without a word. She had her own kit, though *hers* was always clean.

"Ah! Yes!" Stefan took the belt and added it to the mess in his case.

"Where's Father?" she asked.

"Upstairs. There is so much to arrange and we must get there as soon as possible!"

Katy left the chaos of the kitchen and ran up the stairs to Josiah Willacott's study. It was small, as crammed and cluttered as the rest of Rose Cottage, and it was Katy's favourite room in the house aside from her own bedroom.

The walls were lined with books, except where they held glass cabinets full of her father's private finds. As a younger child, Katy had spent hours sitting on the floor behind her father's chair with the notebooks and watercolour sets he gave her, learning the business of looking at things with enough attention to explain them to others. Her father had always had such patience for her, no matter how many times she asked '*But why, Papa?*' or how busy he was with his own work. He had always praised what she produced, whether it be a childish painting of a dandelion with all its parts labelled accurately, or the correctly identified and painted flight feather from a robin's wing.

Katy arrived in the doorway to see that her parents were side by side at the desk, trying to pack another case.

"Father?" Katy asked.

Josiah Willacott turned with a smile. "Katy. Did you enjoy meeting Fran Brocklehurst?"

"What? Oh – yes. Stefan says you are going to Hastings?"

Her father continued his packing. "Yes! We must be off first thing in the morning. The museum wants me there as soon as possible."

"That's wonderful, Papa," Katy said. This would be the first time the museum had trusted her father with a full expedition.

"It really is, isn't it?" beamed Mary Willacott, rubbing an affectionate hand against her husband's shoulder.

"Stefan is going with you?"

41

"Yes, it will be a wonderful opportunity for him to receive proper field training."

"Then – may I come too?" Katy asked. "It will not take me long to pack. My field kit is already clean and ready to go."

Her mother turned to look at her, a pensive look on her face. Her father was too busy arranging books in his suitcase to notice.

"No, Katy," he said, over his shoulder. "This is not a trip for you."

"But why not?" Katy asked. "It is nearly summer, I will have no school! Why should Stefan accompany you but not me? I want the field experience too!"

"Stefan will be my assistant," her father said, still too busy to look at her.

"I can assist you too!"

"This isn't a family holiday, Katy," her father said. "This is important work."

"I know," Katy said, growing frustrated. "And I can help you with it."

"Katy, I don't have time to argue," said her father. "Stefan is older, he will not require the same supervision, and he can share a boarding room with one of the other workers. Taking you is impractical and I will have enough to worry about without having to chaperone my young daughter."

Katy was stung. "You wouldn't have to," she pointed

out. "I would be with you at the cliff face, working beside you."

Her father finally turned around with a sigh, pinching the bridge of his nose between thumb and forefingers. "You are too young, my dear."

"I'm only two years younger than Stefan! Anyway, you've always said I was the more mature one."

"Katy," her father said quietly. "I'm sorry. You know I would take you with me if I could, but you also know how long I have been waiting for this opportunity. I can't appear like an amateur by letting my young daughter come along for my first managerial position. A fossil dig is not a playground."

Katy bunched her hands into fists, the many injustices of the situation sitting heavily in her heart. "I am a better naturalist than Stefan," she said. "I am more observant, I am more meticulous as I catalogue, and my watercolours are better. And you *both* know it."

There was a moment of silence.

"One day, Katy, I hope you will understand," was all her father said. "Until then, I'm afraid you must simply do as you are told."

Katy stormed out of the room. She climbed the ladder into the attic in a fury and stood at the centre of her bedroom with her hands on her hips. Of *course* she knew such opportunities were rare – the rarest, and even more so for her. Katy's gaze fell upon her own desk and the notebook that was open there, full of all the many commonplace finds from Kew with which she had contented herself, believing that it was all good practice for her first 'real' expedition. Would that ever come? How could it, when even her own father would not take her with him? Why had he bothered to spend time teaching her how to do everything she could do if he had not intended her to use those skills? Just so she could have a *hobby*?

Hours later, once the sun had set and after she had repeatedly refused to come down for dinner, once the noise of the house had subsided into sleep, Katy climbed out on to the roof. The Perseids were stirring again, their yearly storm of ice-white fire streaking the dark sky. How Katy wished she were one of them, burning so brightly they could not be ignored by anyone who saw them, even if their brief flames signalled their end.

"Katy," said her mother's voice from the window.

Katy did not answer but Mary Willacott joined her daughter anyway, climbing carefully out on to the tiles beneath the night sky. She set down a plate of bread and cheese between them.

"Please do not think too harshly of your father," her mother said quietly. "He would take you with him if it were possible. You *are* too young, and there is so much resting on this expedition being successful for him."

"It's all right for you," Katy said bitterly. "You've never wanted to go anywhere. You've always been happy staying

44

right here."

Mary Willacott was quiet for a moment. "That isn't true," she said eventually. "There was a time I wanted to travel, to see the world."

Katy, surprised, turned her head to look at her mother's profile, silhouetted by the moon's shadow. "You've never told me that before."

"You never asked me, Katy."

"Why didn't you do it?"

"I was young, and then I met your father, and then I had Stefan and you. I would have found it too difficult to leave my duties here."

"Father doesn't," Katy pointed out.

"That's different."

"How?" Katy demanded. "How is it different?"

Her mother sighed. "Katy, I have a wonderful life here. I have my family, I have this home, I am a *scientist*, respected and gainfully employed. I do not regret any of my decisions. When you are older, you will understand."

"When I am older, I will be the same person that I am now," Katy said. "And I will do exactly what I want."

Her mother leaned over and kissed Katy's forehead. "Don't stay up too late," she said. "It would be nice if you were up in time to see your father and Stefan off tomorrow morning. Try to be happy for him, Katy. He loves you very much."

Chapter Eight

Josiah and Stefan left for Hastings early the next morning. Katy was there to see them off. After all, it wasn't that she wasn't happy for both her father and her brother. It was just that she was sad and frustrated for herself. Her father held her lightly by the shoulders and kissed her on the forehead.

"Perhaps you and your mother can come and visit us for a weekend, once the dig is properly established," he suggested. "Then you shall be able to see it for yourselves."

Katy tried to smile. "That would be lovely, Papa."

Stefan's goodbye was awkward. "I'll keep a fossil for you," he said. "One that you can catalogue yourself. I promise."

Katy smiled. "Thank you, Stef, that's very kind."

"You *are* better at it than me," he said quietly. "I do know that."

Katy felt guilty for the words that had bitten their way

out of her mouth the night before, but even more for the fact that her brother had obviously heard them. She reached out and took his hand, squeezing it. "Only because I spend so much more time practising," she said.

Stefan smiled at her and squeezed her hand back. Then it was time for them to leave. They climbed on to the cart containing their stacked luggage. Katy and her mother and grandparents watched them trundle away up the lane from the front door of Rose Cottage, waving until they were out of sight. Mary Willacott wrapped an arm around her daughter's shoulders to hug her lightly, but Katy stepped away.

"I'm going for a walk," she said. Her mother said nothing and let her go.

"Here's something that'll interest you, Katy," said her grandfather as they sat around the dinner table that night. "Someone left this on one of the benches and I kept it for you."

Ned passed her the folded sheets of a newspaper across the expanse of kitchen table. Home seemed strange without her father and brother. It was so quiet, for one thing. Katy took the paper and turned it around.

Meteorites Fall Over Brazil, the headline declared and then, in slightly smaller type below: *Scientists Suspect Largest Precipitation of Space Matter on Record*.

Katy read on, her heart in her mouth. It seemed that there had been numerous reports of burning chunks of rock blasting through the sky above the coastal Brazilian city of Salvador, in the region known as Bahia. While residents saw many of these crashing into the ocean, other meteorites plummeted into the dense rainforest that surrounded the city.

An expedition is to be launched in haste to recover as many of these meteorites as possible, read the paper. *Led by Sir Thomas Derby, the British Museum hopes to claim these cosmological artefacts for display in the new Natural History wing of that great institution when it opens in 1881.*

"Derby!" Katy looked up from the paper. "Did you read this, Mama? It says Derby is going to lead an expedition."

"Oh, *that* horrible man," said Mary Willacott, with a derisory sniff.

"It's good, though, isn't it?" Katy pointed out. "It'll take him months to get to Brazil and back again. He won't be here to interfere with the running of the herbarium! Maybe he'll forget about it altogether?"

Mary Willacott frowned doubtfully. "Is Derby really going himself?" she asked, looking at the paper over Katy's shoulder. "It's not like him. He usually prefers to manage from the museum and just put his name on the expedition."

Katy pointed. "This makes it sound as if he's going. Look."

At the conclusion of the article was a large advertisement, set in bold type.

By Order Of The British Museum

Renowned Naturalist Sir Thomas Derby
Will Form an Expedition to Brazil
Where He Intends to Retrieve Numerous
Specimens of Meteorite for Scientific
Study Following the Grand Opening of
the New Natural History Museum.

Thereafter followed a paragraph of smaller type:

*In view of the urgency of this undertaking, Sir Thomas Derby
will choose his small expeditionary team from interested
parties of well-disposed gentlemen able to travel immediately.
Experience and own equipment preferred; funds essential.
Please apply to Cpt Roberts, the SS Alerte, Southampton.
Departure expected at high tide on Saturday.*

"Hmm," muttered Mary Willacott. "You're right. How strange."

"What a pity that Father is already occupied in Hastings," Katy said. "It would be a dream of his to join the expedition."

"Derby would never have taken him," said her mother. "Even if we had been able to raise the funds."

"Do you think," Katy asked thoughtfully, "that this is why Father was given the Hastings dig? Because Sir Thomas is otherwise occupied?"

Her mother nodded. "That would make sense. There's never even been a suggestion that your father would be given such a position before. He's just not notable enough, in Derby's opinion."

"If Derby's in such a rush, he'll have a devil of a time finding able seamen ready and willing to sail so soon," her grandfather said, helping himself to another thick slab of bread and smothering it with butter and then jam. "Four days' notice? He'll be lucky to find anyone good and capable. That's likely why he's been forced to go himself. He's taking the *Alerte*, though, which means he's not mucking about."

Katy looked up. "You know the ship?"

"Aye. She's not big. Sixty-four footer, built in Cowes by Ratsey, oh … must be more'n ten years ago now. I saw her out of Portsmouth once. Good, old-fashioned build, she is," Ned said.

"Is she anything like the *Falcon*?"

Her grandfather considered. "Smaller, but not so very different. Faster, that I will admit. The *Alerte* made Sydney from Southampton in one hundred and three days, which is creditable, aye, very creditable indeed." He finished his bread and took up his pipe instead. "If they do leave on Saturday I'd say they'll make that journey in six weeks, weather willing. Derby's keen as mustard, so he is."

"I'm not surprised," Katy said wistfully as she read the advertisement again. She was struck by a sudden thought. "I wonder if Fran will go with them?"

"Well," said Mary Willacott, rising from the table and beginning to help Peg clear the dirty plates. "I can quite believe that she would love to go, but Derby would never allow a woman to be part of his expedition."

Katy got up to help her mother and grandmother. She kept the paper, though, despite the fact that the details were already marked indelibly on her mind.

That night, no one came to join her on the roof. She lay looking up at the pinpoint furies of the Perseids as they shot through the sky. Josiah and Stefan would be asleep at their lodgings in Hastings by now. The *Alerte* would be at anchor in Southampton, waiting to be off on her adventure. All around her, people were moving, travelling, embarking on journeys and reaching destinations that Katy could only dream of.

Extraordinary women, doing extraordinary things.

The memory of Fran's voice returned to her then, as did the stories the journalist had recited. Mary Lacy the shipwright. Eleanor Creesy, navigator of the *Flying Cloud*. Lady Sarah Montague and her daughter Zinnie. Amalie Dietrich, award-winning expeditionary botanist. Ching Shih the fierce pirate queen. Francesca Brocklehurst, riding the pilgrim trail to Santiago alone. All extraordinary women, all doing extraordinary things.

There are more of us than folk think. There always have been.

"I'm going to be one of them," Katy promised herself. "I am. I just need to work out how."

She stared up at the falling stars as an idea planted itself in her mind, the first curling frond of a germinating seed beginning to uncurl.

Chapter Nine

Her plan grew quickly after that. It had to, since she had only four days before the *Alerte* would leave Southampton and once that happened the opportunity would be lost forever.

Katy Willacott would run away and join the crew of the *Alerte*. She would sail the trade winds to Brazil and once there she would find her own meteorite. She would disguise herself as a boy to do it and she would prove once and for all that she was made for more than working in the herbarium, cataloguing what other people had found. She would do this extraordinary thing and no one would ever be able to say she was not capable of doing whatever she wanted ever again.

She concentrated on behaving as normally as possible as she quietly gathered what she would need to take with her. It wasn't just her precious expedition equipment. Katy would need entirely different clothes too. These she took bit by bit from Stefan's room.

"I'll look after them," Katy promised him silently, feeling the shadow of guilt lurking over her.

Katy was careful not to leave a trace of what she was planning anywhere that her family might see, but she had tacked the article that had been in the newspaper on to her wall beside her collection of Fran Brocklehurst stories. Her mother hadn't mentioned it, probably assuming it was as much of a keepsake as the journalist's articles. But then, on Wednesday afternoon, as Katy was assembling everything to put into her travel sack ready to go, she had an unexpected visitor.

"Katy," Mary Willacott called, from the bottom of the stepladder. "Edie is here!"

There was the sound of climbing footsteps and then her friend appeared in the hatch as Katy hurriedly tried to hide what was in her hands.

"Hello!" Edie said as she clambered into the room. "It's a lovely day outside. Will you come out for a walk? I'm going to go down to the—" Her friend stopped. "What have you got there?"

Katy had been rolling up the trousers she'd taken from Stefan's room, ready for packing. She dropped them on the bed instead. "Nothing at all."

Edie picked up the little pile and shook it out. "Why have you got trousers?"

"They're not mine," Katy said, taking them back and tossing them on to her bed as if they were of no consequence at all. "They're Stefan's." She hoped that would be enough of an explanation.

"Oh. Well, will you come out? Your mama says you've been up here all day."

"I can't, I'm busy."

Edie raised her eyebrows, looking around the room. "Really? Doing what?"

Katy shrugged and went to her desk, where she had assembled some of the kit she was going to take with her – her current field notebook and a new one she could start once it was full, her pencils and watercolour tin with its brushes, her clean and shiny dig kit in its smart leather roll. She didn't think Edie would take any notice of them, but her friend stared at the neat pile suspiciously for a moment. Then she looked back at Katy's travelling pack on the bed and back at the kit again.

"Are you going somewhere?" Edie asked.

"Well," Katy said, thinking quickly. "I thought it was best to be prepared in case Papa wrote to say that he needed help in Hastings."

Edie nodded slowly. "I hope he does, Katy. I know how upset you must be that you didn't get to go with them."

Katy looked down at her feet, swallowing an unexpected lump in her throat. "It doesn't matter."

"It *does* matter," Edie insisted. "But I'm sure you'll

get to go with Mr Willacott one day. You just have to be patient."

Katy made an indignant sound in her throat. "Stefan didn't have to be patient! The first hint of Papa managing his own dig and *ppft*! Off my brother goes with him."

"Well," Edie said uneasily. "He is older than you, Katy. And he has been training with your father…"

"So have I!"

Edie sighed. "Come on. Come out for a walk. It'll make you feel better, I promise. Better than moping up here and reading Francesca Brocklehurst's stories over and over again, anyway." She looked up at the newspaper pages pinned to the wall. Then she went very still. Edie moved to look at the piece that detailed the meteorite fall and Sir Thomas Derby's advertisement. A moment later she turned and looked at Katy. Then she looked at the pile of kit on Katy's desk, and then over to the sack on the bed, next to Stefan's crumpled pair of trousers. Her face took on a horrified look.

"Oh no, Katy," Edie whispered. "You can't."

Katy tried to fix an innocent look on her face. "I can't what?"

Edie went quickly to the bed and picked up Katy's bag, shaking it a little. "You're going to run away, aren't you?"

"What?" Katy said, forcing a laugh, her heart jumping unevenly in her chest. "Of course I'm not."

"You are!" Edie pointed a furious finger at the meteorite article. "You're going to try to get to Brazil!"

"Shh!" Katy hissed, glancing at the open hatch. The last thing she needed was for her mother or grandparents to overhear. "Don't be ridiculous."

Edie threw down the bag and stomped back to the desk, glowering at the pile of items on it and then at Katy. "It's not ridiculous. I know you, Katy Willacott, and this is exactly the kind of absurd thing you would try to do, and you can't. You can't just run away to Brazil."

"I'm not!" Katy protested, her heart still hammering. "I wouldn't!"

Edie put her hands on her hips and narrowed her eyes. "Fine. In that case, you won't mind if I go downstairs and tell your mama all about it so that we can all laugh at silly Edie and her daft ideas, will you?"

Edie turned for the stepladder but Katy caught her arm. "Don't! Oh, Edie – don't!"

Her friend whirled around. "I *knew* it!"

"Please don't tell anyone, Edie!" Katy begged. "*Please.* Promise."

"Only if *you* promise that you're not going to do this," Edie said. "You can't, Katy. It's too dangerous."

"It's not," Katy insisted. "It won't be. I know what I'm doing."

"But—"

"I've got to do this, Edie," Katy insisted. "I've just got to. There'll never be a better opportunity. And once I've been to Brazil and back all on my own, Papa will see that I should be on every dig he ever goes on from now!"

Edie bit her lip, looking at the advertisement in the newspaper. "It says you need to provide funds to join the expedition. Where will those come from?"

"I'm not going to join the expedition," Katy said, heading over to the rucksack on the bed and continuing with her packing. "I'm going to get a job on the *Alerte* as a cabin boy so I can work my way to Brazil. You heard what Grandpa Ned said the last time I had a sailing lesson. I'm a natural."

Edie looked even more horrified. "A cabin *boy*?"

"Yes!" Katy shook out the pair of Stefan's trousers that she'd borrowed. "I've thought it all through. On the day I go, I'll leave a letter here to say I've gone to Hastings to visit Father and Stefan. It'll take at least a day for a letter from Mama to reach Hastings, and then the same again for a reply to come back saying that I never arrived. By then I'll be aboard the *Alerte* at Southampton, ready to set sail, miles away in the opposite direction! Before I leave I'll send *another* letter, telling everyone that I'm safe and not to worry. By the time it arrives at Rose Cottage, the voyage will be under way and it'll be too late for anyone to stop me."

Edie shook her head. "But what about your family? They'll all worry, you know they will."

Katy didn't really want to think about that, because she knew it was true. But when set against what she would be missing out on if she *didn't* go, she put her misgivings aside.

"I'll be one of those extraordinary women, doing

extraordinary things, just like Fran Brocklehurst said," Katy replied, ignoring her guilt. "You can't ruin it for me by telling anyone. You're a better friend than that, I know you are. At least I *think* you are." They were harsh words, and Katy felt a stab of regret in her chest as soon as she'd said them.

Edie looked at her, hurt. "I'd be a worse friend if I let you go and something bad happened to you."

"Nothing bad will happen! And I promise, if when I get to Southampton, it all feels too dangerous and difficult, I'll come right back home again."

Edie shook her head, her lips set in a tight line.

"I have to do this," Katy whispered. "I have to at least *try*. I'll be miserable forever if I don't. I'll always be wondering what might have been if I'd just had the bravery to do something extraordinary."

There was another moment of silence.

"If I ever have the misfortune to meet Francesca Brocklehurst," Edie grumbled, "she'll get a piece of my mind, and no mistake."

"Please, Edie," Katy begged her friend again. "Please, please promise me you won't say anything."

Edie sighed. "All right. I promise. But after this, once you're back … I hope that's it, Katy. I hope all the wildness will have worked its way out of you and you'll never want to do anything foolish ever again. But if you don't go, I know it never will. And I suppose," she added with a sigh, "that if anyone can do it, you can."

Chapter Ten

"Mama?"

It was the night before she planned to leave. Katy was hovering at the door of her parents' bedroom. Mary Willacott was preparing for bed, sitting in front of her mirror to brush out her long hair. She turned at the sound of her daughter's voice and offered a small smile. Their argument of a few days before had lingered, and Katy did not want to leave with it still hanging over them. For all their differences, for all the disagreements they'd had over the past few months, Katy still loved her mother with her whole heart.

"Katy," Mary Willacott said, putting down her hairbrush. "I thought you would be up on the roof by now. The Perseids haven't finished yet, have they?"

"No," Katy said. "I thought you might like to join me."

Her mother looked surprised and Katy felt even guiltier. Had she really been so distant from her mother these last few days?

"I'd love to," was all Mary Willacott said, and so together they made their way up to the attic and through the window on to Rose Cottage's rickety tiles.

As they lay side by side beneath the stars, Katy's mother reached out and took her hand, squeezing it hard.

"I love you, Katy, and I believe that you can do whatever you set your mind to," she said, her voice drifting on the night wind like star shine. "You know that, don't you? And if botany isn't what you want, then we'll find you something else. Whatever you do, I know you will excel at it."

Katy's eyes filled with tears. She squeezed her mother's hand back. "I want to make you and Papa proud," she said.

"You already do, my darling," said Mary Willacott. "And so I can only imagine how much we will burst with pride over your achievements in the future."

When the stars fell, it seemed as if the entire cosmos was tumbling to Earth, right over their heads. Katy wondered what she was thinking, running away from this. Here was her home, her family. It was safe and beautiful and she was loved. Was she really going to give it all up to run away to sea?

Fran Brocklehurst would, Katy thought to herself. *Mary Lacy did.*

"I need to go to bed now," her mother murmured. "Will you stay out here?"

"For a little while," Katy said, though she kept hold of her mother's hand for a moment more, squeezing it firmly. "I love you, Mama. Very much. You do know that, don't you?"

Mary Willacott leaned over and pressed a kiss to Katy's hair. "I do, and it means everything to me, Katy. Everything."

Her mother went below to her bed, leaving Katy to watch the stars and think on what she was about to do.

Later – much later, when the hour came for her to leave – Katy almost couldn't. She crept down the stairs in the clothes she had chosen for travel and then dithered in the shadowed hallway, her pack on her back and the letter she had written her family in one hand. Around her Rose Cottage was shrouded in sleep, still and silent. She thought of her mother and grandparents upstairs, all oblivious to her extraordinary plan. Through the small window over the front door, Katy could see how dark it still was outside. Did she really want to step out into those shadows, did she really want to walk away from Rose Cottage, her home and her family, to step into such a great unknown?

If you don't go, Katy asked herself, *what will you do? Follow in your mother's footsteps, walking the same paths of Kew Gardens to the herbarium every day to look at specimens found by other people. Is that what you want? Or do you want to chase the stars and find the ones that fall? Will you ever get another chance like this again?*

Fran's voice echoed to her again.

Extraordinary women, doing extraordinary things.

Katy stirred herself from her indecision and squared her shoulders. She slipped quietly along the hallway towards the door, pausing only to leave her letter propped up amid the chaos of the sideboard, catching a glance at herself in its mirror. She'd gathered up her hair and pushed it beneath one of Stefan's battered old caps, but already wisps were beginning to escape. Katy quietly slid open one of the cabinet's crammed drawers and rooted around until she found a pair of her grandmother's embroidery scissors and slid them into her pocket. She'd have to find a way to deal with her hair properly before she reached Southampton.

She left Rose Cottage and stepped out into the inky darkness of pre-dawn, where the stars still peppered the clear sky and the birds were only just beginning to stir. Katy paused again on the step, her heart beating wildly, fear making her breathless. Was she really going to do this? Could she?

Above her, a skein of light unwound itself and pierced the night with one final, blazing trail. It arced over Katy's head, another Perseid burning its way out of eternity. She hefted her pack on to her shoulder and followed it.

Chapter Eleven

The man in the ticket booth at Kew station squinted at her through the glass with a suspicious look on his face.

"You want a ticket to where?"

"Southampton," Katy said again, wondering if the gruff voice she'd put on to make herself sound like a boy had been a mistake. She'd pulled Stefan's cap low and had made sure all her hair was tucked away but her heart was still thumping. What if someone saw through her disguise? It wouldn't do for her plan to be scuppered before she'd even got out of the village!

"Hmph," the man muttered. "Let me guess. You're all ready to begin a life at sea."

Katy blinked. "Well—"

"Believe me, the high sea's not a place for the scrawny likes of you," the man said as he punched out the ticket.

"Stay in the schoolroom, that's my advice."

Outside on the platform, the dawn was drawing on, painting pale pastel colours over a lead-coloured sky heavy with rain. Katy was surprised by how many people – mostly gentlemen – were waiting for the next train, but then she supposed they were like her father, bound for jobs in the city.

Katy had been on a passenger locomotive many times, but never alone, and the idea that she would be setting foot aboard without any of her family, or indeed any guardian at all, caused a fizz of nerves to start up in her gut.

The sound of the engine came to her through the grey morning, first as the tracks began to rattle with the weight of their load and then with the loud hooting wail of the train's whistle as it grew closer. It chugged towards them, its black funnel belching gout after gout of white steam to add to the general cloudiness of the sky.

The passengers all stepped forwards. Katy did the same and found herself standing beside someone who, to her utter horror, she recognized. It was Mr Palmer, Edie's father. He was an accounting clerk and she had completely forgotten that, just like her own father, he went into the city every day to work!

Katy immediately dipped her head, and then had to clutch at Stefan's cap to keep it over her hair in the gust of wind brought by the arrival of the engine.

The train drew to a hooting, hissing standstill. Doors began to open and everyone surged forwards, top hats bobbing as the men trooped on to the train and dipped their heads to make it through the doors. As the steam dissipated, Katy could see the seats inside filling up and realized she must make sure she was as far away from Mr Palmer as possible. She hurried up the platform to another carriage, but that was busy too.

The guard blew his whistle and Katy began to panic that she wouldn't be able to get on the train at all. Eventually, though, with the guard blowing his whistle again and the train hooting and hollering and belching steam for all it was worth, Katy found herself hefting her pack up the steps and into the belly of the beast. She made her way through the carriages, looking for an empty seat, but they were all full, and she was dismayed to see that if she went much further she would find herself back in the same carriage as Edie's papa.

This was no good. What was she to do? She turned back again, wondering if she could stand in one of the tiny corridors between the carriages and stay out of sight that way. Then Katy spied the sign for the conveniences and made her way towards them, pushing open the tiny wooden door and squashing herself into the small space beyond. She locked the door behind her and dumped her pack on the closed toilet seat, catching her own eye in the mirror above the small sink. Her hair was already beginning to tumble out from beneath her borrowed cap. She looked just as she was – a girl dressed in boy's clothes. If someone looked at her for more than a glance they would be sure to notice, which meant she'd never pass as a cabin boy, not to the crew of the *Alerte*.

She lurched a little on her feet as the train pulled away from the station, but by then Katy was too busy to think about the fact that she was leaving Kew behind. She was concentrating on cutting off her hair with Grandma Peg's embroidery scissors, making it as short as she possibly could.

Chapter Twelve

By the time Katy reached Southampton, she was pleased with herself. Now that her hair was short, she looked surprisingly like her brother Stefan. She'd had to change trains at Clapham Junction and she was able to get a seat near the window, watching as the towns and countryside whipped by, smudged into watercolour blurs by the train's puffs of steam. The journey gave her a chance to rehearse what she was going to say when she found the *Alerte* and Captain Roberts. She'd have to be able to prove she was worthy of joining the crew. By the time the train was pulling into Southampton, Katy was pretty sure she had the perfect speech all ready to use.

The port city itself took her by surprise. Everyone and everything was in furious motion. The station was packed – the railway tracks rattled with new arrivals and fresh departures, the guards blew whistles, the porters shouted as they dragged or carried luggage through the moving throng of passengers. For a moment Katy had to pause and catch her breath. It was a far cry from the peace and quiet of Kew.

Katy asked one of the uniformed guards for directions to the port. His peaked hat and bushy white beard reminded her, with a little stab of guilt, of her grandfather. Would they have realized yet that she was gone?

"Keep going downhill, lad," the harried man said. "Out the front, turn left. Can't miss it."

Lad! He'd called her 'lad'! Katy couldn't help grinning as she left the station.

He hadn't been joking when he'd told Katy she couldn't miss the port. It sprawled out below her along the glinting waters of the estuary, a rippling storm of ships rising and falling gently on the tide. The sound rose towards her too, growing ever louder as she made her way towards this city within a city: the *snick-snick-snick* of lines against masts, the hollers of the dock workers loading and unloading cargo. Katy could taste salt on the wind and somehow felt as if she were coming home.

Once she got closer, Katy realized that she faced another problem. There were hundreds of ships moored in Southampton's port. She had no idea how to find the *Alerte*.

"The *Alerte*?" she asked numerous people, the sun continuing to rise as she searched. "Please, do you know where she is berthed?"

No one seemed to have heard of the ship at all.

Katy paused beside a large pile of goods that looked as if they were waiting to be loaded on to one of the ships lining the dock and tried to work out what to do. She was beginning to worry that by the time she found the ship it would be too late. All the crew spaces would be filled. Perhaps the expedition would even have set sail a day early, taking advantage of the good weather.

"Help you, lad?" said a voice. Katy squinted beneath the morning sun and realized that there was a man standing with the pile of goods, leaning on a barrel. He was eating an apple, slowly carving slices from it using a sturdy folding knife. His hands were tanned and bore the lines and scars that spoke of long hours of work. His face was similarly marked by the sun.

"Do you know the *Alerte*?" Katy asked. "The ship soon bound for Brazil?"

"Oh, aye," the sailor said, nodding his head at the pile of goods beside him. "She's right here, lad."

Katy realized that he wasn't nodding at the unruly stack of boxes, barrels and cases, but behind it. She took a step to her right and saw that there was a ship moored just a few feet from where she stood. Well, you could call it a ship, but it was really little more than a large boat. Next to the larger ships between which she was anchored, the *Alerte* looked more like one of Grandpa Ned's models.

"That's the *Alerte*?" Katy said, dismayed. "*That's* the ship bound for Brazil?"

The sailor pushed away from his barrel, still chewing his apple, and came to stand beside her, surveying the little ship. "Aye," he said. "That's her. What's it to you, boy?"

"I… I am looking for work."

"Work? What sort of work?"

Katy squared her shoulders. "I'm a good cabin boy."

"A cabin boy!" The sailor laughed, finishing his apple and tossing the core into the water. "A scrap of lean gristle like you out on the ocean? The gulls would have you for supper before we'd got beyond Cowes."

Katy turned to him, jutting out her chin in defiance. "I can trim a mainsail single-handed, I can splice a line in five minutes and I bet I can tie a knot faster than you too," she said defiantly. "*Blindfolded.* Tell me where to find Captain Roberts of the *Alerte* and I'll prove it to him."

The sailor held up both hands, still laughing. "All right, all right. No need to go off the deep end, lad. The real question is, can you carry your weight? Or, even more importantly, Sir Thomas Derby's weight?"

Katy frowned. "What do you know of Derby?"

The sailor waved at the boxes and crates stacked up beside them. "Only that he seems to think all this tat necessary for his voyage, and if I don't get it loaded on the ship before the captain gets back, there'll be hell to pay. Give me a hand, and providing you don't tip a crate in the drink, I'll put in a good word, how's that?"

Katy blinked. "You're part of the *Alerte*'s crew?"

"Think I'm standing here for my health?" the sailor asked cheerfully. "I'm first mate. Sent the second mate off to find us some help, but where's the sense in looking a gift horse in the mouth, eh? No promises, mind. The captain's not in the best of moods. Won't be all the time he has to deal with Sir Thomas, I'll warrant."

"I'll help," Katy said. "Just show me what needs to go where."

The sailor grinned, then stuck out one grizzled hand for her to shake. "I like you, lad. I'm Percy. You are?"

"William," Katy said. "William Chandler. Cabin boy."

Percy grinned. "All right then, William Chandler Cabin Boy," he said. "Let's get this lot aboard."

He waved at a crate and together they hefted it between them, making their way up on to the *Alerte*'s deck. She might be small, but she was certainly a pretty ship, kept in good order by her crew. Beneath Katy's feet the wood of her timbers shone in the sun.

"Watch your step," Percy warned as they reached the doghouse, the little wooden hut that could be closed over the stairs in bad weather. "It's steep and dark below."

Chapter Thirteen

Gloom rose to meet them. Below decks the *Alerte* seemed even smaller. Katy could stand upright, but someone taller would be in danger of hitting their head. There was so little space that as soon as she was at the bottom of the stairs, Katy found herself standing beside the mess table, where all hands would be expected to eat their meals. It was smaller than the one in Rose Cottage's kitchen.

Beyond the table was a wooden wall that cut the ship in half, although it had a wide door that could be folded back to open out the space. This was where Percy led her, the crate growing heavier between them by the second. Stepping through the open door, Katy saw that they were standing in the galley kitchen. There was a small, coal-fired stove and a few cabinets crammed into the tiny area. Percy set his end of the crate down and Katy followed suit.

"We'll bring everything down," Percy said. "Then we'll work out where to put it all. Our cook's called Danny – he's off ship at the moment, ordering supplies. He'll need to have a say."

As they went back up and down the stairs, Percy pointed out the rest of the ship's layout.

"The captain's cabin's aft," he said, nodding his chin towards the rear of the *Alerte*. Then he pointed to a tiny room between the captain's cabin and the mess. Inside Katy could see a small table with a map spread out across it. "The chart room's there, see? Well, it's less of a room and more of a cupboard without a door, but beggars can't be choosers, eh? There's one more cabin forwards, right at the very prow of the ship."

The prow was the front of the ship, which would always be ahead of the rest as they set off across the open ocean.

"Whose cabin is that, then?" Katy asked. "If not the captain's?"

Percy pulled a face. "Derby's commandeered that one, which tells me all I need to know of what Sir Thomas thinks of himself compared to the rest of us," he said. "Crew quarters and t'washroom are between the galley and his lordship's gaff."

Katy peered along the corridor towards the cabin that Derby had taken at the front of the boat and saw, built either side of the narrow space, eight narrow bunks stacked two by two. There was a curtain that could be drawn across each, but that was all the room and privacy the crew of the *Alerte* could expect.

"Sure you still want to come aboard for the journey?" Percy grinned, seeing her expression.

Katy nodded firmly. "If I can persuade the captain he needs me."

There came sounds from overhead, the heavy tread of boots and the muffled murmur of strong voices.

"I've a hunch that's him now," Percy said. "Come on."

Katy's stomach churned nervously as she followed Percy back up the stairs. The voices grew louder, and one – the loudest – did not sound at all happy. On deck, two men were standing at the top of the gangplank. One was clearly a sailor – he looked close to Percy's age and was dressed similarly, in a thick blue wool sweater and sturdy trousers. The second also looked as if he was used to life aboard ship; a mountain of a man with wiry red hair and a matching beard protruding from a prominent square chin. His face, shadowed by the large brown leather hat he wore, bore a menacing scowl that he turned towards them as Katy and Percy approached.

"Who the devil's this?" the man demanded as his gaze fell on Katy.

"William Chandler, Captain," Percy supplied. "He's looking to join the crew. He's been helping load the gear while I was waiting for Martim to return."

"All busy," said the second man, who was obviously

Martim. Katy thought his accent might be Spanish. "No workers to be had."

Percy grinned at the captain, who was still stony faced. "You see, Captain? Providence, it was, that brought us Chandler."

Roberts eyed Katy. "Really? Because to my eye the lad's young enough to need a milk ration instead of rum."

"Oh, aye, Captain," Katy said, knowing this was her chance to impress and gearing up to launch into her rehearsed speech. "I can trim a mainsail single-handed, I can splice—"

"Can you, indeed?" Roberts said, raising his eyebrows. "Well, then, it's your lucky day, for I was just discussing our rigging with Martim." He flicked a glance at Percy. "Derby's decided he wants a racing spinnaker," he said. "Darned pointless if you ask me – which he didn't." His mouth drew into a tight line of dissatisfaction. "So, Chandler, here's your chance to impress me. Martim's got the spinnaker there, see? Off you go."

Katy felt a little faint as she looked at the mass of silk folded neatly in the sailor's arms. She knew what a racing spinnaker was – a particularly thin sail that could be rigged in place of the standard mainsail. She'd heard her grandfather describe them before. A spinnaker was usually used on a racing yacht to increase the speed of the boat.

"Well?" Roberts said. "What are you waiting for, boy? Let's see your mettle!"

Katy hurried to take the sail from Martim. She suddenly wished Grandpa Ned was there to help her, but she knew what he'd say even if he were: *Head up, girl. You can do it. Get it done.*

Katy took a deep breath. She *could* do this. She knew how, even if she'd never actually done it before. And if she could show Captain Roberts...

The three men followed Katy to the mast, watching her every move. Katy pulled the ropes (which aboard a ship are called the 'lines') towards her, and checked that they were free of tangles. Then she got to work. In a matter of seconds she had taken down the standing sail. She unfurled the spinnaker, which fluttered in the wind, and in less than three minutes the flimsy form had been raised against the *Alerte*'s mast.

"Good job, Chandler," Percy said quietly. Martim nodded his agreement with a smile.

Katy could hardly bear to look at Captain Roberts in case his face told a different story. In any case, before he could say a thing there came a commotion behind them, a storm of feet thundering on the gangplank. They all turned to see a stout man in a stiff black suit leading a group of men across the *Alerte*'s deck.

Sir Thomas Derby himself.

Katy's heart did a backflip in her chest. She had a sudden panic that he would recognize her – after all, it was barely a week since he'd strode into Hunter House – but it was soon clear that Katy need not have worried. Derby didn't even cast her a glance.

"Aha, the spinnaker is up, I see!" he bellowed across the deck. "Mark my words, this will have us to Bahia in no time! Now, Roberts, we have a few additions to our supplies to bring aboard. See that your men are careful with them, what?"

He strode to the doghouse without waiting for Captain Roberts to answer. His 'gentlemen' followed like an obedient pack of hounds. There were three of them besides Derby himself and Katy would have liked more time to gather a first impression of each. She knew from Percy that their names were Mr Barnaby Levins, Mr Feargus Sholto and Mr Theodore Pickering, but that was all. There was no time to even look them over, though, because Roberts was issuing an order that seemed to include her.

"Jump to it, you three. Bring that new lot of kit up from the dock," he growled. "Derby looks like to sink us with his trinkets, but better that than listening to his bellyaching should we leave anything behind."

Then he strode away, leaving Percy to nudge Katy in the ribs.

"Well, lad," said the first mate, with another grin. "Looks as if you've got yourself a job."

Katy had no time to reflect on her good luck. There was too much to do.

Chapter Fourteen

For the rest of the day and late into the night, the crew moved what Derby and his men had brought with them. Every time they prised open yet another crate or box, Katy expected to see expedition equipment, but instead it was always something else, usually more food and drink. Stacks of sealed silver tins packed with preserved meat and vegetables vied for precious space with just as many bottles of red wine and whisky.

"Well," Danny the cook said in his broad Yorkshire accent, waggling his eyebrows at Katy. "At least if they drink all this lot, our passengers will be no trouble at all! Let's hope they're the share-and-share-alike sort, lad."

But Katy had no interest in the stores. Here she was aboard a ship with one of the world's most renowned naturalists, about to embark for South America! She'd been expecting to see Derby's scientific kit. Where were his specimen cases? Where were his sheets of paper and his watercolours, his research books and preserving materials, his maps and preparatory research? She supposed they must already be stowed inside his private cabin at the front of the *Alerte* and was disappointed. She had been hoping to pick up some tips that would help her in her own quest. What she did find was a crate of shotguns; such large, unwieldy contraptions that Katy couldn't understand why anyone would bring them on a scientific expedition.

"It's the gentry, innit," Percy sniffed, when Katy pointed them out. "Can't go anywhere without bringing a souvenir of the wildlife home with 'em to stuff and put on the wall. Else their friends might think they'd gone down the Thames on a jolly, like."

"But this is a scientific expedition, not a hunting trip," Katy said. "That can't be what they're for."

Percy laughed. "Oh, Chandler. You've got a lot to learn and no mistake."

She was also surprised to find that Sir Thomas Derby was not the only naturalist on the trip. One of the last expedition members to arrive was Doctor John Whitaker, a name Katy knew from some of her father's journals, for he had written several papers on the insects of the Canary Islands. An older gentleman with neatly cropped white hair, Doctor Whitaker arrived on board in a cream linen suit, a matching waistcoat, plenty of his own collecting equipment – and not a single gun.

Katy was puzzled by Doctor Whitaker's arrival, because why would Derby bring another naturalist on the expedition with him? She knew from her father he usually liked to be the only one in an exploring party, so that he could be sure of taking credit for any finds himself. Katy supposed it was because Whitaker had been able to provide the 'funds' that Derby had requested. Whatever the reason, Katy assumed the doctor must be a friend of Derby's, and anyone who was a friend of a man like that must be unpleasant himself.

Whitaker kept out of the way of the crew as they bustled about their tasks, getting the ship ready to sail. Sadly, the same could not be said of Lucas Mazarin, Sir Thomas's private secretary. He was a small, pale man with dark hair and sly eyes. Katy disliked the way he trailed around after Derby whenever his employer was there and kept a close eye on everything on his behalf when he wasn't.

"Sir Thomas wouldn't like that," Katy had already heard him remark to Percy, Martim and even the captain about all sorts of things that he clearly knew nothing about. "You must do it again, and this time do take *care* in your work." He said this as if none of them could be trusted.

Katy very much doubted that Mazarin had any idea of how to do anything aboard a boat preparing for a sea voyage, but that didn't stop him from behaving as if he knew better than any of them. She resolved to avoid him if she could. And hopefully Mazarin wouldn't even notice her – after all, she was only William Chandler, cabin boy, and therefore the lowest of the low aboard the good ship *Alerte*.

By the time Percy finally told Katy to go to bed that night, it was already well past midnight and she was exhausted.

She climbed into her bunk and lay down on the lumpy mattress with a grateful sigh and was just drifting off when she heard voices. Two people, discussing something loudly enough to keep her awake. Katy peeked around the edge of her curtain and realized that the only other curtain not fully closed was Mazarin's, and that he was not in his bunk. Moreover, the door to Derby's cabin was slightly open, the yellow flickering of an oil lamp casting light out into the corridor. Katy shut her curtain again with an annoyed huff. If either of those two had worked as hard as she had all day, they wouldn't be carrying on their natter, that was for sure!

Katy tried to sleep, but the two men's voices continued to drift into her bunk.

"… must be vigilant!" she heard Derby say suddenly. "… spies everywhere … rivals … secrecy is vital … if our true mission were known…"

Katy's eyes snapped open in the darkness of her bunk. What was Derby talking about? What 'true mission'? He was on his way to Brazil to find a meteorite, wasn't he? She strained to hear Mazarin's quieter reply.

"Fear not, Sir Thomas," his secretary said. "I will do everything in my power to ensure it remains our secret."

"You'd better," Derby harrumphed. "For if not, I shall know who to blame."

There were a few more hushed words, which Katy couldn't make out. Then Mazarin slid open the door of Derby's cabin. Katy leaned back as far into the shadows of her bunk as she could go, afraid that he would see her. Mazarin slunk quietly along the corridor to his own bunk.

The ship settled into quiet again, silent apart from the occasional creak of the timbers, the sound of the wind whistling across the deck overhead and someone's continuous parping farts. Katy lay back and stared blankly into the darkness. What were Derby and Mazarin up to? What was this expedition really about, if not that spectacular fall of meteorites?

Katy realized that she was just going to have to investigate and find out. After all, that's what Fran Brocklehurst would do, wasn't it?

Chapter Fifteen

The *Alerte* weighed anchor and slipped away from Southampton docks at 11.58 a.m. on 2 August, 1879, bound for the trade winds that would carry her all the way to the city of Salvador in South America. With her went a cabin boy called William Chandler, who until that moment had never once been to sea.

The breeze continued to freshen as they made their way down the estuary towards the Solent. Ahead, the Isle of Wight stood sentry between the *Alerte* and the wide waters of the English Channel. Around Katy rose the noise of Derby giving a grandiose leaving speech to his four expedition members. She kept an ear open but reasoned that people who conducted secret meetings in the middle of the night were unlikely to shout about them in broad daylight. Instead, she checked and re-checked every line and cleat fastening, determined not to get a single thing wrong.

As the *Alerte* rounded the Isle of Wight they could see the Needles ahead. The curious, jagged white rocks dived away from the land in an uncertain line like the undulating neck of an ancient sea monster disappearing beneath the waves. That was the first time Katy paused in her duties, to take in this wonder as the *Alerte* passed. She wished that she could retrieve her field notebook and pencils from her bunk and make a sketch, but alas she was too busy. She noticed, though, that Doctor Whitaker was swiftly sketching the sight into a notebook of his own. Even Captain Roberts seemed to lose his ornery air for a moment. Katy saw him briefly break into a smile as he looked out to sea. Meanwhile, Derby and the rest of the men were noisily toasting their departure with a second bottle of champagne.

Katy let the salt wind wash over her, exhilarated despite the nagging guilt of what would be happening back at Rose Cottage. The letter Danny had sent for her when he'd gone ashore to get their fresh vegetables early that morning would arrive tomorrow and would hopefully set her family's minds at rest. In the meantime, she was at sea, heading towards a great adventure. The only thing to do was make the most of every moment. After all, when she reached Brazil, Katy would have an expedition of her own to arrange, and between now and then she had an investigation to conduct. She had six weeks or thereabouts to work out what Derby was up to.

Not that she had much time to think about anything beyond work. Katy had thought that her lessons with her grandfather would mean she was prepared for life aboard the *Alerte*, but she was wrong. Katy felt as if she knew nothing at all. She was exhausted already, and they hadn't even spent a night under sail! Her muscles burned with the effort of hauling heavy ropes. Her back ached. Not to mention that they'd only had a bowl of porridge for breakfast instead of a large fry-up like the one Grandma Peg would have made at home. Well, the *crew* only had porridge. Derby had demanded a huge plate of eggs, bacon and sausages, which Danny had served alongside the bread he had baked that morning, despite the fact that as far as Katy could see, Derby had done nothing more strenuous than rise late and walk up on deck to complain to Captain Roberts that the noise of the crew's boots on the timbers had disturbed his sleep.

"I don't care, man," Sir Thomas told the captain, when Roberts had explained that there had been much work to get the *Alerte* ready for departure with the tide. "I know they are all rough brutes with no brains between them, but they should at least show courtesy to their betters."

He really is a horrible man, Katy thought. Worse, Derby's attitude quickly rubbed off on his companions. Mazarin was the worst, but even Levins, Pickering and Sholto ordered the crew about as if they were servants. Although, Katy had to admit, that didn't apply to Doctor Whitaker, who had got up while it was still dark and had declined a fry-up in favour of porridge. All he had asked for was a little honey to sweeten his oats.

The wind dropped as night began to draw in, which did not suit Sir Thomas Derby at all. Katy was on deck with Percy, being given a lesson in how the *Alerte*'s little lifeboat should be lowered into the waves should a catastrophe occur, when Derby appeared and strode towards the tiller.

"This won't do at all," he barked at the captain. "Why have we slowed?"

Captain Roberts gave Derby a steady look, as if trying to work out whether or not this was a serious question. "There is no wind, Sir Thomas. Without wind there is nothing to fill the sails. Without wind, we cannot progress."

Derby made a dismissive sound in his throat. "Poppycock!" he exclaimed. "This delay is clearly your fault, Roberts. You are failing in your duty as captain."

Katy drew in a breath, seeing the thunderous look that rolled across the captain's face.

"I assure you, Sir Thomas, that I have no more control over the wind than you do over the sun."

"We are at sea!" Derby insisted. "There is always wind at sea. A good sailor simply stays ahead of it so that his sails are always full, thus this delay is your fault. We must travel speedily, do you understand? We must! Do your job, man, and do it better – I will not accept excuses!"

"What exactly do you expect me to do?" Roberts asked.

"Blow into the sail?"

"Don't be insolent," Derby said angrily. "You have paid hands aboard this vessel. Get them to row!"

Katy heard a muffled snort from beside her as Percy tried to stifle a laugh at Derby's absurd suggestion. Katy bit her lip.

"Did I hear you correctly?" Roberts asked, his voice dangerously quiet. "You want my sailors to *row* you to Brazil?"

"Of course I don't, you imbecile," Derby said. "They can row us into the wind, where the sail will catch its fill."

There was a moment of silence. Percy and Katy crouched side by side in the lifeboat, trying to smother their laughter.

"We cannot do that, Sir Thomas," said the captain with remarkable restraint. "In the first place we have no oars. In the second, even if we did, it would take more than all the hands aboard – yours included – to move this ship. This is not a dingy, man. The wind will rise again before dawn. I will hear no further foolish suggestions."

"You will hear whatever I pay you to hear," Derby snarled nastily. "And do what I tell you to do."

"Only if what I hear and what I am told to do are sensible, Sir Thomas," Captain Roberts said, showing absolutely no sign of being even slightly nervous of his employer. "I am the captain of this ship. Forget that at your peril."

Percy and Katy were no longer having to stifle their laughter. There was something dangerous in the air now.

Katy could see the two men squaring up against each other like two dogs with their hackles up, ready for a fight.

"We'll see, Roberts," Derby said. "I'm a powerful man. It wouldn't take much for me to make sure this is the last ship you ever command. Be *very* careful."

There were no more words, just a moment of silence. Then Derby strode away.

Chapter Sixteen

Captain Roberts, of course, was right. The wind did pick up again overnight, and by the time Katy was hurriedly eating her porridge the next morning, the *Alerte* was once again racing over the waves. Katy had slept better, so tired that she had fallen asleep quickly after crawling into her bunk. She had tried to stay awake, just in case Derby and Mazarin decided to have another meeting. It was no good, though – she slept like a log, and didn't wake until Percy shook her shoulder, so early that it was still dark and he had to hold an oil lamp up to his face before she knew who had woken her.

"Up you get, lad," the first mate whispered. "There's work to be done."

"You've been to Brazil before, haven't you?" she asked Percy later, as they stood together at the tiller. They were watching as the sun finally began to rise above the horizon, pushing ahead of it a fine bright blush of pink and gold that lit the drifting clouds from below. The last stars were fading into the colours of a new day.

The first mate laughed. "You could say that, lad, yes. I know Salvador like the back of my hand."

"Tell me what it's like."

"Hot. I know this market stall that sells the most amazing *acarajé*. I'll take you there. It's food like you've never tasted before."

"What about the landscape?" Katy pressed. "Outside the city, around it? The rainforest, for example – is it really as dense as they say?"

Percy gave her a strange look. "I've never been further than the coastal cities. I'm a sailor, William. Why would I?"

Katy shrugged. "I thought you might have explored a little, that's all."

"I explore the oceans, lad, not the land. Who has time for that when there's always cargo to be loaded or unloaded, always a ship to be kept in shape?"

This gave Katy something new to think about. She'd assumed that when the *Alerte* reached Salvador she'd be free to do as she pleased for as long as it was docked. What if that wasn't the case? She needed her position on the *Alerte* to get back home again, but if she was going to be kept busy aboard the ship while Derby's expedition went ahead…

"Anyway," Percy said, oblivious to her sudden worry. "If you want to know about Brazil, Martim's the one you need to talk to."

Katy looked up, surprised. "Martim?"

"Aye," Percy said. "He's been at sea about as long as I have, but Brazil is his home country."

"Then he speaks Portuguese!" Katy exclaimed.

"That he does," Percy agreed.

"Do you think he'd teach me a little?"

"I don't see why not. I also don't see why you're so eager to learn all this on top of all the work you already have to do," Percy said, eyeing Katy shrewdly.

Katy looked out over the glinting waves, worried she'd given a little too much away. She had an idea Percy was already suspicious that she wasn't quite what she'd said she was, and Katy didn't want her true reason for being aboard the *Alerte* to get back to Derby. Perhaps if she confessed the truth about one thing, the first mate would forget to wonder about all the rest.

"Percy," she said. "If I tell you a secret, will you promise not to be angry?"

Percy hitched an eyebrow, but his blue eyes still held a smile. "Either way, lad, you'll have to tell me now."

Katy sighed. "The truth is, this is my first voyage," she said. "I'm sorry I lied, but I need this job and haven't I been a good hand so far?"

Percy laughed. "William Chandler," he said. "Did you

really think I didn't already know you're as green as a new corn shoot?"

Katy blinked. "But … you got me this job in the first place!"

"No, William, I didn't," Percy said. "You did that yourself. It's obvious you're a hard worker. You carried just as much of Derby's luggage as I did, and you didn't complain once. You trimmed the spinnaker too and sure, we can all see you're green, but you know what you're about." He clapped a hand on Katy's shoulder. "Keep doing what you're doing, lad, and you'll be right."

"Oh," Katy said, relieved. "Well, now you know why I want to learn about Brazil. It's the first place I've ever been," she pointed out. "I want to know *everything* about it!"

Percy laughed again. "Aye, well, maybe I was the same on my first voyage, though it was so long ago I can barely remember." He raised his voice to call across the deck. "Martim! Chandler has something he wants to ask you."

Martim came directly and smiled as he heard Katy's request.

"We begin straight away," he said, pointing to the waves. "The sea, we call *mar*. Waves are *ondas*. For ship, we would say *navio*."

Katy looked up into the sky, seeing the last hint of a star still lingering in the blooming light of morning. Katy pointed to it. "What's 'star' in Portuguese?"

"*Estrela*," Martim told her.

"*Estrela*," Katy repeated, feeling the strange filigree shape of the word on her tongue. "That's a beautiful word."

"So's *breakfast*," opined Percy. "I wonder if Danny's ready with ours? I'm so hungry I could eat a whale! I want something before that gannet Derby wakes and scoffs the lot."

Katy saw movement overhead – the last of the Perseids falling through dawn.

"What about *shooting* star?" she asked Martim. "What's that in Portuguese? *Estrela*…"

"*Estrela cadente*," Martim told her, looking up too.

"*Estrela cadente*," Katy repeated, and thought that might just be the most perfect thing she'd ever heard.

Chapter Seventeen

For the next few days, Katy barely had time to draw breath. Between the ship's daily tasks and learning a new language, she was kept fully occupied. Martim called out a new word in Portuguese every time they passed each other. She repeated them to herself as she scrubbed the deck and polished the grab rail. Whenever she had a moment to herself she scribbled them down in her notebook to make sure they were firmly fixed in her mind.

"Isn't your head aching with all those new words?" Percy teased. "You'll be dreaming in Portuguese soon enough!"

"I like to learn," was all Katy said, in answer to Percy's question. "It's good to be busy, always, I think."

Percy snorted another laugh. "Oh, aye, because there's a chance that we three might stand idle for a minute aboard this ship – I *don't* think!"

"What's this?" asked a strong voice. "Have none of you work to do?"

Captain Roberts strode across the deck, his customary scowl as dark as the gathering night. Since his argument with Derby about the speed of the voyage, the two men had been at odds. It made for an uncomfortable atmosphere given the tiny confines of the *Alerte*.

"Derby doesn't employ you to stand around gossiping," the captain warned. "If he saw you there'd be hell to pay, and I've already had enough of his whinging. We're still not moving fast enough for his liking, he tells me, although I'd like to see him find a ship that could do better. Percy, Martim, get below and get on."

"A-and me, Captain?" Katy asked. "What are your orders for me?"

"Stay at the tiller, boy. I've to go below and check the charts. I've a hunch the weather's coming about, and not for the good."

Katy looked at Percy, then back at Captain Roberts. "You ... want me to man the tiller, Captain?" The tiller was the lever that controlled the rudder and therefore where the boat moved. Whoever stood at it was responsible for where the Alerte went. It would be the first time that Katy had taken control of the ship alone. She could hardly believe it!

Roberts narrowed his eyes at her. "Don't make me regret it, Chandler."

"No, sir. I won't." Over the past hour, as the sun had set,

the wind had dropped again so that they were barely moving at all. The waves were calm. Katy knew that Roberts was only entrusting her with this task because there was little chance of the *Alerte* needing to change course in the next little while.

"Steady as she goes, Chandler," Roberts said.

"Aye, Captain."

Roberts nodded and then turned and strode away again, the two mates following. Katy watched them all disappear below decks and then set her attention on her task, her eyes fixed on the horizon.

Above her, the night had taken the sky with the absolute darkness of a cloudless evening. The stars had appeared in fits and starts: a pinprick here, a cluster there, as if someone had slowly lit a festival of candles and set them to burn in the clear air. The ship rocked gently beneath Katy's feet, the salt wind brushing against her face.

Katy felt as if the *Alerte* could be the last ship on Earth, afloat on waters that had risen to cover every landmass. She looked up and the sky was full of falling stars, the Perseids once again performing their fabulous cascade, a rain of fleeting ice-fire above her head. It made her think of that last night at home, when she'd lain on the tiles of Rose Cottage beside her mother, and Katy had to blink around the threat of tears. She wished Mary Willacott were with her now. She could do with a hug and she would love for her mother to see how beautiful the stars above the *Alerte* truly were. Just at that moment, she felt very lonely indeed, and very, very far from home.

"*Estrella cadente*," she said aloud. "*Estrella cadente* over the *ondas*."

Footsteps echoed suddenly on the dark deck behind her and Katy jumped as a figure loomed at her through the darkness. She went to light the oil lamp that hung on the mizzen.

"No, no – please don't," said a voice. "It will pollute the night and this is by far the best view I have ever had of the Perseids."

Katy recognized the voice as belonging to Doctor Whitaker. He came closer, until she could just make out his face.

"I think they will reach their peak tonight, sir, or perhaps tomorrow," she said politely.

He looked up at the night sky. "You must have seen some spectacular displays in your time, Chandler."

Katy blinked, astonished. The Doctor knew her name? She'd thought all of the crew were entirely anonymous as far as Derby's men were concerned.

"Yes, sir," Katy said truthfully. She didn't think she needed to tell him that this was her first voyage.

"What was that language you were speaking?" he asked.

"A little Portuguese, sir. Martim, the second mate, is teaching me on our way to Brazil. I thought it best to be prepared before our arrival."

"An admirable endeavour," the doctor said. "I have

been trying to do something similar myself, although with the landscape rather than the language. My wife, God rest her dearly departed soul, would have scolded me for bringing more books than changes of shirts to wear."

"I don't think it is possible to have too many books, sir," Katy said. "On the other hand, I have only two shirts and I would gladly give one away for a new book."

Whitaker laughed, a warm and genuine sound that reminded Katy of Grandpa Ned. "Well, then, I think you and I share a sensibility, Chandler. How about we strike a deal? You can keep both your shirts and you can also take custody of some of my books. I was not expecting my bunk to be quite as small as it is. I am rather overcrowded."

Katy grinned. "I will gladly look after as many as you wish, Doctor."

Whitaker looked at Katy with curiosity. "Perhaps I am doing cabin boys a disservice, Chandler, but you seem an unusual sort to me. I never thought of them as being great readers and scholars before now."

Katy bit her lip. Had she given the doctor a clue as to who she really was, without even realizing it? Was he being nice to her because he suspected something? All of this pretending to be someone else was hard work.

"I was raised to always be curious, sir, that's all," she said, tight-lipped and wishing he would go away.

"Well," said the doctor, sounding a little awkward, as if he had detected her sudden coldness. "I am glad to hear it. And now I will leave you to your work. Goodnight, Chandler."

"Goodnight, Doctor," Katy said.

When she finally got to her bunk in the early hours, Katy found something unfamiliar lying upon the gloom of her blanket. It was a book all about the great rainforests of Brazil, which could only have come from the doctor himself.

Chapter Eighteen

Katy's investigations into the curious conversation she had overheard between Lucas Mazarin and Sir Thomas Derby had failed to progress. She could find no way to sneak into Derby's cabin, where she knew the answers must lie. She tried to keep her ears open in case of more muttered secrets but heard nothing. As the days passed, Katy began to wonder if she had imagined the clandestine meeting.

Instead, every rare spare moment was spent learning Portuguese with Martim or with her nose in the books that Doctor Whitaker gave her. More volumes continued to appear without comment. Katy tried to read a few paragraphs each night before she went to sleep and each morning before she got up, despite how very tired she was. She was extremely grateful to the doctor. It made her think that he couldn't possibly be the bad person she had first assumed because of his association with Derby.

Whitaker hadn't come to join her at the tiller again after that first night, even though it became Captain Roberts' custom to give Katy the last anchor watch before midnight. She loved the new friends she had found in Percy and Martim, but she wished she could talk to the doctor about what he was taking down in his field notebook and compare his observations with her own. She saw him sketching the birds that followed the boat as they pulled up their catches of fish, and indeed the fish themselves once they were landed on deck, flapping and sparkle-scaled. She had once managed to look over his shoulder as she passed him at work and saw that he was drawing the clouds overhead, on a page that was filled with other similar sketches, each with a different date beneath them. Doctor Whitaker seemed to be interested in everything.

Derby, on the other hand, had done nothing of the sort whatsoever. He spent his days complaining about everything, from the speed at which they were travelling to Danny's cooking.

"Says it's only fit for the pigs," Danny grumbled mutinously to Katy, Martim and Percy. "Well, say I, that is only fitting, since pigs is who I is feeding on this tiresome voyage of ours."

"You didn't say that!" Katy said, shocked. "Did you? To *Derby*?"

Percy gave a guffawing laugh and nudged Katy in the shoulder. "Of course he didn't!"

"No," Danny admitted. "I did not. Thought it, though. Right *at* him, so to speak."

Percy snorted. "Oh, aye," he said. "Reckon we've all done that."

"He's a bad sort, though, so he is," Danny said darkly. "Bad tidings travel with 'im."

"Oh?" Katy said, pricking up her ears. "What makes you say that?"

"Too much rum," said Percy, this time nudging Martim instead of Katy. The two hands chuckled to each other.

"It ain't that," Danny said. "There's trouble brewing. Can't ye feel it? And its name is Sir Thomas Stuffed-Shirt Derby."

"It is the weather," Martim said. "Like the captain said. It is changing. The air, it feels heavy. The wind will turn."

"Not too soon, neither," said Percy. "I reckon Derby's about ready to go over the side and start swimming to Brazil."

There was a brief silence as they all looked at each other and then, as one, they burst out laughing, because it was so obvious that they were all thinking the same thing: *That would suit us all just fine!*

On the *Alerte* sailed, ploughing through the notoriously boisterous waters of the Bay of Biscay. Katy got used to the long days and the heavy labour, even though working the ship's ropes left her hands sore and chapped in the salt air. Percy and Martim both looked at her poor burnt palms and laughed to each other.

"Oh, aye," Percy said, slapping Katy so hard on the back that she almost dropped her spoon in her bowl of porridge. "Don't you worry about that, boy. A few more weeks at sea and you'll have calluses on your calluses, just like us seasoned sea dogs."

Doctor Whitaker was far more sympathetic. Once he saw Katy's hands he insisted that she apply iodine and then camomile balm every night before going to sleep. He went to the trouble of bringing the antiseptic and the lotion to her at the tiller.

"Ignore them," the doctor advised, as Katy muttered she was worried that Percy and Martim would think her soft for taking his treatments. "Only a fool would risk infection unnecessarily, Chandler. No self-respecting naturalist would endanger an expedition for the sake of keeping up appearances, eh?"

Katy's heart gave a stuttering jump. "I'm not a naturalist, though, Doctor."

He gave her a kind smile. "Of course you are, my boy. Why else would you be racing through my books as fast as I can give them to you? And every time I get my notebook out I know you'll be hovering somewhere nearby. I was thinking – perhaps you would like a notebook and pencil of your own? I have spares with me."

Katy chewed on her lip. She was heartily tired of lying and didn't want to tell yet another. "I have a notebook," she said quietly. "And a tin of watercolours. I just don't have time to use them."

"Is that so? Well," said the doctor, apparently impressed to hear this. "Really, you are by far the most observant and interested young man I've come across in a long while, Chandler. It makes me wonder quite why you're a cabin boy at all, and not at school somewhere."

Katy's heart thundered and she kicked herself. She'd allowed her liking for Doctor Whitaker lower her guard. She couldn't let Derby discover her subterfuge – goodness only knew what might happen if he discovered there was a *girl* on board. Katy knew it would be nothing good.

"I've been wondering something similar about you too, Doctor," she said boldly, hoping to put him on a different course.

"Oh?" the doctor asked, surprised. "Whatever do you mean?"

"I mean, sir," Katy said. "That now that I know you a little better, I don't understand why you are friends with a man like Sir Thomas Derby."

Whitaker stared at her and for a moment Katy thought she had made a terrible mistake – that he would report her insolence straight to Derby himself and make trouble for her where she could not afford it. Then he gave a loud laugh that held a sharp edge of bitterness.

"Sir Thomas Derby is no friend of mine, Chandler," he said. "When I signed up for this journey I thought that he must be a decent sort, given his reputation, but it did not take long to work out that he has no friends, only people he can use to his own ends. No, it was not his friendship that brought me on this voyage; it was my money. I have wanted to visit the tropics for as long as I can remember and have saved my funds accordingly since my wife died. When I saw the advertisement for this expedition I realized that I could finally fulfil my wish and get the chance to work alongside such a renowned naturalist." He sighed. "Even as a child I wanted to pursue the natural sciences, but my father had already chosen my course for me, and so it was that I became a doctor. It is only since my retirement that I have been able to pursue my hobby to my heart's content. I thought this journey would be the answer to all my childhood dreams. But alas, since our departure, I have discovered that though it might yet be so, I can learn nothing from Sir Thomas Derby. He is really not what I thought a true naturalist would be."

Katy snorted a laugh. "You can say that again. It's nothing new, either."

She immediately regretted her outburst when Whitaker looked at her in surprise. "You have previous knowledge of Sir Thomas, then?"

"Um – no," Katy said, quickly, trying to cover her slip. "Just what I've read about him in the papers. When I saw the article about the meteorites and then the advertisement for his expedition…" She trailed off, realizing she was only making things worse.

Whitaker regarded her with suspicion. "When did you join the crew of the *Alerte*, William?"

Katy felt her cheeks burning red and cursed herself. "Only the day before we left, Doctor."

Whitaker was silent for another moment. Katy's heart pounded in her chest.

Then the doctor gave a sudden smile and patted Katy on the shoulder. "Worry not, Chandler," he said. "You are not the only boy in the history of the world to run away to sea. Your secret is safe with me. Besides, I'm quite sure you will learn more on this journey than in sitting before a blackboard at whatever educational establishment you've escaped from."

Katy was so relieved that she gasped. "Oh, thank you, Doctor."

Whitaker chuckled. "No matter, my boy," he said. "We true naturalists have to stick together."

"And we can't rely on Sir Thomas for that," Katy added.

The doctor's face grew serious. "No, that we can't. Between you and me, Chandler, I am not sure we can rely on that man at all."

Chapter Nineteen

Katy's conversation with Doctor Whitaker about Derby had made her think again about the muttered words she had heard pass between Sir Thomas and Mazarin. *The true mission.* If Derby wasn't really travelling to Brazil to find the meteorite, then why was he going? What could possibly be so secret that he had to cover it with an expedition for the museum? Surely if Derby wanted to go to Brazil he could just … go? In fact, surely he must have been there before? But perhaps not. After all, as Mary Willacott had pointed out, he usually liked to stay at home and send others out for him instead.

"Percy," she said, glancing around to make sure they were alone. They were polishing the *Alerte*'s grab rail beneath the glaring morning sun. "What do you know about Derby?"

Percy gave a snort. "Other than that the man's a pig, you mean?"

"Shh," Katy hissed.

"Ach, it's all right lad," said the first mate. "Did you not hear the lot of them carousing last night? He's sleeping it off. I wager he'll be there till dinner." Percy sighed. "Anyway, to answer your question, how on God's blue waters would the likes of me know anything about a fancy man like that? The captain's who you should ask. Why do you want to know, anyway?"

Katy shrugged. "Just passing the time."

"Oh, aye?" Percy gave her a sharp look. "I've a hunch you never do anything just to *pass the time*, William Chandler. A right busy bee, you are."

Katy said nothing to that, not wanting to make Percy more suspicious. Later, though, as she met Captain Roberts for her night-time watch, she remembered what he'd said.

There was a stiff breeze blowing from the north, buffeting against the sails. The captain let her take the tiller as usual, but tonight he didn't leave her side. Katy was glad, because this was by far the strongest wind under which she'd had to manage the *Alerte*.

"Steady, Chandler," Roberts said calmly, watching her movements. "That's right. The weather's changing tonight, lad. We're in for a rough ride over this next while, but you can handle it, at least for now. I'll come back up myself when I think it necessary."

"Thank you, Captain," Katy said, grateful for his trust in her abilities but also because in turn she trusted him to know exactly the best thing to do in any circumstance. He was an excellent captain, she could tell. She thought that he and Grandpa Ned would get on well. "Captain Roberts," she said, before he could leave. "Can I ask you something?"

He raised his eyebrows at her. "Aye, lad. Ask away but be quick about it."

"It's about…" Katy said, glancing towards the doghouse to make sure that they had not been joined by anyone else, "Sir Thomas."

Captain Roberts' face showed a scowl that transformed him back into the fearsome personage it was easy to assume him to be. "What about him?"

"I just wondered…" Katy said, trying to sound as if she didn't really care one way or the other, although she cared very much indeed, "whether he'd ever been to Brazil before."

Roberts made a sound in his throat. "Oh, he and his like have been to Brazil before, lad, that's for certain, not that it did the country any good."

Katy frowned. "What do you mean?"

"Slavery and rubber, boy. That's how his family made their money back in the day, before the evils of slavery were made illegal. They had a big rubber plantation up near Manaus, a long way from where we're going. The rubber trade in Brazil's fizzling out, though, so I hear. Too much competition from new plantations elsewhere." Roberts eyed her. "But why would a cabin boy need to know about that sort of thing?"

Katy shrugged, keeping her eyes on the dark horizon. "Just interested."

"Aye, well, you shouldn't be," said the captain. His eyes were serious. "You stay away from Sir Thomas Derby, Chandler, do you hear me? He's no good for the likes of us."

Katy blinked, and then nodded. "Aye, Captain."

"Good. Eyes up, Chandler."

"Aye, sir."

Katy watched as he crossed the deck and disappeared below. *Slavery and rubber.* The first word made her shudder just to think of it – that anyone could believe it was right to *own* another person – to force them into the horrors of such servitude – was too awful to think about without feeling sick.

"Evening, William."

The voice belonged to Doctor Whitaker, who appeared out of the darkness to stand beside her.

"Evening Doctor." Katy smiled at him. "I don't think there'll be much to see of the stars tonight, sir. The clouds have gathered."

The doctor looked up. "Ah well, we've had a good display so far, so we mustn't complain, eh?" He shivered a little as a blast of stiff wind gusted across the deck. "The barometer must have dropped, I think?"

Katy felt the tug on the tiller as the wind filled the sail and wrenched at the *Alerte*'s course. "Aye, sir. The captain says we're in for a storm." She heard – and then felt – the first peal of icy rain scatter across the deck timbers. "I'd go below if I were you, Doctor."

Whitaker made a face. "I'd rather be up here for as long as possible. Derby seems set on a repeat of the racket he made last night and I'm not one for such carousing. Do you mind, Chandler?"

Katy was surprised, again, that Doctor Whitaker would even ask. "Of course not, sir. But you must try not to get too cold and wet."

The wind was rising briskly – soon Katy found herself having to fight to hold the tiller steady. The sail was full, the ship lurching over the waves like a drunk staggering over cobbles.

"The captain will be up soon," Katy said nervously. "Or one of the mates."

When they heard footsteps, though, it wasn't Roberts. It was Derby himself, being followed at heel as always by Lucas Mazarin, who bobbed across the deck carrying a lit oil lamp.

Chapter Twenty

"Why is it so blasted dark up here, Whitaker, and where is the crew?" Derby demanded. He spied Katy at the mizzen. "Ah, *finally*," he said. "You, go down to the hold and fetch me more bottles of the claret. The cook has failed to stock the galley with enough, the fool, and I can't be expected to search for it. Be quick about it."

"I…" Katy was taken aback. "I can't, Sir Thomas."

Derby's glower looked devilish in the yellow lamplight. "What do you mean, you can't? I've given you an order, carry it out."

"Be sensible, Derby," said Whitaker. "The boy cannot leave the tiller."

"Pish," Derby declared. "Do as you are bid, boy. I will take the tiller."

"I… I have my orders, sir," Katy said. "From the captain."

"The captain is not the chief of this expedition," Derby barked. "You will carry out my orders this very minute, or you will be put off the ship, do you understand?"

"Derby—" Whitaker protested.

"Do it," Derby commanded.

Katy hesitated, but what could she do? "Only small corrections," she said to Derby, still unwilling to leave the tiller.

"Oh, for goodness' sake," Sir Thomas said, elbowing Katy away from the mizzen. "Get on with it."

Katy ran to the doghouse and dashed below decks, feeling the *Alerte* lurch as she went.

"Chandler!" Captain Roberts bellowed from the door of the chart room, as she reached the bottom of the steps. "What's this? Did you abandon your post?"

"Sorry, Captain, but Sir Thomas – he gave me an order, and—"

Roberts strode towards her. "I give your orders, not Derby."

Katy was desperate. "I know, Captain. I tried to refuse, but he threatened to put me off the ship, and—"

Roberts gave a snarl and stormed up the stairs. Katy hurried to find Danny, who was with Martim and Percy in the hold, trying to lash down the crates of supplies more firmly in preparation for the bad weather ahead.

"Quick," she said. "I need more of Derby's wine. He wants it up on deck."

"*More* wine?" Danny exclaimed.

Martim helped her find four bottles of claret and then followed her back up on deck. They could hear the shouting before they even cleared the doghouse. Roberts and Derby were going at it hammer and tongs. Roberts had taken the tiller from Derby, who stood close by, obviously angry.

"How dare you challenge my authority?" Derby was shouting.

"It does not include the running of this ship while we are under way," Roberts told him. "This was agreed upon, Derby, and you know it."

"It will include whatever I decide, whenever I decide it," Derby bellowed.

Roberts was the angriest that Katy had yet seen him, but now he became still in that strange way that the air grows calm in the last moments before a storm breaks. Speaking of storms, the temperature had dropped quickly, the wind rising into sharp gusts that cut across the deck and sliced through Katy's clothes. The boat was rocking beneath her feet.

Captain Roberts took his hands off the tiller and held them palm up to Derby, as if in surrender. His face was as blank as a clean sheet of paper.

"All right, Derby," he said. "By all means, take the tiller. My crew and I will retire and leave you to manage the *Alerte* overnight. Take us where you will."

He strode back across the deck towards Katy and Martim.

"Leave those," the captain ordered, indicating the wine. "We are not needed."

"Roberts!" Derby shouted from the mizzen. "Where are you going?"

"To catch up on my sleep," Roberts shouted back, disappearing below decks without another word.

Katy and Martim looked at each other. Martim gave a small shrug and set down the bottles he carried. Katy followed suit.

"Wait," said Mazarin. "Pour the wine, damn you!"

Katy hesitated, but Martim caught the sleeve of her shirt and gave her a brief, warning look. Together they followed the captain.

"Fine!" Derby's voice bellowed after them. "We have no need of the likes of you!"

Roberts was waiting for them at the bottom of the stairs. Percy and Danny both stood beside him, their faces unhappy and anxious.

"Get to your bunks, all of you," Roberts said, his voice quiet but firm. "Stay alert. I have a hunch they'll be calling us for help sooner rather than later, but you must not do a thing until I give you the order, is that understood?"

Katy's stomach churned. To her surprise the captain reached out one bear-paw of a hand and patted her on the shoulder.

"Worry not, boy," he said. "No one will lose their positions because of this. Our lives – well, that's another kettle o' fish. But some beasts only respond to brute force, and it seems Derby is one of them. Get to bed, all of you."

They did as they were told, feeling the wind rock the *Alerte* ever more fiercely as they made their way through the ship. Before Katy crawled into her bunk she looked back to see the captain leaning into the tiny chart room. As she watched he straightened up and rubbed a hand over his beard. He glanced heavenward, towards the deck, and then turned and stepped into his cabin, closing the door behind him. Katy heard the definitive click of his lock being turned.

Chapter Twenty-One

The storm grew stronger. Katy lay in her bunk as the ship pitched and rolled. By rights she should not have been able to sleep, but the long day caught up with her. She dozed fitfully, moving with the ship, turning this way and that as distant shouts and thumps from the deck floated to her through the dark of the *Alerte*'s hold. At one point she was sure she heard footsteps run past her little bunk, a voice calling for help, but it wasn't enough to rouse her. She was exhausted.

"William!"

It wasn't until a hand reached in to grab her leg that Katy gasped, opening her eyes into the darkness. For a second, she was utterly confused as to where she was.

"William Chandler!" shouted the urgent voice. "Wake up!"

Katy came fully awake just as a wave hit the *Alerte* with a huge *CRASH*. The force was almost enough to roll her out of her bunk. The shouts on deck became screams. Something heavy rolled across the deck above them, a series of loud, rumbling bangs muffled by the sound of the raging storm.

"William, get up!" Percy yelled again, over the cacophony of noise that filled the hold. "We are going to lose the ship if we do not act! The captain needs us!"

Katy scrambled to the floor. The pitch and roll of the vessel was terrible. Percy went ahead to the stairs, lurching from one side of the narrow corridor to the other as he went. Katy could see torrents of rain lashing the steps that led up to the deck. Getting up them was a nightmare – she kept slipping on the slick, wet wood. The ship lurched from side to side with every new crash of waves against the hull. Rain slashed down upon her with each step, icy cold. It was dark – no light anywhere, just a few sudden white slashes as lightning tore the raging sky overhead.

Percy made it to the top and turned to drag her out. The scene above deck was of utter confusion. More lightning forked and bucked overhead, slicing through a heavy, malevolent sky. Katy was horrified to see that Derby and his men had not taken down the sails. Instead of being safely stowed away, they had been left to the mercy of the storm. The mainsail was straining at the mast, threatening to snap it clean in two.

Derby's men were clinging to anything they could find that was still fixed down. Captain Roberts was at the tiller, his feet planted far apart as he tried to balance on the heaving deck. Wave after wave of icy-cold water crashed over the grab rail. The whole deck was awash.

Neither Percy nor Katy needed orders. Martim was already at the mast. With the sail up the *Alerte* was at the mercy of the storm. It was a wonder she had not capsized already. They had to get it stowed away or they could lose the mast completely. Then they would all be dragged below the waves.

Katy fought her way across the deck with Percy. It was madness to try to lower a sail in a storm, but they had to try. By the time they reached Martim, Katy was already drenched to the skin.

"The sail's stuck," Martim bellowed, his words almost lost to the rage of the wind.

He pointed up the mast. It took a huge flash of lighting for Katy to realize what he was saying. Her heart shrank in fear as she realized that one of the rigging lines had come loose from the cleat that had held it in place. It should have been there for them to use, but instead the wind had lifted the rope and tangled it high above their heads. It was unreachable, and without it there was no way to get the sail down.

"I cannot reach it," Martim shouted again, his eyes desperate.

"Let me try!" Percy yelled back. "Give me a boost!"

Martim and Katy fell to their knees, joining their hands to give the first mate a step to stand on. Another wave crashed against the hull, tipping the *Alerte* at a violent angle. Katy couldn't keep her balance and lurched sideways, crashing to the wet deck. She couldn't find anything to hold on to. The wave caught her, dragging her towards the grab rail. Martim snatched a handful of her shirt and held on. That was all that stopped her from plunging overboard.

The ship crashed down level again, throwing Percy off his feet. The three of them scrambled up as the mast emitted a loud creak, straining against the pressure.

"We have to get it down!" Percy screamed. "We're going to lose the mast!"

"But how?" Martim bellowed back. "Without the line—"

"Find something to stand on!"

Percy began looking around the deck, his movements wild and desperate, but the idea of being able to balance on anything in this storm was ridiculous. Katy grabbed his arm and pulled him to her, yelled right into his ear so that he'd hear over the rage of the weather.

"Knife," she screamed. "Give me your knife!"

Percy snatched his flick knife from his belt and held it out to her. Katy grabbed it and pulled open the blade.

"Help me," she shouted. "I'll climb!"

Percy's drenched face took on a shocked look. "You can't! You'll be thrown off, break your neck – or drown!"

"If I don't, we're all dead!"

"William—"

"What else can we do?" she screamed, as another wave exploded against the *Alerte*. "Help me! Now!"

She shoved the blunt side of the knife between her teeth. She'd need both hands to climb. Percy, his hair plastered flat against his head by the rain, looked at her with wild eyes, but he must have known there was no other option. Martim grabbed her shoulder in a strong grip and nodded at the mast. Then he let her go and knelt on the flooded deck again. This time he put one arm round the mast to hold on as he held out his other hand to Percy. Percy saw what his friend was doing and did the same. The two men clutched at the mast with one arm, and joined their two free hands. It gave Katy a foothold. Something she could step on.

Katy put her weight into the cradle of their hands and launched herself at the mast. She'd climbed trees in Kew before, but never in weather such as this, and they had always provided plenty of gnarled handholds. The mast was smooth and slick with rain. She clung on, the knife heavy between her teeth, the cold of the storm freezing her fingers as she fought to find purchase. She grabbed any tiny crevice she could find and clawed her way skyward into the storm.

She was halfway to the trapped line when she felt a weird sensation, as if the *Alerte* and everyone aboard it, Katy included, had been launched into the air. The ship suddenly swung round, as if the water beneath her had dropped away. Katy glanced into the wild gloom as another lighting flash glinted against a wall of water towering over them. She locked her hands and legs together around the mast and held on for dear life.

Chapter Twenty-Two

The wave crashed down. The *Alerte* groaned. Black water hit Katy square in the face, tearing her breath from her lungs. She almost lost her grip. For a second she thought she *had* lost her grip, that she was already in the ocean, that she had gone overboard and was drowning. Then she gasped in air, forgetting Percy's knife clutched between her lips. It fell but she managed to trap it between her shoulder and the mast before it could be utterly lost. The timber to which she clung creaked and whined – she could feel it bowing and prayed it would not snap. Katy heard the screams of those below her, and still she clung on.

For a moment she was convinced the ship was going over – that they were going to capsize and they'd all drown. But somehow the *Alerte* struggled up, shaking off the worst. The mast swung skywards again with another almighty groan.

Katy ducked her head and managed to take the knife back between her teeth. She could hardly feel her lips, she was so cold. Her hands and arms were numb too. She didn't know how much longer she'd be able to hold on. She could barely see – her eyes were full of stinging saltwater. Katy blinked to clear them and looked up. The trapped line was just a few feet above her. She *had* to keep going. This was their only hope.

When she reached the rope she had to let go with one hand to use the knife, but her fingers were so cold she couldn't get them to grip. She forced the blade between the line and the mast and began to saw back and forth, praying there would be no more waves as bad as the last one. She kept slipping down the mast and having to scramble back up again. Her arms and legs were aching now, burning with the effort. The *Alerte* rocked one way and then the other. Everything was darkness. Katy couldn't even see whether the knife was working. Her fingers were so numb she was terrified that any second now she would drop the blade and it would be lost to the ocean for good.

Another flash of lighting, another staccato dash of vision, and Katy saw that the rope was beginning to fray. Her heart leaped, and she sawed harder, ignoring the pain of her cold fingers, the howl of the wind, the freezing air and waves. Suddenly she felt the rope give, the surprise of it almost throwing her loose. She clung harder still and would have cried with relief if her face hadn't been frozen with cold. The mast was free and the sail could be lowered at last.

Katy almost let go and fell all the way back to the deck, she was in such a hurry to get down again. She felt Percy and Martim's hands grabbing at her once she was in reach, pulling her from the mast. Katy hit the deck and crumpled to her knees, spitting out Percy's knife and coughing up water. She felt as if her lungs might explode. She couldn't open or close her hand, it was frozen in the shape of her sawing at the rope.

Percy and Martim battled against the wind to lower the sail. Once it was low enough Katy moved to help, binding it into its stowed position. The three hands looked at each other, breathing hard, exhausted and soaked. Percy reached out and grabbed Katy to him, squeezing her hard.

"You did it, boy!" he shouted into her frozen ear. "You did it!"

Katy nodded, too exhausted to say anything. She held out Percy's knife but her friend pushed it back towards her.

"You keep it," he shouted over the wind. "As a lucky memento of the day you saved the *Alerte*!"

There was no time to celebrate their small victory. The storm was still upon them. They gathered up Derby's men who were still on deck and helped them get below. Sir Thomas himself was nowhere to be seen and Katy wondered briefly whether he – or any other of his men – had gone overboard into the waves. If they had, there would be nothing any of them could do.

Percy and Martim battened down the hatches as the *Alerte* struggled on against the furious waters.

The storm raged throughout the night, pitch-black waves roiling against the gunwales. Katy was wet through and so very cold. The three hands and the captain helped the *Alerte* as best they could, but she was no more than a leaf blown this way and that in the wind, at every whim of the elements. To Katy it seemed as if the storm would never end, as if this hellish darkness was permanent. The wind would never drop, the waves would never again be anything but mountains pushing up beneath them.

Eventually the wind began to die. The rain lessened. Katy wiped her face free of water for the millionth time and realized that it did not immediately feel wet again. The wind was not quite as vicious. Instead of inky blackness there was a faint light in the sky. Dawn was drawing on, reaching tentative fingers over the horizon, as if feeling to see if the welcome would be a warm one. The pale light spread and swelled, opalescent, into Katy's watery world. The *Alerte* no longer pitched amid towering waves. The sea flattened into a sheet of deep blue velvet, as if it had never been a monster that had tried to swallow them whole.

"Percy!" It was Roberts, shouting from the tiller. The captain hadn't left the tiller for a moment throughout the storm. His clothes were plastered against him, and he had lost his hat, but his face was still as resolute as always. "Take my post!"

As the first mate hurried to carry out his order, Roberts looked to Martim and Katy, "Start getting her shipshape again, lads. I'll be back in a moment."

He strode to the doghouse and unlocked it, shouting something down the stairs before vanishing below. Katy couldn't hear what he'd yelled – there was a swollen ringing in her ears, as if the storm had stolen her hearing.

She and Martim looked around. The deck of the *Alerte* was a terrible mess. Even items that had been lashed down had worked their way loose and were strewn here and there upon the ship's timbers, and that was only if they hadn't been washed clear into the sea. Together, slowly, they began to set her to rights.

Roberts reappeared with Danny behind him, carrying an earthenware jug in one hand and four flagons in the other. He made his way to each of them, first passing out a mug and then filling it with something that steamed as it met the chill, wet air.

"Hot chocolate," Danny said. "Don't let Derby know I've got it or he'll have the lot. Drink. It'll help."

Katy was grateful for the heat. The warmth of the thick, sweet chocolate spread through her as she drank, thawing her from her bones out.

"How went it below decks?" Roberts asked the cook as he drank his own portion.

"Kit's all o'er the place, be a devil to square away," said Danny. "As far as the men go, few scrapes and a knocked head or two, but nowt worse than that. The doctor tended to them all and then made everyone lay as still as they could in their bunks. There's a fair bit of groaning still going on, but let's just say they've nothing left in their stomachs to come up, so we must thank heaven for her small mercies."

"Derby?" the captain asked, the name curt on his tongue.

Danny shrugged. "He's not left his cabin since you came above."

There was the sound of footsteps behind them and the doctor appeared on deck. He looked pale and tired but otherwise composed.

"Doctor Whitaker," the captain greeted him as he came towards them. "I hear you've had scrapes and bruises to see to this night."

The doctor gave a thin smile. "I have, Captain. And now here I am to see whether any of your brave men have need of me." He looked at Katy first. "What about you, young man?"

Katy, still dazed, shook her head but did not speak.

"Well, I'd still like to look each of you over," the doctor said. "You must have had a rough night of it, all of you."

It occurred to Katy that letting the doctor examine her was impossible. Even if she were to remain dressed, she couldn't risk him being able to tell that she was not, in fact, William Chandler, cabin boy.

"Really, sir," she said, passing Danny her empty flagon

129

and edging away a little. "I am fine – no hurts at all. And there is much to do."

"Your first task, Chandler," Roberts said. "Is to change into dry clothes and to sleep. Go below decks and do both."

Katy looked around at the damage. "But Captain—"

"That's an order, Chandler," Roberts said, cutting her off. He glanced at the doctor. "Without him we'd have lost the mast last night. He needs rest. Three hours' sleep, boy, no more. And no less, either."

Katy wanted to protest but found she was so exhausted that her feet were already obeying the captain's order. She stumbled to her bunk, pulled on some dry clothes and was asleep within minutes.

Chapter Twenty-Three

Things were different after the storm. For one thing, Derby rarely left his cabin and when he did he avoided everyone except Mazarin. He even refused to eat with the rest of his party. The *Alerte* ran far more smoothly with only one person issuing orders.

Katy herself had gone up in the estimation of every member of the ship's company through her actions in freeing the mainsail.

"But however did you do it?" one or other of them would ask, over and over.

Katy didn't really know herself and so her answer was always the same. "I just knew what had to be done and did it, that's all."

When she looked up at the mast now, though, she wasn't sure herself how she had managed it. It seemed such a long way to climb with a knife clutched between her teeth in the midst of a raging storm. She wondered what Fran Brocklehurst would say, and could imagine the journalist grinning, tipping her head to one side with a shrug of her shoulder. *Extraordinary women, doing extraordinary things. There are more of us than folk realize. There always have been.* Katy also wondered what the men around her would say if they knew the person who had performed this feat they all found so remarkable was not Mr William Chandler, as they supposed, but Miss Katy Willacott.

She was not quite assured enough of their regard to risk finding out.

On 19 September, almost a full seven weeks after the *Alerte* had departed Southampton, Katy was the first to spot land. It was dawn and she had been given first watch, which meant rising at three to see the sun come up. A fresh easterly had sprung up and they were making good progress after a still night. Katy was scanning the horizon when—

"Land!" she shouted, her excitement overflowing. "Land ho! Land ho!"

Katy heard her shout repeated below decks – Percy calling to the rest of their crewmates, still asleep in their bunks. There immediately came the sound of movement and voices, and a few minutes later everyone, including Captain Roberts and even Sir Thomas, was up on deck.

"It is Fernando de Noronha," said Roberts, standing at Katy's shoulder. "If the wind is in our favour we may sight the coast of Brazil as soon as this evening. If not, then we will certainly see it tomorrow – which means we are but a few days from Salvador itself."

A great cheer went up among the group.

"Splendid!" Derby declared, almost seeming his old self again, as if the events of the storm and his absence after it had been forgotten in an instant. "Then we must make up some of the time that we have lost! Mazarin, we have much to discuss. But first, gentlemen, I think this calls for an early breakfast. Cook? Where are you? Get to work, man, at once!"

Chapter Twenty-Four

The *Alerte* made the port of Salvador in Bahia province, Brazil, as dawn began to break on 22 September, 1879.

With Salvador before them, spirits soared. The city twinkled beneath the pink and orange hues of the rising sun, the walls of the buildings reflecting the changing pastel colours of the sky. Salvador was built against slopes that blended into the rainforest, as if the streets and plazas had grown in the same way as the great trees themselves. From across the water drifted the customary noise of a busy port.

Katy Willacott hauled on the mainsail lines, reefing the great canvas as Captain Roberts called orders for them to dock.

"Gather your essentials, men!" Derby shouted to his assembled gentlemen, and Katy saw that he was clutching something in his hand – it looked like a sealed letter. "I shall send word ahead to the hotel!"

"When will we be allowed to go ashore?" Katy asked Percy as they and Martim dealt with the *Alerte*'s rigging. "It won't be long, will it?"

"If you're desperate to get out there, tell the captain you'll help carry Derby's bags," Percy advised her. "Martim and I can handle things here."

Captain Roberts listened to William Chandler's request with a frown on his face. "You're mighty eager," he observed. "Got a sweetheart down there, have you, Chandler?"

"No, sir," Katy said. "I just want to explore, sir."

The captain's bushy eyebrows shot up his forehead. "Explore, is it? When there's work to do on board?"

"W-well, Captain," Katy stammered. "Th-that is to say…"

Roberts shocked her by breaking out into a wide grin and slapping her on the shoulder. "Ach, get away with you, boy, I'm only teasing. You've worked hard, you deserve to let your hair down. Just don't go getting into trouble. And make sure you're back before we need to prepare for our return. You won't want to be stranded here and I don't want to have to find another cabin boy. Understand?"

"Aye, Captain!" Katy said happily. "Thank you, sir!"

She turned to run across the deck, but the captain's voice stopped her in her tracks.

"Not so fast, Chandler," he said, and she turned back to

see him holding out a small leather pouch. "Here's pay for the journey out. You'll not get the rest of it until we're back in Southampton, so spend it wisely, eh?"

Katy took the pouch, which chinked and jingled as she stuck it into the pocket of Stefan's battered breeches. "Thank you, Captain."

Roberts nodded. "Go on, be off with you."

Katy left the *Alerte* with Derby and his expedition members, hefting two of his leather suitcases with her own satchel on her back. She waved to Percy and Martim as she went down the gangplank and her two shipmates grinned at her.

"We'll find you in one of the inns later," Percy called. "Save enough to buy us both a drink, you young scallywag!"

Katy waved and smiled, feeling a little guilty – after all, she had no intention of meeting her friends later. With any luck she'd already be far away from the city, on her way to find a meteorite.

The Hotel Britannia was an imposing building made of white stone that stood facing the ocean towards the top of Salvador's sloping streets. Derby led their little procession in its direction, striding ahead. All traces of his cowed behaviour in the wake of the storm had vanished now he was back on dry land – he acted as if the world and everything in it belonged to him. Mazarin scurried along beside him, scribbling down notes as Derby barked orders.

Katy tried to take in everything she saw as she passed. There was so much to see, hear and smell that her head spun.

"Isn't it wonderful, William?" said Doctor Whitaker, his face flushed hot from the sun overhead. "We're *here*! Why, my boy, I almost feel as young as you again!"

Katy grinned up at him as the two of them fell a little behind the rest of the group. "What are you going to do first, Doctor?"

"Well," he said. "Derby has told us that he has arranged for guides to meet us at the hotel. I imagine we will get settled and then have a meeting about our journey into the jungle."

Katy's heart sank a little despite her excitement. It sounded as if Derby really did have everything worked out.

"Shall I ask if you can join our expedition as an extra hand, Chandler?" asked the doctor. "I know you are eager to see the rainforest. I am sure we can use the help."

"That is very kind of you, Doctor," she said. "But I think I would prefer to strike out alone."

Whitaker laughed, glancing at Derby, blustering away in front of the party. "That does not surprise me in the slightest, William."

"Behold!" Derby cried loudly from ahead of them. They had reached the smartly painted double doors of the hotel, which were flanked by two liveried footmen. "Relief is at hand, gentlemen, and luxury within after our cramped travails aboard ship." He nodded at one of the footmen. "Tell your manager that we have arrived, my man. We will be expected."

Katy put down the two suitcases, breathing hard in the hot morning air. "If that's all, Sir Thomas, I'll go now."

"What?" Derby looked around as if he'd forgotten she was there at all, which he probably had. "Yes, yes. Go, do."

Katy had taken only a couple of steps when Doctor Whitaker called to her.

"Chandler, wait a moment."

Katy turned back, shielding her eyes in the strong sun. Whitaker held something out to her. It was another small pouch and, just like the one the captain had given her, it jingled a little as she took it.

"Good luck," the doctor said quietly. "And do be careful, won't you?"

"Thank you, Doctor," Katy said, taking the pouch. "And the same to you."

He smiled and turned away, and as he did so Katy saw Mazarin watching them both carefully. She ignored him, pocketing the money and hurrying back down the hill.

She had no time to lose. Unlike Derby and his party, there would be no one waiting to assist Katy. She'd have to find her own help, and she had been thinking about the best way to do that. Katy couldn't speak Portuguese perfectly, not by a long shot, but she thought she could make herself understood well enough to explain what she needed from a guide. Martim had told her Salvador had a great market with many stalls run by people who came from all parts of Bahia every morning. What better place could there be to find out where the meteorites had fallen, and possibly meet someone to guide her there? She had even worked on a sentence in Portuguese that she thought would help here: *Você pode me ajudar a encontrar as estrelas caídas?*

Can you help me find the fallen stars?

Chapter Twenty-Five

Katy stopped dead as she reached the market square. The huge courtyard was laid with a jigsaw puzzle of stone slabs edged by large, imposing buildings. An assortment of merchants and stalls had crowded into the place, hawking goods of all sorts, from food and clothing to animals in cages. Between and around them milled more people than Katy had ever seen in one place before. The space was a jumble of noise, movement and colour, so busy that Katy had no idea where to start. Who should she ask first? The boy herding pigs, or the seller of leather goods loudly shouting her wares? The man holding a brace of squawking chickens in his hands, or the woman with a table full of pastries?

Katy took a deep breath and plunged in.

She spent the morning searching as the sun grew ever higher and hotter overhead but could find no one to help her.

Either they couldn't understand her or they shooed her away. A couple even laughed when they heard what she wanted. After two hours, Katy was already exhausted and beginning to despair.

"Derby won't be having this problem," she muttered to herself as she trudged away from yet another stallholder. "He and the others are probably already on their way into the jungle right now."

An angry shout rose above the general hubbub. A commotion had started up at one of the food stalls. A stallholder was lurching out from behind his wares, lunging towards a little girl who was trying to get out of the way. There was a small black kitten at her feet, eating a scrap of food that had been dropped for him. The girl ran but tripped over the edge of one of the flagstones. She crashed down at the man's feet as he produced a heavy stick and prepared to beat her with it.

"Hey!" Katy shouted. "Don't! Stop! *Pare, pare!*"

She ran to put herself between the angry man and the little girl. Katy held up her hands to ward him off. The man shouted something that Katy didn't understand.

"I'll pay," Katy shouted. "I have money. Just don't hurt her. *Dinheiro!*" she said, finally remembering the right word. "Here." Katy pulled out one of her purses and tipped two coins into her palm.

The man looked at what she offered him with a scowl and then grabbed both coins. He spun on his heel and stalked back to his stall, kicking out at the kitten as he went.

"Hey!" Katy protested. The kitten dodged nimbly out of the way, but Katy picked him up anyway. It was a bundle of skin and bones, with paws too big for its body and startlingly bright green eyes. She kept hold of him as she went back to the little girl.

"Are you all right?" Katy asked, helping her up.

The child gripped her hand and got to her feet. Katy thought she was probably only about seven or eight. Her skin was dark against Katy's and her hair was long and black, loose around her shoulders. She wore a dress that had probably been cut down from a larger garment and beneath Katy could see the bottom of a skirt made of dried rushes. Her face looked as if it could be mischievous, although at that moment the little girl seemed more anxious than anything. She took her hand back and stared at Katy without a word.

"*Você está bem?*" Katy asked, repeating her question in Portuguese this time, wondering where her family were.

There came another angry shout, this time from behind them. Katy looked round to see a boy about her age pushing through the throngs of people.

"Hey!" he shouted. "*Deixa-a em paz!*"

"I didn't—" Katy began, forgetting to use Portuguese, "I wasn't—"

"That's my sister," the boy said, switching to English when he heard Katy speak it. "Get away from her!"

He pushed Katy hard, making her stumble. The kitten wriggled out from beneath her arm and jumped to the ground.

"Celia!" The boy picked the girl up, hugged her, and then held her by the shoulders, speaking in rapid Portuguese that Katy could only just follow. "Are you all right? What did he do to you?"

"Nothing," cried the little girl. "It wasn't him, Theo. He was helping. It was *him*." She pointed at the stallholder, already back at work.

"Why?" Theo frowned. "What happened?"

The little girl hung her head. "Nothing."

"Celia, did you do something to make him angry?"

"No! I just took a scrap, that's all! There was a kitten – there he is, look! – and he was so hungry, Theo, and I didn't have anything to give him and you didn't give me any money, so I just took a tiny bit, that's all, just the tiniest bit, and it wasn't even for me, it was for the kitten!"

"Celia!" the boy said, exasperated. "What did I tell you? The city isn't like home. You can't just take what you want! You'll get us both into trouble."

"But the kitten was hungry," the girl protested. "No one would let him go hungry. Not even in the city. Would they?"

Her brother sighed impatiently. "Never do anything like that again. Now come on. I still haven't found any work. I need to keep looking."

Celia looked at Katy. "Thank you," she said, in English.

"I'm glad you're all right, Celia," Katy said, with a faint smile.

The little girl looked behind her and Katy turned to see the kitten. He was sitting in the dust, washing himself with paws that seemed far too big for the rest of his body.

"Don't worry," Katy said. "I'm going to get myself some lunch. I'll make sure he gets some too."

The little girl beamed a bright smile. Her brother looked a little uncomfortable.

"Sorry," he said. "For pushing you. I just thought – well, you know." He turned away.

"Wait," Katy said. "Please, just a second."

The boy turned back, a guarded look in his eye. "I haven't got time. I've got to find work."

"I can pay for your time," Katy said, taking out one of her purses.

The boy eyed the little leather pouch. "I wouldn't wave that around too much. You won't keep it for long if you do."

Katy took out a coin and held it out. "I need some information, that's all. I'm looking for something."

The boy took the coin and slipped it into his pocket. "What are you looking for?"

"Meteorites," Katy said. "A couple of months ago, there were … stars that fell from the sky. Did you hear about that?"

"I saw them!" Celia piped up, excited to have something

144

to add to the conversation.

"*Everyone* saw them," her brother added. "It was all anyone talked about for days."

"Grandfather said it was the sky falling in," Celia added. "He said it was a punishment from the jungle spirits. The sky didn't fall in, though," she added, as an afterthought.

Katy's heart soared. "Well, that's what I'm looking for," she said. "I need to find someone who can take me to where they fell. Can you do that? Or do you know anyone who could?"

Theo looked doubtful. "I haven't heard anyone say anything about seeing a burning star on the ground."

"It wouldn't look like a star," Katy said. "It would just look like a rock, although it would be much heavier."

Theo's stared at her. "You're ... looking for a *rock*? In the *rainforest*?"

Katy's brief moment of excitement faded fast. "Well ... it would probably be darker than a normal rock. It would have burned through the atmosphere, you see, so the outside would be scorched. And it would have impacted the ground at speed, so it would be embedded into..." She stopped, seeing their blank faces. "Can you at least tell me what direction I would need to take through the jungle?"

Theo and Celia looked at each other and then together they turned and pointed to the south, where the great expanse of trees closed in around Salvador. Katy refused to give up.

"Where were you when you saw the meteorites fall?"

Katy asked. "Were you here, in Salvador?"

"No, we were still at home then," Celia said. "In the village."

"And where's that?"

Celia pointed to the south again as Theo said, "It doesn't have a name. It's on the river."

"Which river?" Katy asked. "Could I take a boat there?"

"That wouldn't be a good idea," Celia said, with a frown. "Not if you don't know it. The river runs very fast."

"Have you got your own boat?" Katy asked, feeling a sudden flare of hope.

"No," Theo said, firmly, giving his sister a forbidding look. "We don't. Look, we've got to go."

"Wait," Katy said, following. "Please. Could you take me to your village? I might be able to find the meteorites from there."

"We've just come from there," Theo said. "We can't go back. Not without earning money first."

Katy saw a flicker of something dark pass over his face. Celia frowned too.

"I'll give you all the money I have," Katy said, pulling both purses from her pocket and holding them out. "Everything. Count what's in there. If it's more than you were going to earn, that's got to be a good deal, hasn't it?"

Theo looked doubtful, but Celia tugged at her brother's sleeve. "It would mean we could go back to the village and grandfather straight away. You said you didn't want to be away long. Theo—"

"All right, all right," Theo said with a sigh. "But no guarantees that you're going to find what you're looking for. I don't know how anyone could."

Katy thought of Derby and felt sure that his expedition would already be under way and they probably knew exactly where they were going. "I've got to at least *try*," she said.

Theo held out a hand. "We'd better introduce ourselves properly, then. I'm Theo Monroe. This is Celia."

Katy smiled and held out a hand, remembering just in time that she was still undercover. "William," she said. "I'm William Chandler."

"Come on then, William," said Theo. "There are supplies we need to gather before you can go anywhere at all."

Theo headed deeper into the market. Katy went to follow but Celia grabbed her sleeve.

"Look!" Celia said, pointing behind them. Katy turned to see the kitten, following along in the dust at their feet, blinking up at them with his bright green eyes.

"Ahh," said Katy. "He's still expecting lunch." She saw a stall selling whole roast chickens and nodded at it. "Let's buy one of those. He can have some, and we'll save the rest for our own dinner."

Chapter Twenty-Six

The kitten continued to follow them around the market even after he had wolfed down two chicken legs.

"You can't have any more," Celia told him, as if she expected the creature to understand. "The rest is for us!"

Theo, meanwhile, gathered what they needed for the trip, which included a hammock and food.

"How long will it take to reach the village?" Katy asked as she watched.

"If we're lucky, two days," Theo told her. "But it could take three. It's always best to be prepared."

Katy wondered when Captain Roberts, Percy and Martim would begin to wonder where she was. What would happen when they couldn't find her? She thought about Derby's expedition too – what if they found a meteorite very quickly, and the *Alerte* left to return to

England without her? How would she get home?

Extraordinary women, doing extraordinary things, Katy told herself. She'd come this far, she couldn't stop now. Whatever happened, she'd find a way to deal with it.

"We should head out," Theo said. "We've got a long way to go."

"We hid the canoe on the riverbank," Celia explained as they left the market. "Theo was worried it would be stolen if anyone found it. He doesn't think much of the city and the people here." She beamed a glowing grin. "I love it, though, don't you? I've never seen so many people!"

Katy smiled at Celia's enthusiasm. "You don't come to the city very much, then?"

"Never!" Celia said. "I wish we did."

"There's nothing for us here," Theo said.

"Have you always lived in the rainforest?" Katy asked. "How is it that you speak English so well?"

"England is where our papa was from," Celia declared. "From somewhere called Norfolk."

"Our father was a naturalist," Theo said. "James Monroe. He always said that the best way to understand a place is to learn from the people who live in it. That's why he came to live in the village and that's how he met our mother."

"So – you were born in the rainforest?" Katy asked. "What an amazing place to grow up! Your parents must be very interesting people. I can't wait to meet them."

Theo and Celia were quiet and Katy sensed she'd said something wrong.

"They both got ill two years ago," Celia said, her fingers twining around each other as she looked at her feet. "Dengue fever. They died." The little girl said this quickly, as if that was the only way she could get the words out.

Katy felt the air leave her lungs in a rush. "Oh," she said. "Oh, I'm so sorry."

There was a moment of silence, in which Theo stared ahead into the jungle and Celia dipped her head, twining her fingers together. Katy didn't know what to say.

"Do you ... do you have any other family?" she asked eventually.

"We have an older brother," Celia said, with another beaming smile. "He was already born when our mother met our father. His name is Ubiratā. He's the strongest and bravest person I know! He taught Theo how to hunt. He's the best hunter in the village!"

Katy smiled at the pride the little girl had in her older brother, glad that her new friends had someone to look out for them. "Then I look forward to meeting him!"

Celia's face fell a little and she glanced at Theo, who had picked up a stick and was poking at the ground with it as he strode. "He's ... he's not with us at the moment," she said. "He and some of the other villagers went to find out—"

"Our brother is away from the village at present," Theo said brusquely, cutting Celia off in an oddly formal tone.

"On an extended hunt deeper in the rainforest."

"I see," Katy said.

"Grandfather lives with us as well, though," Celia said brightly. "He stayed in the village. He looks after us and we look after him."

Katy tried to lighten the mood. "I live with my grandfather too. His name is Ned."

Celia smiled at her. "I'd like to meet him one day. When we come back to England for a visit."

Katy smiled back. "I'm sure he'd like to meet you too. Do you visit England often?"

"No," said Celia. "We've never been. I would love to though. I really want to see what it's like, and—"

"Come on, you two," Theo said, cutting off Celia's chatter with a touch of impatience. He strode on ahead, as if he was trying to leave the conversation behind. "Stop dawdling!"

They had reached the edge of the city, the grand buildings shrinking away into a rough shanty town. Thin-looking dogs prowled around, eyeing them and the kitten that Katy realized was still trailing along in the dust at her feet.

"Go on, shoo," she told him. "Go back to the market, you'll be better off there."

"You should give him a name," Celia said, sounding happier again.

"No!" Katy said. "He's not mine."

"But you fed him, didn't you?" Celia said in her sing-song voice, skipping along almost as lightly as the little cat. "That means you're his."

"I'm going on an expedition into the jungle," Katy pointed out. "I can't take a pet with me!"

Ahead of them the river came into view, curving out of the line of trees to run alongside the rough road they were on. It was wide, mud-coloured and choppy with a swift current.

Katy and Celia caught up with Theo as he made his way on to the riverbank and began pushing his way through the undergrowth beside it. The sun was already falling from its peak, starting its long, slow slide towards dusk, and the shadows beneath the dense mass of trees ahead gathered in pools that seemed darker than night. The air smelled familiar and yet like nothing Katy had ever experienced before. It was the rich, loamy scent of many plants growing beside each other, fed by a warm sun and plentiful water. It was the smell of the Palm House at Kew but amplified far beyond anything that walking into the great glasshouse could provide. She was surrounded by miles and miles of the greatest rainforest on Earth, and it was already, even on the outskirts, more magnificent than anything she could have imagined. It was *real*.

Celia went ahead of her, tracing the narrow route opened up by Theo, and Katy tried to put her feet into the same places that they had trodden ahead of her. Both of her companions moved quickly, even though they were barefoot. Katy's own worn-out shoes were beginning to rub, and she thought how much more convenient it would be not to bother with them at all. How long would it take for her feet to get used to going without, she wondered? The kitten still followed behind them, silent, determined and utterly unafraid.

The canoe that Theo led them to was made from thin strips of pale wood shaped around a similarly light frame. It barely weighed anything. It wobbled precariously in the fast-flowing current as Katy got in. For a moment she thought she was going to end up in the water, along with all manner of creatures she was fascinated by but would rather not meet up close, or at least without the benefit of a net and a specimen jar.

"Did you make this?" Katy asked Theo as he held the canoe steady for Celia to climb in. The water was already pushing at it, wanting to wash it downriver. It sank even lower as the little girl settled in the middle of the boat.

"Yes, with Ubiratã. Grab that paddle," he said, pointing towards a whittled oar beside Katy's feet. "I need you to hold the canoe still while I get in, and then help me get us back upstream."

As soon as Katy put the paddle in the water, she felt the power of the river trying to drag them downriver.

"Paddle!" Theo said as he leaped into the canoe and dropped into a cross-legged position at the front of the boat with his back to her and his oar plunged deep into the water. Already they were being carried away from the shore. "Paddle as hard as you can, William!"

Katy thought the little black kitten had finally decided to leave them. Surely he would not want to strand himself on water? He stood on the bank, watching them with those bright green eyes.

"Goodbye!" Katy called to him as they fought the current. "I hope you find a home, little one!"

The kitten blinked once and then jumped into the water.

"No!" Katy shouted, horrified.

The kitten swam against the current for a moment, then went under before coming up again. Celia knelt up in the canoe, reaching for him.

"Celia, sit down!" Theo shouted. "You'll tip us over!"

"I can reach him!"

The canoe gave a precarious wobble, water splashing over the sides as Celia grabbed at the kitten. She fished him out, bedraggled but apparently unperturbed, and then grinned at Katy.

"You're lucky," she said. "He likes you."

Katy shook her head, her heart beating fast. "I thought cats were supposed to be clever?"

"Concentrate!" Theo shouted. "Or we'll all end up in the river!"

Chapter Twenty-Seven

Weeks of hard work aboard the *Alerte* had made Katy's arms strong but paddling against the river current was another world of effort. The water surged around them, constantly pushing against the tiny boat. At times Katy thought her arms would be pulled out of their sockets – it was so hard to hold the paddle still in the water, let alone help to drive them upstream. They paddled for hours, completely enclosed by the jungle, the trees curving over the water to touch branches above their heads, creating a vibrant, deep green tunnel. Light fell in dappled patches on the murky water, glinting like gems on the ripples made by the canoe.

Katy was far more exhausted by paddling upstream than she had ever been on the *Alerte*, even in the wake of that huge storm. The heat was draining, the air so humid and heavy that it felt like a warm, wet blanket over her face, making every breath a huge effort. She was determined not to ask Theo for a break, but Katy wasn't sure how much more she could take. She wondered how long it would be until they stopped to pitch camp for the night. The thought of sleep was glorious.

The riverbank alternated between foliage that rolled gently down to the water and steep, dry slopes that gave the impression that the river had cut a channel directly into the earth. Trees hung low, wreathed in leafy creepers. Katy was sure she saw at least one snake dangling from a branch, its lithe, green body stretching down towards the water. She wished she'd been able to stop and watch, to see what it would do. Was it drinking, or fishing? Could it breathe underwater? Was it a species known to science, or one that had never been recorded before? Did the local people have a name for it? There were so many questions to ask, and yet no time to ask them. Theo was concentrating hard, avoiding floating logs and rocks that stood up out of the flow. Celia had shifted on to her side and gone to sleep with the kitten curled tightly up against her stomach.

Then an acrid smell reached Katy, a choking, cloying scent of burning. She looked up through the knitted branches to see that the sky above their heads was smudged with roiling black smoke. Celia woke and began to cough. Theo barked something at her over his shoulder, using a language Katy didn't recognize – she didn't think it was Portuguese. Celia pulled something from her pack and leaned over the side of the canoe to dip it quickly into the water, wringing the cloth out before tying it around her face to cover her nose and mouth.

"Theo," Katy shouted. "What—" The smoke caught in her throat and she coughed, her eyes watering. Celia pulled another strip of cloth from her bag and passed it to her.

"Quickly," the girl said, her voice muffled. "Before you breathe in too much."

Katy followed Celia's example and dipped the scarf before tying it around her face. It didn't help with the smoke in her eyes but it was still better. Katy blinked through stinging tears and saw that Theo had pulled his shirt up to cover his nose. The kitten hunkered down as low in the canoe as he could get, trying to find fresh air.

A few minutes later Theo turned to shout to her, his voice muffled by his shirt.

"Ahead. We make for that."

Katy saw that they had reached a wider part of the river that curved to the left. Straight ahead was a smaller channel of water that separated from the main river. For a few minutes Katy and Theo battled to turn the canoe in the stiff current. Katy's arms burned and she really thought they would finally give out, but between them they managed to make for the tributary. As they passed the river's wide bend Katy turned to look down the main river. Her breath caught in horror.

Further up, a large tract of the riverbank had been torn away. There were no trees blocking out the sky, no green foliage at all. The land had been cleared, with nothing but low stumps left in the dry, trampled black dirt. A wooden jetty had been constructed that took up half the river. It was loaded with wooden barrels stacked high. From beyond it, too distant for Katy to see what was burning, billowed the thick, ugly black smoke. Great gouts of it belched into the air, sending up poisonous fumes that threatened to block out the sky itself. Here, the rainforest was no longer scented with loam. Katy thought that it smelled not just dead, but as if death was being carried in that smoke and on every gust of wind that brushed through her short hair.

She turned away as they passed into the tributary's waters, but the sight lingered in her mind.

"What is it?" Katy asked. "What's going on back there?"

"Rubber," Theo said shortly, over his shoulder. "It is a new plantation, only a few months old."

Katy knew what rubber trees looked like – there were some in the Palm House at Kew, grown from seed sent back from an early expedition to South America. "But the trees we've passed so far – they aren't rubber trees."

Theo was quiet for a moment. Katy stared at his back as he continued to paddle, wondering if he was going to say anything else, or if he was just too tired by the journey.

"Some are," he said eventually. "They cut down everything to find them. They burn what they don't want. Then they will plant more – only rubber trees – and later they will cut those down too."

Katy tried to understand this. "They're – they're cutting down the rainforest?"

"Yeah," Theo said, his voice fringed with bitterness. "They are."

"Rubber was in those barrels? But … there was so much of it. If they're cutting down enough rainforest to harvest that much rubber…" She trailed off.

"People think the trees go on forever and that the rainforest will always be here," Celia said forlornly into the silence. "But they're taking too much. They don't let the other trees grow back and the animals don't understand what's going on…" The little girl hung her head. "It's horrible."

"What about the smoke?" Katy asked. "*That* was horrible. It didn't smell like burning trees at all."

"Whoever owns this new plantation is doing something different. We don't know what," Theo said wearily. "Before, when they burned the trees, it was bad enough, but not like this. Now they do something to the rubber before they put it in the barrels and take it away. Whatever it is causes the smoke. It poisons everything. It's terrible."

He lapsed into silence. Katy imagined waking up in Rose Cottage one day and looking out of her window to see that a huge part of Kew Gardens had been destroyed. Her heart clenched at the thought. She knew how she would feel. Angry, devastated. Helpless at the thought of what had been lost.

"Who?" she asked. "Who is doing all this?"

She saw Theo shrug. "The person who owns the plantation and the river, I suppose."

"What?" Katy said, shocked. "But how can anyone own the river?"

Theo said nothing more. Celia stroked the kitten's head, her shoulders slumped. Katy took a deep breath, and even though they had left the acrid smoke behind, she could still smell it. It lingered in her hair, her clothes, her eyes. It had coated her throat and was stuck there, sour and cruel.

"There's a clearing coming up," Theo said suddenly. "We should stop for the night, the jungle only gets thicker from here."

They paddled to the bank and pulled the canoe up out of the water. Katy looked around. The trees surrounding the small clearing they'd stopped in grew close together, hundreds of them, tangled around and into each other, looking for all the world like a huddle of friends leaning together for a chat. Katy wondered how old these trees were, how long they had stood here and what had been here before them. More trees, she supposed, and probably more trees before them too. Then she tried to imagine what it would look like if the trees were all stripped out and there was nothing left but stumps and the last dying leaves of a felled jungle. The thought was too awful to even imagine. The smell of burning stuck in her throat, making her feel sick and sad, and this place wasn't even her home. *How much worse must it be*, she thought, *for Theo and Celia.*

Chapter Twenty-Eight

Katy had never slept in a hammock before. Theo and Celia had ones they had made themselves and brought with them from the village, but Katy's was new. She helped Theo sling it between two trees so that it hung about four feet from the ground. Celia giggled at Katy's ungainly attempts to get into it.

"Here," said the little girl. "You do it like *this*."

In one swift movement Celia gripped the edge and swung herself into the hammock so that it barely rocked at all.

"You've had a lot more practice than me," Katy grumbled as she tried again. It took her three more attempts before she managed it. Then she draped her mosquito net so that it hung like a transparent tent around her. She looked up at the patterns of the leaves criss-crossing above her, still not really believing that she was actually here, in a jungle in Brazil.

Theo hung his own hammock so that together their three beds formed a rough triangle, with a square of bare earth in the middle. Here he lit a fire and roasted some of the corn he had bought from the market, while Katy pulled out the leftover chicken from earlier in the day and shared it between them all, including the intrepid kitten. The little cat's ears remained pricked as he ate, his green eyes flicking from shadow to shadow, listening to noises that the rest of them could not hear.

"Should I take him with me into my hammock overnight?" Katy wondered.

"He'll keep you awake," Theo said. "He'll want to be out among the trees, doing cat things."

"But what if he gets lost?"

"He won't. If he doesn't come back, it'll be because he doesn't want to. And you said he wasn't yours, didn't you?" Theo pointed out.

The three of them sat and ate in silence, listening as the night jungle came awake around them. The fire attracted flying insects of all sizes, moths and beetles with fluttering wings and iridescent carapaces that shone in the flickering light. Katy got up and went to her pack to pull out her notebook and discovered a huge moth with patterned wings resting on the canvas. She held her hand beneath it and it crawled on to her finger. A moment later the moth fluttered lazily on its way and Katy watched it meander into the shadows. Around them the jungle was now a thick wall of darkness. Katy returned to the circle of firelight with her notebook and pencils.

"What's that?" Celia asked as Katy flipped to a blank page and began to make notes about the day's events.

"It's my field notebook. Where I write and draw about things I've seen during the day. See?" Katy held up an open page for Celia to look at.

"Oh, I've got our mother's one of those," Celia said. "It's really big. I think she got it from a trader who passed through the village once, years before I was born. She used it to collect flowers and then write about them."

Katy looked up. "Really?"

Celia nodded. "I'll show it to you when we get home. It's how our father started to learn our language."

"What do you mean?" Katy asked.

"Mama told me once that our father was so excited when he found out about her book that he begged to see it, and then he kept asking her to explain what she had written. She got fed up with having to translate it." Celia laughed. "She said she didn't have time to tell him everything. I don't think she liked him much when they first met! She just thought he was like any other trader, only interested in what the rainforest had that he could take for himself and sell."

"Anyway," Theo said, taking up the story. "She started to write her notes in English as well, so that Father could read them and so that she wouldn't have to translate them. He started comparing the notes in both languages. Then, when she realized he was serious about learning as much as he could, she started to help him."

"That's how they got together," Celia explained. "They both loved the rainforest and Father always said that Mama knew everything there was to know about the flowers and trees here. *I* don't have any notebooks as pretty as yours, though," the little girl added, with a tiny touch of envy. "Just the paper we make ourselves. I've been copying Mama's notebook page by page. In a way that makes me feel as if she's still here, teaching me about the jungle and the plants in the same way she did Papa."

"That's lovely," Katy said. "I can't wait to see it – both your mother's journal and yours, Celia."

Theo stoked the fire and then tossed the husk of his corncob into it, sending sparks spinning helter-skelter into the air. "We should sleep," he said. "Tomorrow will be a long day and we should be up early."

Katy and Celia climbed into their hammocks. Katy tried to get the kitten to join her but he squirmed away.

"Please, be careful," Katy warned him. "Stay near the fire where you'll be safe."

The cat just sat looking up at her, those green eyes gleaming as bright as emeralds in the firelight.

Katy lay in her gently rocking hammock and watched the flames of Theo's fire from beneath her mosquito net.

She thought again of that terrible sight they had passed on the river, of the destroyed trees and black, billowing clouds of choking smoke. How could anyone do such a thing? *Why* would anyone do such a thing? Despite how tired she was, Katy lay awake for a long time.

Chapter Twenty-Nine

They were in the canoe again before the sun was fully up the next morning. The dawn air was cool and fragrant with leaf and loam as they cut smoothly through the water. The river here was far calmer than the one they had navigated the day before and it was easier for Katy to observe what was around her. She was surprised by how quiet everything was. There were no birdcalls, no sudden splashes from fish leaping from the water to snap bugs from the air. She kept expecting floating logs to be hidden crocodiles, but no – they were just logs. In the books she had read the rainforest was always teeming with life, so much so that it often appeared suddenly and in unexpected ways. But not here, it seemed.

Unlike the day before, when the kitten had sat quietly in the bottom of the canoe, today he would not be still. He paced from prow to stern, clambering over their provisions, his gaze firmly on the riverbank, his ears flicking this way and that.

"What is it?" Katy asked him as he pawed his way over her crossed legs. "What can you see?" The cat ignored her, turning round to pace his way back towards Theo.

They had been paddling for several hours when Theo declared they needed to stop.

"We'll have to walk from here," he said as they pulled the boat up on to the dry earth.

"What will we do with the canoe?"

"We leave it here."

Katy looked around. To her, the section of riverbank they stood on looked the same as every other inch they had passed by that morning. She couldn't imagine how Theo proposed to find it again for their return journey. But he was already unloading their provisions. She had to trust he knew what he was doing.

Striking directly into the jungle was a different experience from paddling through it on a river. Katy had to watch her step to stop her feet tangling in undergrowth. Although the trees close to the river had been smaller, just a few metres in they shot up to fantastic heights as they competed for light. Katy found she just wanted to stand and stare up at the distant gleams of sun that dropped through the tiny gaps left between the leaves. It felt like a different world. It *was* a different world.

"Is it always this quiet?" Katy asked, breaking the silence that swelled around them, struck again by the stillness of the jungle.

Celia, walking a little way ahead, looked back at her. "Everything hears us coming," she said. "And nothing wants to meet us. Not since the rubber men came."

"Shh," Theo hushed from the front of their little procession.

Katy wanted to ask why they couldn't talk but decided against it. She concentrated on keeping her footing on the uneven ground and trying to remember everything she saw instead. The kitten stayed beside her, slipping in and out of view as he ducked smoothly under leaves or leaped over them, depending on their height. There was an extraordinary variety of flora and Katy wondered how the foliage down here managed to thrive with so little light.

Mama would love this, she thought to herself, and wished suddenly that Mary Willacott was with her. Katy's heart clenched a little, and it occurred to her that even if there was no time to stop and sketch them now, she could collect specimens and press them into her notebook for later inspection. She could take them home for her mother to see for herself.

She fumbled with her pack, pulling out her notebook. Then she began to gather examples of leaves, seed pods, stems – whatever she could. The more she looked, the more things she saw that Katy thought vital to collect. She scrawled quick notes too because her mother had often said that the notes of when and where a specimen had been collected were as important as the plant itself. Katy also tried to make a note of the colours of each plant to be as accurate as possible in her descriptions.

"What are you doing?" Celia asked.

"I want to collect some plants myself," Katy told her. "The way your mother did, so I can take them back to my own mama in my notebook. If I show you what I've found, can you tell me what they're called locally? That would help my mother identify them."

"I won't know all of them." Celia frowned. Then she brightened. "But we could look them up in Mama's notebook when we get to the village."

"That's a great idea," Katy smiled.

After that, they collected specimens together, with Katy showing Celia the best way to handle each plant they found.

"Come on, you two," Theo grumbled, more than once. "We're travelling too slowly. Get a move on!"

Celia stuck her tongue out at her brother. Katy was suddenly reminded of Stefan and was struck by another wave of homesickness. As annoying as her older brother was, she loved him. She wondered what he was doing at this moment – were he and Father still in Hastings? How was the dig progressing, all those thousands of miles away? Katy wished she could find out, but not even a telegram would reach her here, in the middle of the rainforest.

Blinking away her melancholy, Katy paused to collect a small species of vine that grew near the base of a tree. Kneeling, she glanced through the undergrowth beside her and saw a tiny glint of vivid red. It winked at her through the cascade of varying greens and then disappeared. Katy stilled and then moved back a little, tilting her head, and there it was again. It was as if the dappled light from the tree's canopy overhead was catching against the facets of a ruby. She carefully put the leaves in her hand between two pages of her notebook. Then she put it back in her pack and reached out to part the leaves before her, trying to find the source of that elusive glint. It was deep within the thicket, almost impossible to reach. Katy pushed forwards, crawling on her hands and knees, trying to avoid becoming tangled in the jungle flora.

What had caught her eye was a small flower on a tiny stem peppered with dark, glossy leaves. It was reaching out like a vine to wind itself around the nearest branch, but the whole plant was so small it could have fitted into Katy's palm. The jewel-like bloom basked in a thin shaft of sunlight and Katy saw deeper flecks of scarlet running along its petals, a circlet of frond-like stamens standing out from its centre like a tiny crown. It was beautiful and unlike anything she'd ever seen before.

"Celia?" she called over her shoulder. "Can you tell me what this plant is called?"

There was no answer. Katy thought she'd probably crawled too far into the undergrowth to be heard.

Katy pulled her pack from her back, rummaging around inside until she found her tool kit. She unrolled it, took out the trowel, and then carefully dug around the whole plant until she had scooped it, roots and all, out of the soft earth. Then she slung her bag over her shoulder again and crawled clumsily back to the path, the tiny plant cradled carefully in one hand.

When she reached the path, there was no sign of her companions. Katy got to her feet, looked around and realized that she could no longer even hear the crunch of Theo and Celia's footsteps. It was as if they had been swallowed by the jungle. The kitten had vanished too. After a moment, Katy wasn't even sure which direction she should move in order to catch them up. Had she crawled out of the thicket in a different way to how she'd gone in? She didn't think so, but perhaps she had? Katy turned in a circle, but everything looked the same. She tried not to panic, even as her heart began to beat hard in her chest.

"Theo!" she shouted. "Celia! Where are you?"

There was no answer. The rainforest was entirely silent.

"Celia!" she tried again. "Theo!"

Something appeared at her ankle, a lithe black shadow with green eyes. The kitten had come to find her. Katy was so relieved that she dropped to her knees.

"Where did you *go*?" she asked.

A moment later she heard footsteps and looked up to see Theo.

"Oh, thank goodness," she said. "I thought—"

"Shhh!" Theo hissed, putting his finger to his lips. "Be quiet, please!"

He reached her side with Celia close behind him. Together they pulled Katy behind a large tree trunk and down into the shadow of the dark green leaves.

"What—"

Theo clapped his hand over Katy's mouth, his eyes wide. "Please," he whispered. "Be *quiet*."

They crouched there for a few minutes, but nothing happened. Katy still had the little plant in her hand and didn't know what to do with it other than slipping it as gently as she could into the pocket of her jacket. She was about to ask what was going on when she heard something. The sound of voices and the tramping of feet, accompanied by the crack of branches and undergrowth being crunched underfoot.

Katy peered through the leaves, trying to see who was coming. It was difficult to make out anything amid the dappled shadows of the jungle but then she spied movement. There was a group of men spread out through the trees, moving in a line towards them. They each carried at least one gun. Two of them had bulky sacks slung over their shoulders, and although Katy couldn't see what was inside them, one of them had a bloom of scarlet blood seeping through its pale weave. The sight made the hairs on the back of her neck prickle. She turned to stare, wide-eyed, at Theo.

173

"Hunters," Theo said, his voice barely there. "They'll shoot at anything that moves. Stay as still as you can."

The men continued on, barking orders to each other. They all seemed to be searching for something, their eyes scanning the ground as they marched. Every now and then one of them would pause and drop into a crouch, scrabble about a bit, and then stand up and continue on. *Are they tracking something,* Katy wondered?

The strange party grew closer still. Katy felt a knot tightening in her stomach.

The kitten, crouched beside her, grew bored and stood, arching his long back in a stretch. Katy's heart turned over and she reached for him, but he batted her hand away, thinking she was playing. The kitten backed away, dancing skittishly through the leaves, out from the safety of their hiding place.

"No!" Katy whispered. "Kitten, come here!"

Theo clamped his hand on her arm again before she could move, shaking his head. Katy watched helplessly as the little cat continued to move further away. The men were moving quickly, she told herself. The cat was just a tiny shadow, they probably wouldn't even—

CRACK!

The shot rang out, shattering the silence. Katy only just managed to stop herself from screaming. Smoke drifted in the air in the wake of the blast.

"That's mine!" one of the men yelled in Portuguese. "No

174

one else touch it, it's mine!"

"Yeah, yeah," said another, also in Portuguese. "If you hit it, it's yours."

Theo held Katy back closer to the tree trunk as thunderous footsteps ran towards the space where the kitten had been just moments before.

"Where is it?" the man demanded. "I hit it!"

Katy watched in horror as the man scoured the ground, expecting at any second that one of them would pick up the poor kitten's body.

"I *must* have hit it!" cried the man, frustrated now. "I *never* miss!"

His comrades began to jeer and laugh.

"You're not as good as you think you are, eh?" laughed one. "Better luck next time! No payday from the *senhor* this time!"

"No!" blustered the man. "It'll be here somewhere…"

The search went on, but it turned up no sign of the kitten. Eventually the man gave up and the group went on their way.

Katy, Theo and Celia stayed where they were hiding as the men crashed away from them through the jungle, leaving in their wake a mass of trampled foliage. After a few minutes another distant shot rang out, echoing into the leaves, followed by another shout. Then eventually, there was quiet again. Theo got up slowly, holding out a hand to make sure Celia and Katy didn't move, checking they were alone.

Then he crouched again.

"We have to go, quickly and quietly," he said in an urgent whisper. "Celia, are you all right?"

Katy realized that Celia was crying. There were tears on the little girl's cheeks, but she nodded silently.

"All right. Come on, then."

Katy wanted to say that she couldn't leave, that they needed to look for the kitten. What if he was hurt? She hated the thought of him lying somewhere, needing help but with no one coming. But Theo was right. Those men – whoever they were – would shoot at anything that moved, and they must think about Celia.

They moved softly through the undergrowth, quickly putting as much distance between them and the men with guns as they could. Katy kept looking around for the kitten, hoping against hope that she might see the little black shadow of him following behind her, but there was nothing. The jungle had fallen utterly silent.

Chapter Thirty

It took them the rest of the day to reach Theo and Celia's village. The night was drawing on when a clearing appeared, in the centre of which was a collection of small huts built from leaves, rushes and cut branches. The place seemed quiet, as if it had been abandoned, but what surprised Katy the most was the fact that it stood on the banks of a river.

"What river is this?" she asked.

"It's the one we came in on," Theo told her. "It loops around in an arc from where we entered the tributary."

"Then why didn't we stay on it?" Katy asked. "Surely it would have been quicker and we could have avoided those madmen back there!"

"We aren't allowed to use the river. Not without paying."

"What do you mean?" Katy was becoming more confused by the minute. "No one can stop you using the river!"

Theo gave a short, bitter laugh. "And of course, you know so much about it, don't you?" He went to move away, but she caught his arm and made him stop.

"Theo," she said. "I'm sorry. I'm just trying to understand. Please, tell me."

"The hunters we saw today work for the new rubber plantation. The owners have staked a claim for the land on the other side of the river from here," Theo said. "They say that their claim covers the part of the river that crosses it as well as the land. They won't allow anyone to use that section of the river without paying a fee. We can't fish from it or travel on it without them demanding money from us. We don't have any money, so we can't use the river."

"That's awful," Katy said, horrified. "They can't do that!"

Theo shrugged. "But they have."

"You have to tell someone!"

"Who?" Theo asked.

Katy didn't have an answer to that.

"When we saw those men," Katy said. "They were on *this* side of the river. *Your* side of the river."

"Yeah."

"But that means the plantation men are trespassing on *your* land!"

Theo shook his head. "It's not our land. It's not anybody's land. Nobody owns the rainforest, because everybody owns the rainforest. That's what our tribes believe. We don't have a claim in the same way that the people who own the land over there do. There's no piece of paper that says our village paid money for this side of the riverbank. They wouldn't give us one even if we asked for it, even if we had the money to pay for it, which we don't. We don't own it, so it's not trespassing, is it? Not according to *those* rules. The plantation men can go wherever they like to kill whatever they want."

Katy frowned. "What exactly were they hunting for out there?"

Theo shrugged. "They've been hunting everything lately. They kill everything, and then they take it away. That's why there are no animals. They've killed so many that the rest have run away."

Katy looked around the village. "Is that why there's no one here? Have the people gone away too?"

Theo looked down at his hands. "The ones that haven't been caught, anyway."

"What do you mean, caught?"

Theo looked at her, his eyes sad and angry all at once. "What do you *think* I mean? People that look like me and Celia. Like Grandfather and Ubiratã. They get taken to work harvesting the rubber or clearing the land to plant more rubber trees. Even if they don't want to go. And they never come back."

Katy stared at him, feeling a sudden cold chill. "*Slaves?*" she whispered, in utter horror.

Theo looked away.

"But why are you still here?" Katy asked, looking around the village again. "Why haven't you left, Theo? They were so close to the village! What if they come here, what if they—"

"Why should we?" he said angrily. "This is *our* home! And anyway, if we left, how would Ubiratá find us when he comes back?"

"I'm sorry," Katy said. "Theo, I'm so sorry."

Theo looked away.

"Theo!" Celia appeared, calling from the door of a hut right in the centre of the village. "You and William must come and see Grandfather!"

Inside the hut was an old man sitting on a low stool. His shoulders were broad and although he was sitting, Katy could still tell that he was tall. His face was lined in a way that reminded her of Grandpa Ned, but when he smiled the expression matched Celia's and it was easy to see the family resemblance. He waved a hand at Theo and Katy as they came in, bidding them to sit. Theo settled cross-legged on the floor and Katy did the same, sitting beside him with her pack between her knees. The old man reached out both hands to Theo, who took them, smiling properly for the first time since Katy had met him.

"Grandfather," Theo said in English. "I'm so glad to be home. I've—" He stopped and laughed, as if realizing something, and then carried on speaking in a different language, one Katy didn't know at all. Her Portuguese would be useless here, she realized, and felt foolish for not thinking about the fact that not everyone in Brazil spoke that language. *Of course* they didn't. *Of course* there had already been languages here before the Portuguese arrived hundreds of years ago. Katy felt suddenly ashamed – she had assumed that Portuguese was Theo and Celia's own language, and had felt proud she was able to talk to them in it, even though they also spoke English as well as she did. But it turned out that neither had been the language her two new friends spoke most regularly at home. The only people doing favours to anyone had been them, helping her.

The old man laughed too and for a few minutes Katy watched as they talked back and forth. Seeing Theo with his grandfather like this, Katy felt another sudden rush of homesickness. Rose Cottage was so very far away.

She heard the words 'William Chandler', then the old man was looking directly at her and Katy realized that she had been introduced. It was strange, but she had become so used to her boy's guise that Katy had almost forgotten she was anything else. She smiled and held out her hand to take Grandfather's when he offered it. His grip was reassuring in its strength.

"It is very nice to meet you, sir," she said, and Theo translated.

"Grandfather invites you to stay in the village while you search for your meteorite," Theo told her.

"That's very kind, thank you."

"There is no one else here," Theo added. "He says the last family went hunting yesterday but haven't returned. There is still some cassava left from the last time the field was harvested. I'll add that to what we brought from the market and cook dinner for us."

"Thank you," Katy whispered, but she was thinking about that family. Had they simply decided to move somewhere else? Or had something happened to them, out there in the rainforest? It was a horrible thought. From the look on Theo's face, he was wondering the same thing.

"Come on," said Celia. "I'll show you where you can sleep."

Celia led Katy to one of the other huts, inside which was a cot with a colourful blanket laid on it.

"Are you glad to be home again, Celia?" she asked the little girl.

"Yes, but I wish the others would come back," Celia said. "I miss them. So does Grandfather, I can tell." She scuffed her toe into the ground. "We could go after them, but Theo won't. I won't leave without him and Grandfather won't leave without us."

"Theo won't leave because of your brother, will he?" Katy asked. "That makes sense. You can all go together once he's back."

Celia gave her a look. "He's been gone for almost a year now."

"A *year*?" Katy said, shocked.

Celia nodded.

"Celia," Katy said. "When you told me about Ubiratã before, you were going to say something about where he had gone, but then Theo stopped you. Will you tell me now?"

The little girl sighed. "When the men came to start clearing the land for the new plantation, he was angry," she said. "He and some of the others went to find out more about it."

Katy nodded silently.

"Theo's convinced he's still going to come back," Celia said, her voice sad. "But... I think he would have by now, if he could." She immediately looked guilty. "You won't tell Theo I said that, will you? He'd be upset with me. He's convinced that Ubiratã could return any day. It's why he hates going away from the village."

"I won't say a thing," Katy promised. "Your brother hasn't sent any word back, in all the time he's been gone?"

Celia down looked at her hands. "No. No, he hasn't."

Chapter Thirty-One

Later, they all went back into Grandfather's hut to eat the food that Theo had prepared. The old man wanted to hear all about the city and their journey. Between them they told the tale, with Katy joining in to detail the return trip upriver and through the rainforest. Then Grandfather told Theo that he wanted to hear Katy's story of how she came to the jungle in the first place.

"Oh," Katy said a little awkwardly, because even though the version of the truth she could tell them was eventful enough, she still wouldn't be telling them the whole story. "Well, I came on a boat."

"A canoe, like ours?" Celia piped up.

"No, it was much bigger. Big enough to cross an ocean."

Theo relayed this to Grandfather, who wanted to know more. "He wants to know everything," Theo said. "In the same way we told him about the trip into the city and back. Come on, William. Start right at the beginning, when you were still at home."

There was that name again. Katy shifted uncomfortably because she didn't like the idea of telling her new friends a lie, and yet she had been living one since she met them, and could not tell the whole story of how she had ended up in Salvador without revealing her truth. She thought about how to start. As she looked up she noticed that Grandfather seemed to be watching her very carefully. Did he know? Had he seen through her disguise in a way Theo and Celia – and everyone else she'd met on this journey – hadn't?

"All right," Katy said eventually. "Well, I live in a place called Kew, in a botanical garden…"

She told them as much as she could without giving herself away completely. She described how she got the job aboard the *Alerte*, because Derby was coming to Brazil to find a meteorite, just like Katy wanted to herself. When she got to the storm, Celia gasped. Theo looked at her with a new sort of respect.

"Did you really do all that?" Celia whispered.

"Yes," Katy said. "Now I'm here with you and more than anything I want to find a meteorite to take back with me for the museum. Do you think your grandfather would be able to help me?"

Theo relayed Katy's question and then frowned at his grandfather's answer, asking more questions before finally turning to Katy.

"He says one fell in the Old Place," Theo says. "I think he just means the rainforest, but he's never called it that before."

Katy's heart sank. "He doesn't know where exactly?"

Theo shrugged. "You've seen the rainforest. What do you think?"

The old man seemed to understand their discussion, because he got up and went to the door. The three of them followed him outside. It was dark now and above the little clearing where the village stood, the stars shone brightly. Grandfather walked a few paces and then pointed into the dense wall of jungle to the east, speaking as he did so.

"He's saying the Old Place again," Theo said.

"Could he show us where?" Katy asked.

Theo asked, and his grandfather tipped his head to one side, as if considering his answer.

"He says he will," Theo told her, once the old man spoke again. "But it is a long way from here. We will have to start early."

After they had finished eating, Katy went back to her hut and got out her field notebooks. She had collected her specimens as well as she could, but they needed to be preserved properly if they were to survive the long journey back to England. In any case, keeping busy stopped her thinking about the little black kitten. Her heart clenched every time she remembered the sound of that shotgun going off. She thought about what she'd overheard the hunters say as they searched for the cat. Didn't one of them mention getting paid for it by the '*senhor*'? Katy supposed that must be the plantation owner – but why would he want the bodies of dead animals? With a shiver, Katy remembered the crate of guns that Derby had brought with him on the expedition. She would never understand how anyone could think shooting animals was a good sport.

"Can I help?" Celia asked, appearing in the doorway of the hut, carrying something between both hands.

"I just need to make sure these are all drying properly," Katy explained, pushing thoughts of Derby aside. "What have you got there?"

Celia looked down at what she held. "It's Mother's notebook. You said you'd like to see it."

"Oh yes!" Katy told her. "I'd love to. Will your grandfather mind if we go back to the fire in his hut? There'll be more light there."

"No, he won't mind," Celia said. "He's gone out to hunt tonight, anyway."

They settled beside the fire and Celia passed over the large, hand-bound book. It held many pages of thick paper and as Katy carefully opened it, she saw that an example of a plant had been carefully stitched on to each one. Around these specimens were neat notes written in two different languages – English and another that she could not read. At the top of each page was the name of the plant, also in both languages, but underneath this was written another name, in Latin, which seemed to have been written by a different hand.

"That was Father," Celia explained, when she asked about the names. "Mama just called the plants by what they have always been called here in the village, but he said each should have a scientific one as well, so he made them up and wrote them in beside what she had written. That's why they all have *Anahí* included in them – he named them after her. He said that if they were to ever take the book back to England they would all have to be checked before being verified as new discoveries, but he thought a lot of them were unknown anywhere else."

"This is wonderful," Katy said, awed by the amount of work, detail and knowledge that was contained within the pages she held. "This is sure to help us identify what we collected today."

"Shall we see?" Celia asked, holding out her hands for the book. "We can check your specimens against Mama's pages."

They spent some time doing this, matching up the plants Katy had collected with Anahí's notebook specimens. Katy put each of her own specimens between fresh sheets of the thick paper that Celia had made herself, which would absorb the plant's fluids as they dried. Katy would need to rewrite her notes carefully once this was done. She wished she had a proper collecting press, but Celia got Theo to bring them some large, flat stones from the riverbank and they would have to do. They stacked these up beside the fire, in the hope that the heat would help them to dry more quickly.

Katy tried not to be too disappointed that she and Celia were able to find a match for every one of the plants Katy had collected in Anahí's notebook. Secretly, she'd hoped she'd be taking a treasure trove of new plants that she had found herself back to Kew, but it seemed that would not be the case.

Theo stuck his head into the hut as they laid the last stone on top of the pile of papers. "Are you two finished? We really need to get some rest."

"Is that everything?" Celia asked Katy, yawning.

"Yes," Katy said, yawning too as the long day caught up with them both. Then a sudden thought struck her. "Oh! No – it's not. There's still the little red flower I found. I forgot all about it. I put it in my jacket pocket when we hid!"

She went back to her sleeping hut to get it, gingerly retrieving the little clod of earth she'd dug up from where she had tucked it. Katy carried it back to where Celia waited, relieved that it had somehow avoided being crushed.

"Here it is," Katy said. "Do you recognize it?"

Celia frowned. "I don't think so. What about you, Theo?"

Theo shook his head. "I don't think I've ever seen a plant like that before."

They went through every page of Celia's mother's notebook but couldn't find a match for the tiny flower.

"We should ask Grandfather about it tomorrow. I'm sure he'll know what it is," Celia said confidently.

"Good idea," Katy agreed. "For now, though, have you got a bowl I could put this in with a little bit of water?" The plant still seemed to be happily alive, its small red flower bobbing gently.

"I'll get you one," Theo said. "But then we really should go to sleep, or we'll never get up in the morning."

Chapter Thirty-Two

Theo came to get Katy before the sun was fully up and the little expedition ate breakfast in Grandfather's hut before they set out with him in the lead. This time Katy put her notebook and a pencil into the pocket of Stefan's trousers. That way, if she saw a specimen she wanted to preserve, she could slip it between the pages without delay.

They walked for hours as the sun drew overhead. The rainforest was just as quiet as it had been the day before. Katy longed to see some evidence that they were not alone out there, but there was no noise but them and the occasional buzz or whirr of an insect meandering through the sultry air. At one point they came across a column of determined ants, thousands of them, all marching in a stream across the narrow path.

Katy stopped to watch for a moment, fascinated. Looking around, she grabbed a large stone and pushed it gently into the stream of tiny creatures. The ants immediately changed direction, eddying around it as water would, until regaining their original route, all without losing step with each other.

"Step over them," Theo said from behind her. "Be careful not to get in their way – they bite!"

"Where are they going?" Katy asked.

Theo shrugged. "To make a new home somewhere else, I expect. Even the insects want to leave now."

Katy could feel the sadness of his words. Would the animals come back, she wondered, if the men with guns were the ones made to leave?

When the sun was at its peak they stopped to eat, although Grandfather ate nothing, instead keeping a watchful eye on the trees around them. Katy would have loved to ask him questions about his life, but this walk had been conducted in a different kind of quiet. Katy felt as if they had entered a kind of cathedral. It was that sort of hush, which wasn't only around them but also between them and inside them, and she didn't want to disturb it with too much chatter. In any case, Grandfather seemed thoughtful and withdrawn. He wasn't as smiling and warm as he had been in the village. Katy wondered if he was regretting his decision to take her to the 'Old Place' and didn't want to do anything that might make him change his mind.

As it was, the further they walked, the less Katy was convinced that they were heading somewhere specific. It wasn't that she didn't believe Grandfather knew where they were going. But she wondered whether, as Theo had suggested, the Old Place was the rainforest itself. That would mean they were already at their destination, and Grandfather wanted her to see it – to see the rainforest rather than searching for something within. After six hours of walking, Katy was half expecting that they had gone in a circle and any moment she would find herself back at the village.

As she was thinking this last thought, there came a swift, sharp whistle, almost like a birdcall. Katy looked up to see that Grandfather had disappeared from the front of their column. Celia turned, a worried look on her face.

"That's Grandfather," she whispered. "He wants us to stop and be quiet."

Theo stopped too. The three of them stood close together, but there was no sign of Grandfather.

What Katy heard chilled her blood. There came the sound of voices, the trampling of undergrowth. It was the hunters who had killed the kitten, coming right their way.

There came a whole series of quick, melodious whistles, moving away from them. Theo gave one short, quick whistle back.

"We have to hide," he whispered.

"What about Grandfather?" Celia asked.

"He's going to try to draw them away."

"No," the little girl said tearfully. "They'll *get* him."

Theo gave her a quick hug. "You know he's too quick for that. He'll just confuse them, that's all. Come on," he whispered. "Follow me. Keep low and keep moving."

They ducked and weaved through the jungle as the men came closer but before they had gone very far, a gunshot rang out. Celia screamed, a sharp sound that she cut off by clapping a hand over her mouth, eyes wide in horror, but the damage was done.

Chapter Thirty-Three

"There!" came a shout in Portuguese. "What was that? An animal?"

Theo pushed Celia and Katy ahead of them. "Run," he hissed. "Both of you – that way. I'll distract them."

"No," Celia said, horrified. "You can't—"

But Theo was already drawing away. "William," he said to Katy. "Keep my sister safe. Go!"

Katy grabbed Celia's hand and pulled the little girl after her as Theo disappeared in the other direction. Katy had no idea where she was going, but she ran in a zigzagging line through the jungle, trying to keep herself and Celia ahead of the hunters. A shot rang out and she heard it slicing through foliage somewhere behind them. *They must know that there are people out here, not just animals,* she thought. *Yet they shoot at anything that moves. Who would pay them to do that, and why?*

Another shot rang out, echoing through the rainforest. The bullet thudded into a tree beside them, far too close for comfort. Katy kept on running, pulling Celia with her over tangled roots and through dense underbrush. Anyone would be able to see where they had gone, she realized, just by looking at the trampled leaves and branches they were leaving in their wake, but she didn't know what else to do. They couldn't slow down, and there was nowhere good enough to hide.

Something darted across the ground in front of them – a fleeting shadow that shot from the shelter of one bush to another. Katy thought it was her eyes playing tricks. Behind her Celia stumbled, her toes caught in a gnarled tree root. The little girl cried out as she fell. Katy spun back to haul Celia to her feet. They ran on, but the sounds behind them were louder now, closer. It sounded like a storm wave crashing towards them, and there was nowhere they could go to escape.

"I can't run any more," Celia said, gasping for breath. "I can't—"

"You can," Katy urged her. "You must!"

Even as she said it, Katy realized how hopeless their flight was. The brush around them had grown denser, more tangled, slowing them down. Every step was a fight. She glanced behind, knowing how close the men must be now. Any minute one of them would see them, and then...

The shadow flickered again, beside them but a little

further ahead, drawing Katy's eye. By the time she looked at it, it had vanished, but in its place was a bare patch of earth, somewhere level she could put her feet. The shadow appeared again, showing another flash of dusty earth, then another and another. Katy followed, seeing now that there was a path. It was narrow, so overgrown that it was barely there. Still, the shadow kept flashing before them, showing her where it was.

She kept following, kept holding on to Celia, kept running for dear life. Behind them, the sounds of the men began to fade. Katy kept going, but now the shadow had vanished too.

"William," Celia gasped. "I can't—"

The little girl's words were cut off as the ground disappeared from beneath them.

Katy flailed, letting go of Celia as she lost her footing. She plunged down a hidden slope, bright sunlight beating down from above, crash-landing on her side and beginning to roll. Bushes and grasses battered her until she reached the bottom and finally came to a stop, Celia sliding to rest beside her.

Katy lay on her back, stunned, staring up at the sky. Her head ached, her back ached, *everything* ached. She couldn't catch her breath, but she didn't think anything was broken. Beside her Celia gasped and coughed.

Katy levered herself up. "Are you all right?" she asked Celia once she found her voice. "Are you hurt?"

The little girl's hair was full of broken twigs and bits of leaf. There was a scrape on her forehead. She sat up slowly, touching it with a moan. "My head... Ow!"

"It's all right," Katy said, relieved to see that Celia was moving and speaking. "I think it's just a scratch. You'll have a bruise, but—"

"Oh!" Celia said, eyes wide, pointing past Katy. "Look!"

Katy turned. The shadow that she'd followed was sitting a few feet away. Except, of course, it wasn't a shadow at all. It was the kitten that had followed them all the way from Salvador, looking at them calmly with his bright green eyes.

"You're alive!" Katy said, shocked. "Oh, kitten, we thought they'd got you!"

The cat seemed completely unperturbed by his brush with death. He licked one big paw and began to lazily clean his ears.

Katy and Celia got to their feet. The slope which they had rolled down was the side of a large, deep, vaguely circular bowl in the ground, like an empty pond. Katy didn't think this had ever held water, though. There were no trees inside the bowl, or at least none of the same height as the ones that towered around the edge of it at the top of the slope. Above them the sky was a solid sheet of azure blue, not a cloud to be seen. The ground at the base of the slope was mostly covered with short grass, with tufts of larger plants beginning to grow, as if many feet had trodden over the space so often that the foliage had been kept down, a bit like the land that had been cleared where Theo and Celia's village stood. As she looked around, Katy realized that the plants here had grown over slabs that had been laid like pathways arranged in circles, one inside the other, with straight paths joining them together like the spokes on a cartwheel. Each of these 'spokes' led to the edge of the bowl and at the end of each spoke loomed a huge, oblong stone. They stood like guards over each path. It didn't seem possible to Katy that they had ended up there naturally. Each massive stone looked as if it had been moved from somewhere else, a very long time ago.

Between two of these standing stones, jutting out of the sloping wall of earth itself, she could see another structure – almost like a triangular porch, this too made of grey rock. Katy moved closer and saw intricate carvings marked into these stone lintels – the faces and forms of creatures: big cats, huge birds, crocodiles, even fish. It looked for all the world like an entrance to something, but if there had been a door inside it once, it was now blocked up and inaccessible. Was there something under there, she wondered? If the earth and rocks that filled it were cleared away, would she find a passageway leading directly into the earth, beneath the jungle? It was impossible to tell.

The whole place seemed old – very, *very* old.

The Old Place.

Chapter Thirty-Four

"Have you ever been here before?" Katy asked Celia. She wasn't worried about talking now. It felt, somehow, as if her words would not carry beyond the clearing in which they stood. There was no sign or sound of the men that had been chasing them. Katy thought that this place would be impossible for them to find even if they managed to reach the very edge of the slope above Katy's head.

Celia shook her head, her eyes wide.

"It must be an old settlement," Katy said. "I wonder when people last lived here? Those stones, and the carvings—"

There was a rustle of leaves from the top of the slope above them and Celia's grandfather stepped into the sunlight. He stood looking down at them for a moment, and then smiled slightly. Then the foliage beside him parted and Theo appeared too.

"Theo!" Celia cried. "Are you all right?"

"I'm fine." Her brother scrambled down to join them, worried when he saw Celia's scraped head. "Are you?"

"I'm OK. Where did those men go? Are they still looking for us?"

"We led them away, towards the river. They won't be back today, at least."

"Theo," Katy said. "Do you know this place?"

Theo looked around, shaking his head. "I've never been here before. How did you find it?"

"We didn't," Celia piped up. "The kitten brought us here. Look, Theo! He's still alive!"

"What do you mean, he brought you here?" Theo asked, with a frown. "That doesn't make sense."

It didn't make sense to Katy, either, but she understood exactly what Celia meant. "He ran in front of us," she said. "Because of him we found an old path and that's what led us here. It must have been there for years, gradually becoming hidden beneath the undergrowth." She looked around. "Like the rest of this place."

Grandfather had been silent until this moment, leaning on his long stick as he stood at the top of the slope, as if reluctant to properly enter the clearing. Now he spoke.

"He says the kitten is the spirit of the rainforest," Celia said.

"And that he knows all its secrets," Theo added.

"We've *got* to give him a name now, William," Celia

insisted. "He saved our lives and brought us here! We can't just keep calling him 'kitten'."

Katy looked at the little cat, who seemed to be listening to their conversation.

"Shadow," Katy said. "Shadow is a good name for him."

Celia clapped her hands, delighted. "Yes! Shadow! That's perfect."

"Can Grandfather tell us about this place?" Katy asked Theo. "Where are we? Is this the Old Place?"

Theo looked up at the old man and asked a question in his language. Grandfather nodded and replied, lifting one hand in a gesture that indicated the circle in which they stood.

"He says it used to be a dwelling place," Theo relayed. "A very long time ago, for a tribe that is no longer here."

Katy went to the triangular stone portal and traced her fingers along the lines of one of the carvings. The stone was faintly warm, having absorbed the heat from the sun overhead. "What were the people called? Where did they go?"

Theo asked Grandfather the question. The old man shook his head and spoke a few more words.

"He says the tribe no longer exists," said Theo, a troubled look on his face as he translated Grandfather's words. "He says the first white men to come here brought with them many diseases that the people here could not survive. They all died. The ones that did not die were killed by the invaders."

Katy looked around, taking this in, feeling the weight of the words and what they meant settle on her shoulders. "I... That's awful," she said quietly. "I... I don't know what to say."

Grandfather spoke a little more and Theo listened carefully before translating for Katy.

"Grandfather says that the other tribes have agreed that this place should remain undisturbed out of respect," Theo said. "No one else will live here. No one will hunt here. It is only visited very rarely."

"Then I am very honoured that your grandfather brought me here," Katy said carefully. "It is very kind of him, especially given what this place means. But ... why *did* he bring me here?"

Grandfather lifted his walking staff and pointed it at the opposite side of the clearing.

Katy turned to look but didn't understand what he was telling her. Grandfather said something else and she looked back to see that he'd moved the staff to point into the sky. As she watched, the old man drew the stick down through the air with slow deliberation, until it was once again pointing across the clearing.

A sudden prickle shot up Katy's spine as she realized what Grandfather meant.

"William," Theo said, at the same moment. "I think what he means is—"

"Yes," Katy said, feeling a spark of excitement. "He

means this is where the meteorite fell. Right here, in the clearing. Into the Old Place!"

Celia looked around. "But where?"

Grandfather was still holding out his stick. Katy imagined an arrow shooting from the end of it, forming a line that crossed the clearing. She walked in that direction, which led along one of the overgrown paved paths towards another huge pillar of standing stone.

Katy felt a strange sensation sweep up through her body as she realized that unlike the other standing stones, this one had a huge crack that radiated up from where it was embedded in the earth. Katy held her breath as she got closer.

Then she stopped.

The meteorite had struck the very base of the stone monolith, splitting it with the full force of its plunge from space. It had impacted the rock with such vigour that it had become part of the pillar.

Katy fell to her knees. With shaking fingers she reached out to touch the meteorite, a rock that had crossed such a vast and empty distance to land in this very spot. It was larger than Katy had expected – the size of her two fists set beside each other. It was very dark – black almost, shot through with a single seam of silvery grey. It was uneven yet smooth to the touch; any sharp edges it may once have had melted by the heat and fury of its fiery passage through the Earth's atmosphere.

"Is that it?" whispered Celia.

Katy nodded but couldn't speak.

Theo reached out and touched the rock too, and then ran his fingers around its circumference, where it met the pillar. "How are you going to remove it?"

Katy pulled at it, but it wouldn't budge. Theo tried too, but that didn't help, either. The two of them tugged at it together, but the meteorite wouldn't move. Katy took out the knife that Percy had given her from her pack and tried to fit the blade between the meteorite and the stone, but it was no good. Try as she might, she could not pry the meteorite free.

A shadow fell across them and the pillar too. Grandfather had finally come down the slope into the Old Place. He stood over them and spoke in a clear voice that seemed to fill the clearing, though his voice was very quiet. Katy looked at Theo to see a look of dismay on his face.

"What is he saying?" Katy asked.

"Grandfather says that the meteorite is part of the Old Place now," Theo replied. "You cannot take it. You *must* not."

Chapter Thirty-Five

Katy suddenly felt light-headed, the blood draining from her face. She looked down at the meteorite beneath her hand: this elusive rock that had fallen so far to reach this spot and that she herself had travelled so far to find.

"But … I *have* to take it back," she said. "This is the whole reason I came here. I *have* to. If I don't there was no point to my journey at all!"

Grandfather spoke again and Theo listened in silence before translating his words for Katy.

"He says that not everything is for you, even if you think it is. He says that perhaps your journey was not about the meteorite after all, but about you, yourself."

"I can't go home with nothing," Katy said, her voice breaking a little as she reached out to touch the stone once more, trying again in vain to tug it free.

Celia put her small hand on Katy's wrist, stopping her. "You heard what Grandfather said. This place is left alone out of respect for the tribe that lived here. We can't change it just so that you can take something back."

"But the meteorite doesn't belong here," Katy pointed out. "It came from *space*."

"Then how will you get it out, if you can't just pick it up?" Theo asked. "Will you knock down the pillar and drag it through the jungle with you?"

"No, of course not," Katy said. "But if I had a chisel…"

"You'd cut it out? Leave the Old Place with a hole in it?" Theo asked.

Katy's hand fell still on the melted skin of the meteorite.

"That's what those men with the guns would do," Katy said quietly. "Isn't it?"

"That's what all the rubber barons do," Theo agreed. "They destroy whatever they feel like to get the things they want, because it suits them."

"Because they can," added Celia. "And because they think everything is for them. Just like those first white men who came here."

Katy sat back. They were right, of course. Who was she to suddenly decide that what Grandfather said was less important than what she wanted?

"Does Grandfather know of any other meteorites?" she asked. "You said that everyone saw them falling – the meteoroid they came from would have broken up in the

207

atmosphere and scattered far and wide, but there might be others quite close by. Perhaps Grandfather could take me to one of those?"

Theo asked, and Katy listened to the old man as he answered, the words of his language blending perfectly with the rainforest.

"He says he doesn't," Theo said, after a moment. "If there are more, the jungle itself has claimed them. He doesn't know how we would find them."

Katy nodded. It was as she'd expected. And if Grandfather didn't know how to find them, no one would. Katy could spend years searching and never find another. She knew this.

She pushed away from the pillar and stood up.

"I just need a minute or two to myself," she said quietly.

Katy went to the other side of the clearing and slowly climbed the slope that edged the ancient settlement. She sat cross-legged, facing into the Old Place. Shadow came to sit beside her and for once the kitten did not duck away when she reached out to stroke his head.

"Well," she murmured. "Grandfather is right, of course. I came to find a meteorite but I found so much more than that, didn't I? I found you and Celia and Theo, and Grandfather too. What does it matter that I'm not going to arrive back in London and cover myself in glory? Who cares about that sort of thing anyway? People like Derby, that's all, and people who hunt animals just so they can put a head up on a wall and boast about killing it. I don't want to be someone like that."

She sat for a little while longer and thought about the journey the meteorite had made, and where it had found its resting place. She imagined how long it had been travelling through space, how ancient it was and how ancient the standing stones were that she could see from where she sat. How long had the stones been here themselves? It was fitting, really, that two such ancient rocks had become one.

At length she got up and went to find the others, who had left the clearing to pitch camp just outside it.

"Theo, can you please ask Grandfather if I can draw the meteorite and the Old Place?" she asked. "I won't try to take the meteorite, but I would like to record it properly, and where we found it."

Theo asked and Grandfather answered. "He says yes," Theo said. "But you should only ever show your drawings to people you trust. He is afraid that if other white people knew about the Old Place, they would come here and take it away."

Katy thought about this and knew that Grandfather was right. If Derby knew about the Old Place, it wouldn't stay here for long. That carved door lintel, for example. It would be shipped back to the British Museum, so that people like her family could visit it on sunny weekend afternoons and imagine the history that it represented without truly knowing anything about the tribe who it really belonged to, or the place it had come from.

"I understand," Katy said. "And I will be careful, I promise. Can you tell me how to say thank you in your language? In – what is the name of your language?"

"It's called Tupí," Theo said.

"Tupí," Katy repeated. "Can you teach me?"

Theo smiled and recited a short series of words, which Katy repeated until she hoped she was saying them correctly. Grandfather waited patiently.

"Thank you, Grandfather," she said to him directly when she thought she could say the words in Tupí well enough. "Thank you."

Grandfather watched her for a moment and then nodded. Then he turned away to talk to Celia. He trusted her, Katy realized. She must make sure that trust was not misplaced.

Katy spent the rest of the afternoon drawing and painting the meteorite, trying to commit to paper as accurate a record of how it looked and its composition as possible. She made notes on size, colour and texture. Then she did the same with the Old Place. Theo and Celia helped her to measure the size of the clearing and the stones, to make sure she had seen every one of the paths beneath their feet. They discussed at length each of the carvings on the stone doorway and the names of the animals they could see. Katy asked them to tell her what the names of these would be in their language, and she noted this beside the name they would be called in English. Then Katy began to draw them too.

She sat there in that ancient place for so long that the shadows lengthened around her. Katy kept working until there was no longer enough light in the sky for her to see.

Chapter Thirty-Six

They started back to the village the next morning, packing up their small camp before the sun was fully up. Katy spent a final few minutes sitting cross-legged in front of the meteorite, thinking about all the challenges she had undergone to find it. Leaving it here was difficult, but it was part of the jungle now and would remain so. Something about that seemed right to Katy, even as she thought about how she would be returning home with nothing to show for the extraordinary journey she had taken.

Grandfather did not follow as they set off back through the jungle. Instead, he stood between the two largest pillars and watched as the rest of the party left the Old Place behind.

"He's not coming with us?" Katy asked.

"He said he has another path to take," Theo told her. "I think he wants to watch out for the hunters."

In fact, the journey back to the village was uneventful. The jungle was still quiet, the warm air filled with the scent of impending rain and the buzz of insects. Shadow ran ahead of them, following a path that he seemed to be able to see as easily as Katy saw the leaves that obscured every step she took. She thought about how he had led her and Celia through the undergrowth and towards the Old Place amid that horrible pursuit. *Surely I must have imagined that*, she told herself now. But still, what had Grandfather said? That Shadow was a spirit of the rainforest, and surely a spirit knows things about a place that defies logic and science?

The village was as abandoned as it had been when they left it.

"What will you do?" Katy asked as she, Theo and Celia prepared dinner that evening. "You can't stay here, just the three of you, can you? It's not safe and there's so little for you to eat. You could come back with me. Both of you. You must have family back in England – your grandparents on your father's side?"

"*This* is home," Theo said angrily. "*Grandfather* is our family. I won't leave. How would Ubiratä ever find us again if we did that? Besides, if the village was empty permanently it would give the plantation men a chance to take over this land as well. Is that what you want?"

"Of course it isn't," Katy said. "But I'm worried about you. What will you eat if there is nothing left to hunt or fish? How will you survive?"

Theo stared into the embers of their fire. "I'll earn the money somehow and then they won't be able to stop us fishing or going further upriver to hunt. I won't let them win, and I won't give up on my brother. That's all there is to it, so let's talk about something else. When do you want me to take you back to the city?"

Katy was a little shaken at the thought of returning to Salvador so soon.

"Tomorrow, I suppose," she said.

"Don't you want to search for another meteorite?" Celia asked hopefully.

Katy shook her head. "This time I had both of you, Shadow *and* your Grandfather to help me, and he knew exactly where it was. What chance do I have of finding another without that?"

"All right," Theo said. "Tomorrow, then."

"I'll come too," Celia said.

"No, you won't," said her brother. "We've had close calls every time we've been out on long journeys through the rainforest lately. It's not safe."

"But *Theo*!" Celia protested.

"No buts. You're not coming and I bet Grandfather will agree with me."

He was right. When Grandfather finally reappeared, he did agree. He said nothing about where he had been, just joined them to eat and then retired to his hut. Celia disappeared into the one she shared with Theo, and at first

Katy thought the little girl was sulking. She soon reappeared, though, this time with a small package under her arm.

"This is for you," Celia said, holding it out. "It's Mama's notebook."

Katy was shocked. "Oh no, Celia," she said. "I can't take that!"

"I want you to," Celia said quietly. "I want you to take it back to England," she said.

Katy frowned. "But it's an important family memento."

Celia nodded. "It is. But Theo and I talked about it and we both think you should take it. Mama spent a long time writing all of her notes and collecting as many plants as she could. She wrote down everything she knew about each one, especially the ones we use for food and medicine. What you told us, about your mama and the work she does in her laboratory? Perhaps there will be plants in there she hasn't seen before. Besides, I told you – I've been making a copy of my own. I've finished the last page now. I've had to make sketches of the plants instead of having actual specimens. But I've decided that from now on, I'm going to find new specimens to go with each of the entries." The little girl patted her mother's book again. "This one, though – it should go back to England, to your mother. This way… other people will know about *our* mother's work, won't they?"

Katy finally took the notebook, feeling humbled by the responsibility. "Thank you," she said quietly. "I will look after it. And I know my mother will be really delighted to see this. She will learn such a lot from it. And when you do come and visit us in England, it'll be there waiting for you. I'll keep it safe until then, I promise."

"I know you'll look after it, William." Celia beamed a bright smile. "I trust you. We all do."

Guilt crept over Katy. Theo and Celia were her friends. They were trusting her with a precious possession. But she hadn't even told them her true name.

"Do you think the man you told us about – Derby – do you think he'll have found a meteorite himself by now?" Celia asked.

"I don't know," Katy said. It was something she'd been trying not to think about. "Maybe."

Celia reached out and squeezed Katy's hand. "I'm sorry you can't take one back with you."

Katy smiled and squeezed her hand back. "It's all right. I saw one, in the most amazing place I've ever been. I met you and Theo and Grandfather." She lifted Anahí Monroe's book, safely wrapped in its cloth. "This is a whole store of scientific knowledge that I would never have come across if I hadn't made this journey. It's those things that are important."

Chapter Thirty-Seven

Katy woke early the next morning and went out to sketch the village. It had rained in the night. The air held that wonderful smell that was always released when a downpour fell on soil after a long dry spell: earthy, leafy, fresh and cool. The rainforest was full of the sound of raindrops sliding from the leaves of the trees. The sun was still rising, light slanting at strange angles. A sound reached her above the pitter-patter noise of dripping rain, a faint splashing coming from the riverbank. Katy made her way to the water, just in time to see Shadow wading out of the river with a large silver fish, almost as big as he was, clamped in his jaw.

"Shadow! You caught a fish!"

The little cat jumped nimbly on to the muddy riverbank and padded over to her, dropping the fish at her feet.

"Oh, I don't need that," she said. "That's your breakfast. You eat it."

I've never seen a cat fishing before, Katy wrote in her notebook as she watched the kitten devour his catch. *Yet Shadow seemed to know how to do it through no more than instinct. He's not afraid of the water at all – in fact, I think he likes it.*

Watching Shadow eat, seeing his sharp teeth tear easily through the silver scales of the fish, reminded Katy of something. She turned back to the sketches she had made of the carved stone lintel and looked again at the cat-like creature that had been part of it. The animal in the carved image had a long, wide snout, more like a lion's or a tiger's than a house cat. Katy looked from her sketch to Shadow and back again. They looked similar, and Katy wondered what that meant.

"Perhaps you really are a spirit of the rainforest," Katy murmured. She was sorry she'd have to say goodbye to her accidental pet when she left the village but this was clearly where Shadow belonged. She just hoped he would stay close to the village – he'd used up two of his nine lives when he'd avoided being shot by the men with guns not once, but twice, and he was still only a kitten.

Katy got up and was about to head back to the village when one of the trees on the riverbank caught her eye. She went closer with a frown, not sure what she was seeing. It looked as if there was a burn mark on its trunk, as if something had charred a furrow into its bark at an angle. She shifted her gaze to the tree next to it and saw another burn mark in the same shape but lower on the trunk, as if whatever had caused it had passed both trees in a downward trajectory. Her heart jumped and then started to beat fast. Something had sped through these trees, heading for the ground. Something that had travelled very fast indeed and had been extremely hot – scorching, in fact.

Katy pushed into the jungle, parting leaves and branches, trying to follow the path the object had taken. She saw broken branches, more scorch marks on more trunks. She held her breath. The rainforest became denser the further she got from the riverbank and Katy feared that at any minute, she would lose the trail. But then she pushed aside one more branch and...

Half buried in the loamy jungle earth was a clump of blackened rock about the size of her fist. Its surface looked pockmarked and uneven but smooth, as if it had passed through a furnace that had melted all its rough edges. Katy stared at it. She felt all the blood drain from her face and for a split second she actually thought she might faint. It couldn't be... She couldn't have found...

"Theo!" she bellowed at the top of her lungs. "Theo! *Celia!*"

Katy kept shouting, all the time keeping her eyes on the meteorite. She couldn't look away in case when she looked back, it had vanished. Part of her couldn't believe it was there at all. There came the sound of running footsteps towards the riverbank and then voices raised in confusion – Theo and Celia, looking for her.

"I'm here!" Katy shouted again, but she still didn't turn around, afraid to move a single muscle. "Here!"

"Katy!" Theo shouted, not far behind her. "What happened? Are you hurt?"

"No," she said, feeling a sudden, crazy urge to laugh. "But I need my dig kit. Could you get it for me, please? I can't move."

She heard the sound of more running, and then the sound of someone pushing through the undergrowth to her side. It was Celia.

"Look," Katy whispered. "Can you see it too?"

The little girl gasped. "Is that another meteorite? You *found* one?"

Celia's words broke into Katy's reverie and then she did laugh. "Yes! Completely by accident! Isn't that incredible?" Now she could move again, Katy made her way through the last few branches and knelt over the fallen rock. Theo reappeared a few minutes later with Grandfather. They both pushed into the jungle to join Katy and Celia, Theo holding out the leather roll that held Katy's expedition kit.

"Wow," he breathed, staring at what Katy had found. "I can't believe it!"

Katy shook her head. "Neither can I." She took out her trowel and hesitated for a moment, looking up at Grandfather.

The old man nodded, a slight smile on his face. Katy lost no time in getting to work. The meteorite came out of the soft soil easily, as if it had just been waiting for someone to find it. Katy prised it out and held it up in both hands for them all to see. It was smaller than the one in the Old Place, but very heavy. She couldn't believe she was holding a rock that had travelled through space for millennia before finally crashing through the atmosphere to land somewhere she would find it, completely by accident.

"Oh, William," Celia said, her eyes full of tears. "You found it! You really found it!"

Katy felt a little sniffly herself.

"But … how?" Theo asked. "How did you know where to look?"

"I didn't," she told him. "I just happened to see the burn marks on the trees, and I followed them."

Theo shook his head. "Amazing."

Grandfather started to speak in his melodious language and Theo listened for a moment before translating.

"You respect the rainforest and so the rainforest respects you," Grandfather told her, through Theo. "It sent you one of its spirits to guide you and now it gives you what you came to seek, because you did not take more than it was willing to share."

"Th-thank you," Katy stammered. "I don't know what to say…"

"Do not thank me," said Grandfather, as Theo translated again. "Thank the rainforest."

Theo crouched beside her, touching his fingers to the rock. "The jungle always gives us what we need. It does that for all of us, as long as we look after it."

Katy thought about that awful black smoke, the burning trees, the men with guns shooting anything that moved. "What happens if the rainforest isn't respected?"

Celia gave her a strange look, as if the answer was obvious. "Then *everyone* suffers."

Katy desperately wanted to stop what was happening to their home, to the people that lived here, to the animals that lived around them. But how could she do anything? Especially when her friends didn't even know who she really was. As they made their way back to the village, the heavy meteorite still cupped between both of her hands, Katy made a decision.

"Theo, Celia," Katy said, slowly. "Look, I have something to tell you. About … me."

Theo frowned. "What do you mean?"

Katy felt her stomach churning. "It's about who I really am. I'm not… I'm not William Chandler."

Theo and Celia stared at her.

"Everything I told you, when Grandfather asked to hear my story – that was all true," she went on, her heart racing as the words tumbled out. "I live in Kew Gardens, with my family. My mother is a botanist in the herbarium. My father works for the British Museum. I travelled here aboard a ship called the *Alerte* to find a meteorite. All of that is true."

Celia looked puzzled. "Then what *isn't* true? That's everything, isn't it? Everything that matters, anyway."

Katy swallowed hard, almost wishing that she'd never started this. "My name isn't William Chandler," she said. "It's Katy. My name is Katy Willacott."

There was a silence.

"You're … a girl?" Theo asked.

Katy nodded.

Celia was even more confused. "Then why pretend you're not?"

"Because to get on the ship and come here, I had to be a boy. The *Alerte* would never have taken a girl on a trip like this."

Celia screwed up her nose. "That's stupid."

"Yes, it is," Katy agreed. "But true."

"Katy," the little girl said, trying the name out. "*Katy Willacott*. It's a good name, I like it."

Katy laughed. It felt strange to hear someone say her name after so long. "I do too!"

Theo still hadn't said anything. Katy looked at him nervously, unsure of how he would react. She was relieved when he met her eye with a smile and shrugged.

"Makes no difference to me," he said. "You're still the same person."

Katy let go a breath she hadn't realized she'd been holding.

"I'm glad you think so."

Theo smiled. "And we're glad you came. I promise, when my brother returns and we all visit England, we'll come and find you, Katy Willacott."

Katy smiled back, wishing more than anything that Ubiratã would one day return. And after all the wondrous things she had seen and experienced in the jungle, who was Katy to say he wouldn't?

It was difficult to say goodbye to Celia and Grandfather. Katy couldn't believe that she had known them for only a few days. She realized that the old man had been right. Her journey through the rainforest had changed her. She listened more now, and while she had always been good at observation from a scientific point of view, Katy felt she saw more too, and from a wider angle. The rainforest was made of many different things, none of which worked without every other component. You couldn't just look at one of them, like a lone flower picked and pressed between pages. You needed to see it all at once, as a whole, to even begin to understand it.

"I've got something for you," Celia said as they prepared to leave. "A present." She pulled her hands out from behind her back. She was holding what looked like a very small wicker basket, except that the sides were very high and tapered together at the top, where there were two tiny handles. "I made it for your red flower," the little girl explained. "This way you will have something to carry it in and it won't get squashed."

"Oh, Celia, what a brilliant idea!" Katy exclaimed. She'd tucked the plant inside the top of her pack, but now she opened the bag and took it out, slipping it into Celia's basket. It fitted perfectly. "Thank you, that's wonderful."

"You can tie it to the outside of your pack," Celia said. "That way you can give it a splash of water whenever it needs one."

"It's perfect," Katy said. "Actually, I've got a present for you too." From her pocket she took out the extra field notebook she had brought with her and her tin of watercolours and brushes. "I want you to have these. You can continue your mother's work if you want to. Then when you come to visit Kew you can bring your own specimens to the herbarium."

Celia took her gifts with eyes as round as saucers. "I will," the little girl said, before throwing her arms round Katy and hugging her, hard. "I'm going to make Mother so proud of me, Katy! I will!"

Katy hugged her back. "I know you will. You'll look after Shadow for me too, won't you?"

Celia sniffed and wiped her eyes. "He won't stay with me, you know. He'll follow you again. I told you, you belong to him."

Katy crouched and held out a hand. Shadow butted her fingers with his head.

"You've got to stay with Celia and Grandfather," she told him. "Do you understand, Shadow? I can't take you with me. Besides, Celia needs you for company."

A sound rumbled from the kitten's chest as Katy stroked his head. "He's purring," she laughed.

"Come on," Theo said. "We must go. We need to make good progress before we pitch camp tonight."

Katy lifted her pack on to her shoulders. She had wrapped the meteorite in Stefan's spare shirt and laid it at the bottom of the bag. It would be heavy to carry all the way home, but she had no complaints. She was going back to England with what she had come for. Katy knew how lucky she was.

Katy nodded to Grandfather, who smiled and waved them away. Then she and Theo set off once more into the jungle. Katy looked back from amid the trees and waved. Celia waved in reply. Shadow sat at her feet, as if he'd understood every word Katy had said.

Chapter Thirty-Eight

Katy used the trip back through the rainforest to collect more specimens of her own, spurred on by the riches of Anahí Monroe's finds. Katy folded every flower, leaf and stem carefully into her now very full notebook. She wondered if, when she reached Salvador, she could find a store of blotting paper to take with her on the *Alerte*, now that she had given her spare field journal to Celia. Then she could spend whatever time she had between ship's duties better preparing her finds.

She was carefully freeing the seed pod of a sturdy grass from a vibrant green stem when Theo dropped to a crouch beside her, a frown on his face.

"Someone's coming," he said quietly.

Katy stopped and listened but could hear nothing. "Is it the hunters?"

Theo frowned again. "I don't think so. Wait here."

Before she could protest, he disappeared into the shadowy greenery. Katy put her notebook away so she'd be ready to run. Then she crouched, still and silent, listening to the buzz and whirr of insects around her.

Something rustled in the leaves beside her knee and Katy jumped. Two bright green eyes stared at her.

"Shadow," she hissed. "What are you doing here? You were supposed to stay with Celia!"

The cat sauntered out from beneath the leaves, looking pleased with himself.

Theo reappeared. "It's not the men with guns," he whispered. "But it is a hunting party of some sort. Six people."

Katy's heart turned over. Could it be Derby, out here on his own expedition? If it was, she didn't want to have to explain what a lowly cabin boy was doing out here in the jungle. She certainly couldn't tell him she'd found a meteorite, or where she'd been if it meant risking revealing the Old Place! "Can we avoid them?"

Theo shook his head. "I don't think so. They're close. Let's just stay hidden and wait until they've passed." Then he saw Shadow. "What's *he* doing here?"

"He must have followed us," Katy said.

Theo sighed. "Let's hope he's at least clever enough to stay out of sight this time!"

"Where do you think they're going?" Katy asked quietly as they waited for the party to appear.

Theo made an unhappy face. "They're probably rubber prospectors, looking for new trees. Shh – they're coming."

Katy could hear the tramp of multiple pairs of feet now. Whoever these people were, they were going to pass very close to where she and Theo were hiding. Katy could see glimpses through the foliage – an arm here, a leg there, a boot or the corner of a pack on someone's back. Then she saw a flash of someone's face, and Katy's world turned entirely upside down.

"We really need to pick up the pace you know, chaps," said Francesca Brocklehurst loudly. "We're dawdling a bit here, don't you think?"

"Fran!" Katy gasped, standing up, forgetting everything except for the extraordinary coincidence of seeing someone she knew right here and now.

Theo's hissed warning cry of "*Katy!*" was drowned out by the commotion that Katy caused by appearing without warning. Fran stopped dead, her hands on her hips. Her gaze settled on Katy's face. Katy held her breath. Had she heard what Theo had called her? Had any of the other people with Fran heard?

"Do I know you, young sir?" Fran asked.

Katy realized with relief that even without her boyish disguise, after weeks at sea and another week trekking through the jungle, she was probably unrecognizable.

"Um," Katy said, thinking quickly, and then said, without lying, "You interviewed my mother once for an article you wrote. We were introduced then. But it was over in a moment. I'm not surprised you don't remember me."

Fran narrowed her eyes and then nodded. "What a strange coincidence to meet you here, then."

"Not a coincidence at all," said another voice, and Doctor Whitaker stepped forwards. Katy was shocked – she hadn't even noticed he was one of the party. "Hello, William."

"Doctor Whitaker!" she said. "What are *you* doing here?"

"Looking for you, my boy," he said. "Derby's ready to leave and the *Alerte* won't be in port for much longer – Captain Roberts doesn't want to leave without you but he's running out of ways to stall the ship's departure. Miss Brocklehurst was determined to trek into the jungle and I persuaded her to allow me to join her party in the hope of finding you before it is too late."

"Indeed, Mr Chandler," added Fran Brocklehurst. "You've got your crewmates very worried. What do you mean by running off into the jungle alone like this?"

"He wasn't alone," Theo piped up, stepping out of the bushes. "He had me as his guide."

"And who might you be?" Fran asked.

"Theo Monroe. I live in a village further upriver."

Katy saw Fran's eyes widen a little.

"Wait a minute," she said, and Katy could almost see the cogs turning in her mind. "Monroe. There was an anthropologist called Monroe who came out here to study

230

how the people in the rainforest lived. Is that your father?"

"It is."

"But … that was years ago," Fran said. "No one's heard from him since. You mean, he has a family here?"

"My sister's back at the village. My parents…" Theo swallowed, hard. "They both died."

"I'm sorry to hear that," Fran said softly. Then she clapped her hands together. "Well, it seems we've all had a long day. Why don't we pitch camp together? There was a sort of clearing back by the river. Let's retrace our steps. It seems I have a lot of stories to hear."

Chapter Thirty-Nine

Fran Brocklehurst spent most of the evening talking to Theo about his life in the jungle, barely sparing Katy even a glance. This was a relief to Katy, who was worried that the more time she spent with Fran, the more likely it was that the journalist would see through her disguise. It wasn't Fran she was worried about, but if Doctor Whitaker discovered her real identity Katy might really be in trouble.

"Derby must have found his meteorite, then," Katy said, as she and the doctor talked after a dinner cooked by Fran's local guides. "If he's so eager to leave."

Whitaker gave a snort. "Meteorite! No, he hasn't found a meteorite. He barely even looked for one."

"Whatever do you mean?"

The doctor shook his head. "He didn't come here to find a meteorite, William – he just came to hunt! Can you believe it? The only time he and his pals went into the jungle at all was if they were carrying a gun and had a good chance of bagging some poor animal as a trophy."

Katy was stunned by this revelation … and yet, as she thought about it, she realized she wasn't actually that surprised. It made her think, though, about the hunters that had shot at Shadow. Could Derby have been the 'senhor' they had talked about? He certainly hadn't been there himself, at least not right then. She would have recognized his horrible voice.

"When I finally insisted," Whitaker went on, "we did go on a short trip with the aim of specimen collection, but Derby complained about the heat, the insects, the walking – everything. After that, he declared he had better things to do with his time. He put posters up all over the place, offering money to others for bringing him a meteorite instead. And no one, Chandler, seems to have found one. At least not that they're willing to sell to Sir Thomas Derby."

"But … I don't understand," Katy said. "He could have just done that from London, couldn't he?"

"Well, there's the thing. He and that weasly secretary of his have clearly got something up their greasy sleeves," said the doctor. "They made a trip upriver that they would not allow me to join them for. They've also been receiving wooden crates and barrels at the hotel. Lots of them, all sealed but with Derby's name stamped in predictably large letters on the side."

"Crates and barrels?" Katy said, mystified. "Of what?"

"I've no idea," the doctor said bitterly. "I asked and was told it was none of my business. The poor crew is trying to load them all on to the ship as we speak. Honestly, Chandler, I feel hard done by, and no mistake. This is the first time I've been able to properly journey into the rainforest at all. I paid for part of Derby's trip here and have precious little to show for it. I wish I had asked to join you that first morning, my lad. It seems you've had far more of an adventure than I. I expect your field notebook is full to bursting, isn't it?"

Katy smiled. "It is."

"I would love to see it," Whitaker sighed. "Well, I'm glad for you, Chandler. And grateful, in fact. Without your intrepid nature I think it possible I wouldn't have seen any of the deeper rainforest at all. I'm lucky that Miss Brocklehurst was willing to undertake this journey."

Katy looked over at the journalist, still talking to Theo on the other side of the fire. "What's she doing here anyway?"

The doctor shrugged a little. "Following up a story she got wind of in England, she said. She wouldn't tell me more than that. But I think she was intrigued when I explained what I knew of you and where you had gone."

Fran stood. "Well, my friends," she said. "I think it would be a good idea to turn in. We've a long way to travel tomorrow."

They settled for the night in a circle around the fire.

Katy found it hard to sleep. She wondered where Shadow had disappeared to, though she worried less about him now. Despite her scientific mind, part of Katy thought that Grandfather was right. Shadow *was* a spirit of the rainforest, and perhaps he could turn into smoke and drift away into the night whenever he wanted. She thought again about how strange it was to bump into Fran Brocklehurst all the way out here in the Brazilian jungle. If Fran wasn't here because of Katy, then why *was* she here?

Katy was finally drifting off when a rustle jerked her awake again. She froze, holding her breath.

"Katy," came a tiny whisper, right beside her. "I know you're awake. We must talk."

The sound of her real name came as a total shock. Katy turned so quickly in her hammock that she almost ended up on the jungle floor.

"You know who I am!" Katy breathed.

"Shh," Fran whispered. "Follow me, quietly."

Katy felt her slip away and climbed silently down to the ground to follow Fran into the darkness of the trees. They stood close together with only the faint, wavering light of the moon through the leaves above them.

"Of *course* I know who you are, you silly goose," Fran said, still whispering. "I'm here because of you. Did you really think it was just a coincidence? Your poor parents are going spare – and they blame me!"

"What do you mean?" Katy asked, confused.

"They think I talked you into running away and coming to Brazil. They tracked down my editor and told him so."

"But you didn't!"

"I know that, kid, and you know that, but that didn't help me much when you were off playing deckhand on the high seas, did it? Anyway, I said I'd come out here, find you, and bring you back as quickly as I could."

"Edie," Katy realized. "It must have been Edie that told them where I'd gone."

"Only when she realized how upset your folks were," Fran said. "She thought she was doing the right thing. She *was* doing the right thing. Katy – you should never have worried them so."

"I was going to write to them," Katy said. "Before the *Alerte* left Salvador. To tell them I am safe and coming home."

"What would have been better," Fran whispered, "is if you had never left home at all. What were you thinking?"

"About extraordinary women, doing extraordinary things. And how wonderful it would be to find a meteorite."

There was a momentary pause, and although it was too dark to see, Katy thought that Fran was grinning.

"Tell me," said the journalist. "Did you find one?"

"Yes."

Fran gripped her shoulder and squeezed. "You've got some guts, kid," she said. "I'll give you that. Where is it?"

"In my pack," Katy whispered.

"Listen, you can't let anyone else know you have it, especially not anyone on the expedition. Derby will have it off you in a shot if he knows you've succeeded where his lazy posters have failed. When we get back to Salvador, I'll send a telegram to my editor and he'll let your parents know you're safe. We need to preserve your cover as William, though, as I don't have enough money to buy us both passage and I don't think Sir Thomas Derby will be best pleased to discover – Oh!" Fran stopped suddenly. "What was that?"

"What was what?"

"Something brushed up against my leg – there!" Fran pointed. "What is it?"

Katy looked down and saw something lithe moving around them in a circle. Just for a moment the moonlight caught against green eyes.

"It's just Shadow," Katy said.

"It's *what*?"

"A stray kitten that followed me from the city. He was supposed to stay in Theo's village, but he's got a will of his own."

Fran was silent for another moment, and then she reached out to squeeze Katy's arm again. "You really are one of a kind, Katy Willacott," she said. "Now let's get back before we wake the others and cause ourselves a whole new set of problems."

Chapter Forty

Shadow reappeared again as they were loading the boats early the next morning. Even though she'd known he was still around, Katy had thought the kitten might decide not to get into the canoe that she and Theo were to share. She thought he might disappear back into the rainforest once and for all. Instead, Shadow waited until they pushed off and then waded after them before leaping nimbly in, trailing the river from his sleek black coat as he landed between them.

"I can't take him with me on the *Alerte*," Katy told Theo as they paddled downstream. "I know he likes the river, but he'll hate it if he has to spend weeks with no trees, no jungle. He *must* stay here, with you."

Theo shrugged as they manoeuvred into the middle of the river. Behind them the canoes carrying Fran, Doctor

Whitaker and the rest of the journalist's party followed suit. "He goes where he wants to go. Haven't you learned that by now?"

Katy sighed and then leaned forward to talk directly to Shadow, who was sitting primly in the centre of the canoe. "You've got to stay in the rainforest," she told the cat solemnly. "Do you understand? You've *got* to, Shadow."

Shadow just blinked at her.

Paddling with the current instead of against it was much quicker. The canoes flowed with the water, away from the great gouts of evil-smelling smoke swamping the rainforest and the sky where they joined the main river, heading for Salvador so quickly that Katy felt the wind on her cheeks. The various greens looked like splashes of paint from an artist's brush. Even though she spent all of her time at Kew Gardens, Katy had never realized there were quite so many shades of this one colour.

"Your friend asked me all sorts of questions last night," Theo said as they flowed with the current carrying them towards the city. "She wanted to know all about my life in the rainforest and about my brother and where he went. She wanted to know about the black smoke too, and the new plantation."

"That's what she does," Katy said. "She's a journalist. She investigates stories and then writes about them so that other people can understand. Did you tell her about the people of your village all disappearing and those men, the hunters?"

"Yes. She said she wanted to know more and I told her I didn't know more. She said in that case, she'd have to find out for herself."

"That could be really good, Theo," Katy said. "If she tells people back in England what's happening she might be able to get it to stop."

"Why do you think people will care?" Theo asked. "We're all the way over here, on the other side of the world. We don't matter to them. If we did they wouldn't have come in here in the first place to take what we have."

"*I* care, don't I?" Katy said. "Fran will care too, I know she will. We won't be the only ones."

Theo looked down at the river, setting his jaw. "I just don't see what difference that will make for us. What I need is money. Then we can fish in the river and the people will come back to the village, and then when Ubiratã gets back, everything will be fine again."

Katy didn't see how that could possibly be true, but she said nothing. Who was she to tell Theo she knew better?

Salvador soon rose ahead of them on the horizon, with its outer ring of slums and its inner buildings of gleaming white. Beyond was the cerulean blue of the ocean, as wide and bright as the green of the jungle. The clouds over the water were huge and white, great islands in the air. The travellers stopped and pulled the canoes out of the river at the same bank of rushes from which Theo, Katy and Celia had left nearly a week before.

"We must go straight to the *Alerte*," Doctor Whitaker said. "Time is short, William, and I'm worried that we may already be too late."

"You don't need to go back upriver yet, do you, Theo?" Fran said. "There is something I would like to discuss with you."

"No," Theo said. "I'd like to see the *Alerte*, anyway."

They set off through the city, the kitten sticking to Katy's side, darting along beside her as if he really was her shadow. She was going to miss him when he was no longer there. She realized just how much bigger he had grown since they'd left the city – his head was now level with her knee.

They reached the last slope and the port opened out before them with its mass of anchored ships. Katy searched for the *Alerte* and found her bobbing on the harbour's gentle tide. Despite how much she had loved the rainforest, Katy found she was actually looking forward to being back aboard ship. As they got closer, they could see piles of provisions on the dock, ready for loading. She could see some of the crates that Doctor Whitaker had told her about too – a stack of wooden boxes of varying sizes that really didn't look as if they could possibly fit on the little ship. There were barrels too. What on earth could it all be?

"It doesn't look as if they're quite ready to leave yet," said Doctor Whitaker, at Katy's side. "That's a relief. We should—"

"*You!*"

The shout came from ahead of them. Katy saw Derby storming towards them with Mazarin at his side. Sir Thomas held something in his right hand – it looked like a thick roll of paper.

"You! *Girl!*"

Katy looked at Fran, but Derby shouted yet again.

"Not her. *You*, you little troublemaker! *Katy Willacott!*"

Derby was almost upon them now. He shook out the roll of paper in his hand and Katy saw that it was a newspaper.

"Oh yes," Derby declared, incensed. "You've been exposed for what you really are, my *girl!*"

Chapter Forty-One

Derby reached out and snatched at Katy's cap, flinging it away before she could grab it. The wind caught it and threw it out of reach before dropping it into the port waters.

"Thought you'd make a fool of me, did you?" he demanded, leaning closer, right in Katy's face. "You and that country bumpkin father of yours? Oh yes, I know where you come from, girl. He put you up to this, didn't he? You're a disgrace! Both of you – *all* of you! A shameful disgrace!"

"Sir Thomas," Fran protested. "Really, this is unnecessary!"

"As for *you*," Derby spat in Fran's direction. "I have nothing to say to you."

"Are you sure of this, Sir Thomas?" Doctor Whitaker ventured, stepping forwards with a frown. "I have just been travelling through the jungle with this young man and saw no sign that what you say is true."

"Yes, well," Derby said, his tone dismissive, "Proper observation requires a true naturalist's skill, Doctor, so your deficiencies in this respect do not surprise me."

Doctor Whitaker's face flushed. "I beg your pardon?"

Derby ignored him, thrusting the newspaper in Katy's face. "Look here, girl, and see how thoroughly you have been exposed."

Katy stared at the front page. *Girl Impersonates Cabin Boy*, screamed the headline. *Joins Prestigious Scientific Expedition to Brazil!*

Fran made a sound of dismay. "They promised me they wouldn't publish before I got the whole story!"

"Well?" Derby demanded. "What do you have to say?"

"Yes," Katy said, keeping her voice as steady as she could. "Yes, it's true. My name isn't William Chandler. It's Katy Willacott. My father is Josiah Willacott, an archaeologist—"

"A mere *assistant*," Mazarin corrected her, with a sniff.

"—with the British Museum and my mother is Mary Willacott, a botanist at Kew Gardens. My parents had nothing to do with this. I wanted to join the expedition, and this was the only way I could."

"Goodness me," Doctor Whitaker murmured. "I don't know what to say."

Derby's face twisted in an ugly sort of triumph. "Well," he hissed. "Now we know why we had so many difficulties on our journey here. Was it merely female incompetence, I wonder? Or deliberate, conniving sabotage?"

"*What?*" Katy said, flabbergasted.

"Steady on, Derby," said Doctor Whitaker, from behind him. "We all know how William … *Katy* … saved the *Alerte* in that storm."

"Poppycock!" Derby spat. "Do you really expect me to believe that a mere girl could have performed that feat?"

"But I did," Katy said, utterly bewildered. "You *know* I did."

"I know nothing except that you are a liar, a cheat and not to be trusted or believed in anything," Derby said venomously. "I always knew there was something off about you, Chandler – or whatever you're calling yourself."

"That's absurd," said Fran. "You can't blame Katy for your failures, Derby. Trust me, I've made sure to keep one of your posters as an example of how you conducted this so-called scientific expedition."

"Silence!" Sir Thomas shouted. "I will not be spoken to in this fashion! In fact, I will no longer be spoken to by you at all. Be gone, both of you."

"But I'll be joining the *Alerte* again," Katy said. "For her voyage back to England."

"Oh, really?" Derby said. "You can pay for your passage, can you?"

Katy looked past him, towards her shipmates, who were watching from the deck. "I – no, but … I'll be working. As a cabin boy…"

Derby looked triumphant as she trailed off. "But you're

not a cabin boy, are you? And since I know the pitiful state of your family's finances, I think we can safely assume you'll be staying here."

"Derby—" Fran began.

"You too," Derby said, dismissing the journalist with a flick of his fingers.

"Wait," Fran said as he turned away. "Katy needs to get home as soon as possible. I'll pay her passage."

"But you said you didn't have enough for both of us," said Katy.

"I don't," Fran said. "But I won't be coming back with you. Not straight away, anyway." She looked at Theo. "There are stories here that I need to investigate."

"Then it seems you will have an assistant," said Derby. "For passage or not, I don't want her."

"Sir Thomas," said Doctor Whitaker. "Please consider, for a moment." He indicated the paper, still clutched angrily in Derby's hand. "The papers will be eager to continue such a sensational story."

Derby huffed. "What of it, man? What do I care?"

"Nothing, of course," the doctor went on quietly. "You are absolutely right. She will have to return home some other way, alone among strangers. She does not deserve the selfless care of a great man such as yourself. The papers must simply accept that you are far too busy with greater concerns than returning a troubled child to her distraught parents. The journalists can waste their time interviewing the crew of whatever vessel she finds to take her and print their story instead. I'm sure they will be kind in their words about you, regardless. Although, if they weren't..."

Doctor Whitaker said no more, but Derby's face had taken on a frown of contemplation. He looked down at the headline again and then scowled at Katy.

"Very well. I will do the Christian thing and return you to your feckless parents. But you will stay entirely out of my sight, do you hear? Or I'll have Roberts and his ruffians set you adrift in the lifeboat."

He turned and marched away. Mazarin shot Katy a look of pure dislike and followed.

"Thank you, Doctor," Fran said. "That was quick thinking. I'm grateful to you."

The doctor made a disgusted sound in his throat. "Appealing to the man's vanity and ego is evidently the only way to get him to do the decent thing."

Katy turned to Fran. "I don't want to go back without you!"

Fran squeezed her shoulder. "You're going to have to, kid. It's going to be awful, I know it is, but you can do it. And you've got the doctor here to talk to, at least. You'll be a friend to Katy, won't you, Doctor Whitaker, regardless of her true identity?"

Doctor Whitaker smiled at them both. "The ghost of my late wife would haunt me as a cowardly fool were I to do anything less."

Fran turned back to Katy. "There. And listen to me – when the journalists come – and they will, make no mistake about it – don't you dare let Derby speak for you. You hear me? Your story is a thousand times more interesting than his. Don't let him tell it his way. We both know it'll all be nonsense if he does."

Chapter Forty-Two

The crew of the *Alerte* carried on loading Derby's mysterious collection of cargo, but Katy was not allowed to help.

"You are not permitted on the ship until it is absolutely necessary," Mazarin said sniffily, moving to block her way before Katy could set a foot on the ramp. "That is Sir Thomas's decree. Anyway, why would they want you? Go away and find a pretty cake to eat, silly little girl."

Katy was about to snap something angry back but stopped when Fran's hand landed on her shoulder with a light squeeze.

"Come on," said the journalist. "There's no point wasting our time."

Katy reluctantly followed Fran, Theo and Doctor Whitaker, although they didn't go far. Fran found a low wall to perch on and the rest of them did the same. From there they could still see what was going on aboard the *Alerte*. For the first time Katy noticed that there was a new boy on board, small and lithe, younger than she was but quick with it. Katy's heart sank. They had replaced her already.

There was clearly no more room for Derby's cargo in the hold, because the last of the wooden boxes were being stacked on deck. Katy watched as Percy and Martim hauled a heavy canvas sheet over their bulk and secured it as a protection against bad weather.

"Those crates," Fran muttered, watching too. "What on earth is in them? Where have they come from?"

"I'll try to find out on the homeward journey," Katy said. "There's a story there, isn't there? I want to know what it is."

Fran grinned and squeezed her shoulder. "I knew I could rely on you. Just be careful."

"Don't worry, Miss Brocklehurst," said Doctor Whitaker. "I'm going to make it my duty to be sure that Miss Willacott reaches home safely."

"I can look after myself," Katy said indignantly. "Really, it's as if everyone's forgotten that I worked as hard as anyone on the journey out."

Doctor Whitaker looked suitably chastened. "Of course. My apologies. I only meant that I'll not tolerate any rudeness directed at you, Miss Willacott, that's all."

"It's all right," Katy said gloomily. "I'm grateful to you, Doctor, really I am. I just wish the crew were as kind." She watched as Martim and Percy disappeared below decks.

She had thought they were her friends.

"Remember, you're a paying passenger now," Fran pointed out. "The worst they can do is ignore you."

The idea that her old crewmates might do that was deeply upsetting to Katy. She had no idea what she'd do for the weeks of the ship's journey if no one but the doctor would talk to her and she couldn't work.

There was no other choice, though. Fran had paid her fare and Katy felt she'd already caused her friend more than enough trouble – not that the journalist saw it that way. Fran's excitement about travelling back into the rainforest glowed in her cheeks and glinted in her smile.

"With Theo's help, I'm going to find out exactly what's causing that hideous black smoke, and who's behind it," she said. "I'm going to look into the land issues too – Theo's told me about his village not being able to use the river, which is just awful. And these hunters, taking all the game. Someone's responsible and the world needs to know who. This is exactly my sort of story, Katy – the kind where my writing about it might actually do some good. I'm so glad you brought me here."

Theo seemed rather bemused by Fran's enthusiasm but was warming to the idea of taking her back with him to the village, especially as she was also determined to find out what had happened to Ubiratã. Fran was like that – so exuberant, so keen to learn, that it was hard not to be caught up in her excitement.

"Will you come and see me as soon as you return to England?" Katy asked. "I want to know everything."

"Of course I will!" Fran exclaimed. "Apart from anything else I shall want to know what you found out about those crates, not to mention how it is received when you reveal—" Fran stopped herself suddenly and then tried to cover, "Your journey into the jungle!"

Doctor Whitaker didn't seem to notice her slip, which was a relief. Katy had no intention of getting the meteorite out before she reached home. She trusted Doctor Whitaker, but the fewer people aboard the *Alerte* who knew about it, the less chance there was of Derby finding out.

By the time the tide was high, the *Alerte* was ready to depart. There was the usual commotion as Derby and his men returned to the dock, acting for all the world as if they owned it. Katy and Doctor Whitaker stayed out of the way until they had all blustered on to the ship and below decks. Then Captain Roberts appeared at the grab rail, raised one large hand to cup his mouth and shouted.

"All aboard," he bellowed, over the hubbub of the port.

Katy and Doctor Whitaker looked at each other, knowing this yell was for their benefit.

"Come on," Fran said. "Time to go."

Together the party returned to the ship, stopping at the bottom of the gangplank. Fran pulled Katy into a brisk hug.

"Everything's going to be fine," she told her. "You've had a great adventure, and I don't think for a moment that it's going to be your last, Katy Willacott. Chin up and I'll see you soon. I promise."

Theo hugged her too. "I'm glad to know you, Katy," he said.

"And I you, Theo – thank you for everything," Katy told him. "Without you, Celia and Grandfather my expedition would have been nothing at all. I promise I'll look after your mother's journal."

Theo pulled away and smiled. "I know you will."

Katy looked down at Shadow, sitting at their feet. He was so much bigger than he was the day he'd brought Katy, Celia and Theo together at the market.

"I can't take him with me," Katy said to Theo. "I just can't. Will you take him back into the jungle? That's where he belongs."

Theo nodded. "I'll try."

Katy crouched in front of Shadow, who regarded her with solemn, unblinking green eyes.

"Stay with Theo and Fran, Shadow," Katy told him clearly, because she completely believed that he understood everything she said. "Thank you for following me for as long as you have. Thank you for keeping me safe. But there are no jungles like yours where I'm going, and I don't think you'd be happy there. I don't think you'd be safe. Please stay here."

Shadow lifted a paw, licked it with his pink tongue, and polished one ear. Katy wasn't sure if he was ignoring her or agreeing.

"Final call!" yelled Percy from the deck above them. He threw a brusque, unsmiling nod to Katy.

"Go," Fran said, giving her a small, encouraging push. "You'll be fine. I'll come and find you when I get back."

Chapter Forty-Three

Katy and Doctor Whitaker hurried on to the ship as the captain's voice bellowed from the tiller.

"Weigh anchor! Set the mainsail!"

The ship's mates rushed to do as they were bid, and Katy almost dumped her pack on the deck and joined in, but it was obvious they had no need of her. She watched, dejected, as the new boy hauled on the halyard rope to hoist the sail, and she knew there was no chance she would play any part in the *Alerte*'s journey home. She was, as Fran said, a passenger and no more.

"Godspeed!" Fran shouted as the *Alerte* moved away, trailing the last lines. She and Theo waved. "I'll see you soon, Katy. I will!"

Katy waved too but could not find the words to call anything back. Her eyes welled with tears. This wasn't how her adventure was supposed to end.

They had almost cleared their moorings when Shadow suddenly burst into life. He shot across the dock and leaped out over the water, his lithe body stretching into a sleek black line. The cat caught the ship's last trailing rope and clung on, several feet above the bow wave that bubbled beneath the *Alerte* as she pulled away from dock.

"Shadow!" Katy shouted, leaning over the grab rail to see where he was. "No! Go back!"

The cat clung on, even as Theo and Fran called to him. The *Alerte* began to swing into the deeper channel of Salvador's harbour, ready to depart. Katy was terrified that however well the cat could swim, if Shadow fell into the water now, he'd be crushed beneath the ship.

She needn't have worried. Shadow had no intention of falling. Instead he clawed his way up the trailing line as easily as scaling a tree and jumped on to the deck.

"Shadow," Katy said, aghast. "You can't be here!"

Heavy footsteps thudded behind her and Captain Roberts himself loomed over her shoulder. Derby was just behind him, clearly curious about her sudden cry.

"What's this?" the captain asked, spying Shadow as the cat sat nonchalantly on the deck boards to wash his ears.

"Nothing," Katy said, too quickly stepping in front of Shadow.

The captain glanced back at Derby, and when he turned back there was a scowl fixed on his face, as fierce as Katy had ever seen. "Doesn't look like nothing to me," he growled loudly. "It looks like an animal. On *my* ship." He raised his voice to a shout. "First mate, I have need of you!"

"It's a *cat*!" Derby exclaimed, wrinkling his nose. "Disgusting creatures. Won't have 'em in the house, won't have 'em anywhere near me. Get rid of it, Roberts, immediately."

"For once, Sir Thomas, we are in agreement," the captain said.

"It's only a stray," Katy said. "We can just let him back on to the shore."

Roberts glowered at her. "Oh, can we? Giving me orders now, are you, missy?"

"No," Katy said miserably. "I didn't mean to do that. But—"

Percy arrived at the captain's side, paying no attention to Katy at all. "Cap'n?"

Roberts jerked his bearded chin at Shadow, who seemed completely unperturbed. "We've got an unexpected passenger. Give it the royal treatment, would you?"

Something flickered across the first mate's face, just for a second. "The royal treatment, Captain? You're sure?"

Roberts's scowl deepened still more. "Did you hear me?"

"Yes, Captain."

"Then you've got your orders. Carry them out."

"Aye, Captain!" Percy hurried away.

"What are you going to do?" Katy asked fearfully.

Roberts eyed her. "Stay out of the way, girl. There's work to be done."

Percy returned, this time with Martim, as well as a large hessian sack and a stick.

"Ah, capital," Derby said, with glee. "Be rid of the blighter in a jiff, what?"

"Let's get him in, then," Percy said, still ignoring Katy.

"Wait," Katy said. "Please don't hurt him. Please—"

Shadow fought and spat as the two hands cornered him and forced him into the sack. Even once they'd closed and tied it around him, Katy could still hear him yowling and she felt sure his sharp claws would tear through the rough fabric, but before he could break out of his prison, the two mates had jammed a stick through the knot and used it to lift the sack between them.

"Wait," Katy said. "*Please.* What are you going to—"

"Do please stop this pathetic whinging," said Sir Thomas with disdain. "It grates on my nerves, it really does." He raised his voice to Percy and Martim. "Hurry up and put the wretched creature overboard."

Katy gasped.

"Just a minute," protested Doctor Whitaker, who had appeared on deck to see what the fuss was about. "Is that really necessary?"

"Wait! Please!" Katy appealed to Derby in desperation. "It's not just a cat, Sir Thomas. I think it's a…" She came very close to telling him what she had come to suspect – that the kitten she had fed as a stray in the market in Salvador was actually a young black jaguar.

"It's a what?" Derby sneered.

Something told Katy to hold her tongue. "Nothing. It doesn't matter. But Shadow—"

Derby snorted again. "Shadow. What is it about women and their incessant need to give their pets absurd names?"

From behind them came the sound of a loud splash. Katy whipped around, her blood running ice-cold. Percy and Martim were against the grab rail at the boat's stern, dusting off their hands. The sack containing Shadow was nowhere to be seen.

"No!" Katy shouted in horror as she rushed across the deck, pushing past her old workmates. "Shadow! No!"

She leaned over the grab rail but could see nothing in the water but an empty barrel bobbing in their wake. The sack – and poor Shadow, tied inside it – had sunk without trace.

"Good riddance to bad rubbish," came Derby's loud voice, from behind her. "If only we could deal with all such worthless articles so easily."

The *Alerte* sailed on, leaving the city of Salvador behind.

"Oh, Miss Willacott," said Doctor Whitaker. "I am so very sorry."

Katy didn't move for a long time, her tears dashed away by the wind.

Chapter Forty-Four

"You should get below, miss."

The voice at her elbow wasn't one she recognized. Katy looked down to see the new cabin boy – the new *her* – standing there in the darkness.

"I'd rather stay on deck."

"Captain's orders, miss." The boy looked apologetic, shifting from one foot to the other.

"What's your name?" Katy asked.

The boy looked surprised, as if he wasn't used to being asked such a question. "Arthur," he said.

"Arthur what?"

He shrugged. "Dunno."

Katy sighed. "All right, Arthur. I'll go."

Arthur nodded, relieved. He scurried off towards the doghouse. Katy realized that the sun had set completely as she'd stood at the rail. The watch at the mizzen mast had changed too. There was no sign of Captain Roberts. Percy stood there instead, his back to her.

Below deck, the noise from the galley was rowdy. Doctor Whitaker had already retired but Derby and his men appeared to be in high spirits, despite the failure of their quest to find a meteorite. Katy tightened her cold hand on the strap of her pack as she came down the stairs, thinking about the prize she had hidden away there. At that exact moment, Lucas Mazarin cast a look her way. He scowled at her.

Katy's heart sank even further as she realized she was going to have to walk past all the gentlemen to get to the bunks. She squared her shoulders and took a step in the direction of the sleeping quarters but Arthur caught her sleeve.

"Not that way, miss."

"What do you mean?" Katy was puzzled. "That's where the bunks are."

"Aye, miss, but you've got the captain's quarters now."

"*What?*" Katy said, shocked. "That can't be right."

"Captain's orders, miss."

Katy looked back along the corridor, past the galley. She couldn't take the captain's quarters! Where would he sleep?

"This way if you please, miss."

"I can't," she said. "All I need is a bunk. That was fine for me on the way out; it'll be fine for me on the way back. I don't need the captain's quarters."

There was the sound of movement from the chart room.

Roberts loomed out of the doorway, glowering at her.

"You're a paying passenger and a female one no less," he said gruffly. "You can't bunk with the menfolk. It's unseemly. You'll take my cabin."

"I won't," Katy said. "I'll sleep on deck."

"In the storms that we'll be passing through? Not likely."

"I will," Katy said stoutly. "I'll lash myself to the mast so I can't be washed overboard if I have to."

For a second Katy thought she saw a flicker of amusement pass through the captain's eyes, but it was gone in an instant, replaced by the familiar forbidding look. "Open my cabin door, boy," he said to Arthur.

Arthur did as he was told, his eyes wide.

"In you go, Miss Willacott," said the captain.

"I *won't*."

"You will," Captain Roberts said quietly. "Either you'll walk yourself or I'll push you, but one way or another you're going in. And hear me now – if I have to put you in there myself, I'll lock the door after you and throw away the key, do you understand?"

Katy stared at him for a second. The captain stared back, as resolute as a rock. Without a word, Katy walked into the cabin. The door shut behind her with a sharp click.

The room in which Katy found herself was small and strangely shaped. The widest part of it was where she stood with her back against the door. On either side of her the walls curved inwards to a point. To the left of where she stood there was enough room for a narrow bunk, which had been raised against one wall. To the right was a table, under which was pushed a small wooden chair. Above the bed was a small porthole.

Katy stood still for a moment. Then she took the pack from her back and set it down on the bunk. The sound from the galley was muted here, and she realized just how long it had been since she'd had a door she could shut against the world. She was suddenly intensely relieved to have a space of her own. Captain Roberts had granted her a great favour, even if he had only done it out of spite. She tried not to care about that, or about the way Percy and Martim would no longer even look in her direction, as if she had become entirely invisible.

Katy perched on the edge of the bunk and became aware of two things at once. On the desk's surface was a piece of folded paper, on which had been written, in spiky, untidy lettering, her name: *Miss Katy Willacott*.

Meanwhile, from the shadows beneath the desk stared two bright green eyes.

Katy slid from the bunk with a cry, dropping to her knees on the floor.

"Shadow?"

The cat slipped from beneath the desk, separating from the darkness in one fluid movement. He padded the two steps it took to cross the space to her and rubbed his head against Katy's own.

"I thought you were drowned," Katy whispered, lowering her voice as she remembered the gathered men not far beyond her tiny door. "How did you survive? How are you here? Did you get out of the bag and climb back into the ship? Oh, you clever cat!"

After another head bump Shadow apparently grew tired of the attention. Instead, he leaped on to the bunk and stared out of the porthole at the inky darkness of the night beyond.

Katy got up and picked up the folded paper on the desk. It opened to reveal a letter, written in the same spiky handwriting that had been used to spell her name.

Dear Miss Katy Willacott (it said),

Please accept my apologies for whatever rudeness you have been forced to endure up to this point. The crew and I are all your friends but are being forced to play a part in front of Sir Thomas – he has threatened us all with the loss of our promised pay if we show you anything more than the barest courtesy. In giving you my cabin I hope to make the crossing easier for you. This is also the only way to conceal the fact that we did not dispose of your cat, which Derby certainly would have done had he been given the chance. You must keep him concealed. If Derby finds him out, he will be doomed for certain and the crew's pay forfeit. Speaking of Sir Thomas, on hearing that I was giving up my cabin he demanded that you be kept in it indefinitely. We will try to find a way to get you out when we can, but for now, you are confined to these quarters.

I have left you with paper and writing implements. The doctor has donated his tin of watercolours and brushes. We hope these will provide you with some occupation.

Yours sincerely,

Aurelius Roberts (Captain; The Alerte)

Katy read the letter twice, her sense of amazement slowly giving way to relief. Then she looked at Shadow again, who was still staring out of the tiny porthole. How could she keep a cat in such a tiny space for weeks? How would he be kept fed?

But at least he's alive, Katy reminded herself. *And at least you have friends.*

Chapter Forty-Five

Since she could not leave the cabin, Katy turned to Anahí Monroe's notebook. It was a perfect example of meticulous record-taking. Each specimen had been perfectly preserved and had with it clear, neatly written notes. Mrs Monroe had also been an excellent painter, and each page included a beautifully detailed watercolour of the living plant. She'd also been sure to include multiple examples of each specimen in different stages of its life cycle, from bud to full flower to seed. Besides the usual dry scientific notes about habitat and seasons and so on, there were notes describing the different ways locals in the area used each plant, as well as any connected myths and Mrs Monroe's own thoughts on how these might have developed. It really was a treasure trove of knowledge about flora of the area and Katy found herself grateful to Theo and Celia's mother for writing such an absorbing account – one that helped her pass the tedious hours stuck in her cabin.

Anahí's book also inspired Katy to work on her own specimens. She sat at the captain's desk with the plants she had collected on her journey through the rainforest and set about creating exactly the kind of specimen sheets that her mother had taught her how to make back at Kew, using Mrs Monroe's examples to remind her of exactly what to do.

First, she laid out each example on a clean sheet of paper, recreating the plant as she had seen it in the wild as best she could. Katy also began to rewrite all of her quickly made observations into clearer notes. These included the date on which she had collected the plant and what the area was like where it had been growing. As she copied these down, Katy added her observations of what the plant had looked like in life, because the colours changed as the specimen dried and there had been no time for her to paint them first. To do this she took out her battered copy of *Werner's Nomenclature of Colours* and checked all her descriptions against the ones she had made at the time of collection. The *Nomenclature of Colours* was a book that contained many little squares of watercolour paint, with clear descriptions of what that colour was beside it. Each colour had also been given a name, which meant that anyone with the book could see exactly what colour the plant had been, even if the dried specimen's colour had faded entirely. Werner's was what Charles Darwin had used during his voyage aboard the *Beagle*, and Katy felt pleased to be able to do the same aboard the *Alerte*.

Also in her expedition kit was a reel of brown cotton thread and a pack of sharp needles. These she used to carefully fasten the samples to the paper, sewing a few neat stitches over the fragile stems to hold them in place.

Katy was so engrossed in her work that it was only when Shadow began to silently prowl this way and that in the tiny cabin, brushing against her chair as he passed, that she looked up. She realized how quiet the rest of the ship had become. Gone was the sound of raucous laughter and chat from the galley. Derby and the rest of the gentlemen must have all gone to bed. All she could hear was the creaking of the small ship's timbers and the rumbling of her own empty stomach. She wondered if anyone had thought to save her some food. Surely Danny would?

There came a soft knock at the door. She opened it to see Percy on the other side. Behind him, the ship was dark. He motioned with one finger to his lips that she should be quiet and follow him. He nodded at Shadow too. Katy looked back at the cat, his eyes glowing in the yellow light from the candle. She blew out the flame and followed Percy, Shadow by her side every step of the way.

Up on deck, Katy shut her eyes as she felt the salt wind in her face – how she had missed that! She could see a lantern swinging against the mizzen mast, and saw a group of figures gathered there, outlined by the dim light.

"Miss Willacott," said Doctor Whitaker, with a smile. "We thought this way you and your pet might get some exercise – and some company."

They were all there – Martim, Danny and even Captain Roberts.

"Thank you," Katy told the crew gratefully. "For saving Shadow and for not … for not hating me."

Percy clapped her on the shoulder, as if to him she was still William Chandler, cabin boy. "Ach," he said. "You earned your place fair and square on this voyage, boy or no boy. Martim and me, we just feel bad that we teased you about your hands. Wouldn't have done that if we'd known you were a girl."

"If you'd known," Katy pointed out, "I wouldn't have been allowed to do anything at all."

"Aye, and we'd be lost to the storm because of it," Captain Roberts rumbled.

Katy looked at him. "Forgive me, Captain," she said carefully. "But … out of all of those aboard, I am surprised that you are not more angry with me."

Roberts raised one bushy eyebrow and for a moment Katy thought she had offended him. Then he grinned, a slightly sinister expression despite its intent.

"My mother, God rest her good soul, was a herring lassie," he said. "She gutted those fish from sun up to long after sun down. She followed the fleet more miles than I care to imagine. She could haul a net over her shoulder as if it were nowt but a bairn. She could handle a dingy in heavy weather too. She was as strong as the day is long, and if I could tell her about you, she would have nodded and puffed on her pipe as if there was nothing out of the ordinary to mention. If I dared to treat you the way Derby is, she'd have boxed my ears. You did as good a job as any I've seen in the twenty-five years I've been a captain on these waters, Katy Willacott, and I'll tell that to anyone who has the sense to listen."

Katy smiled. "Thank you."

"Here," Danny said, holding out a bowl of something that had a spoon sticking out of it. "Eat that before it goes stone cold, eh?"

Katy took the bowl, which smelled like beef stew. She looked down at Shadow, wondering if she should share her meal with him.

"Boy," Captain Roberts called. "Have you hauled up that line yet?"

There came the faint sound of effort from the grab rail and Katy realized that Arthur was leaning over it, struggling with something.

"I'm trying, Cap'n…"

"Be quick about it," said Roberts. "We've got a hungry shipmate here!"

Martim and Percy went to help. Between the three of them they hauled a line out of the water and on to the deck. Glints of silver dangled, flapping, at intervals along the rope. Shadow pounced on one.

"Fish!" Katy realized.

"Fish," agreed Doctor Whitaker. "We've got to find a way to keep your cat fed. Arthur here had the idea of dragging a long line rigged with hooks behind us throughout the day. By night there should be enough of a catch to feed Shadow."

Katy turned to the boy. "Arthur, that was a brilliant idea!"

The boy beamed at the praise.

"Don't give him a big head," grumbled Captain Roberts. "Get below to bed, Arthur. You've earned it."

The boy dashed away across the deck, eager for sleep.

"You can both come up here after dark each night, once the others have gone to sleep," Whitaker said. "We'll let you know when it's all clear. That way you should be able to avoid Derby completely and keep Shadow a secret. I'm afraid that does mean you'll be confined to the cabin all day."

"That's all right," Katy said, tucking into her meal. She was starving. "I'm going to spend the time properly cataloguing everything I found during my trip with Theo and Celia."

Doctor Whitaker looked wistful. "I wish I had something so worthy to keep me occupied. I'm afraid this entire journey has been a waste of time for me."

"Don't say that," Katy said. "If you hadn't come, we would never have met, would we?"

The doctor smiled warmly. "That's true. And I am very glad that we did."

"As am I," Katy said, and she meant it.

Chapter Forty-Six

Katy and Shadow's trips up on deck became a night-time ritual. Once the rest of the ship was asleep, someone would tap lightly on her door. They would go up quietly, where Arthur's plan to feed Shadow worked time and again. This arrangement suited Shadow, as he was naturally disposed to sleep during the day and hunt at night. It also meant that both Katy and Shadow got to sleep in the tiny bunk, because Shadow curled up on it for most of each day, which left it free for Katy to use at night. Often, the cat remained on deck with whoever had the night watch, prowling about on the *Alerte's* timbers until the first streaks of dawn lit the horizon. He seemed to understand that this was his cue to return to the cabin. The first few times Shadow stayed on deck without her Katy could barely sleep for fear that Derby or one of his party would spy him up there, but she couldn't keep him confined to the cabin. It would be cruel, especially since he really was getting bigger by the day. After two weeks had passed, she was convinced he would soon be too big to fit in the bunk to sleep. His teeth had grown too, into points as sharp as daggers, set in a jaw powerful enough to bite through a fish in one go.

Her stray kitten had become a black jaguar. By the time they reached England, Katy thought he would be almost fully grown.

"What are you going to do with him?" Percy asked one night as they watched Shadow devouring his supper. "I don't think he's going to fit at your parents' hearth. Not unless they own Windsor Castle!"

"I don't know," Katy admitted. "I just have to get him through this journey safely first. I'll worry about everything else once we get to port."

Meanwhile, Katy hadn't forgotten what she'd said to Fran about finding out what was in the crates and barrels that Derby had loaded on to the ship.

"Do you know what's in them?" she asked Percy and Martim one night.

"Not a clue," Percy said. "Only that there's about a thousand of 'em, and they were a devil to get aboard!"

Katy went over and rested a hand on the rough wood of one of the stacked boxes. "Are they heavy?"

"Some," Martim said. "Others, not so much."

"They're all different sizes," Katy observed. "That

probably means they've got different things in them, doesn't it, rather than one particular item?"

Doctor Whitaker even tried asking Derby again, but to no avail.

"He's not budging," he told Katy heavily. "Just warns me off being interested in things that do not concern me."

"Can't we open one?" Katy asked Captain Roberts. "They're right here on deck! We could nail it back down again afterwards. No one would know."

"No chance," Roberts said. "That nincompoop Mazarin checks each and every one of the crates up here every morning."

"Captain's right," Percy added, with a sigh. "He'd notice for sure, however careful we were."

"What about the ones in the hold?" Katy asked. "Does he check them too?"

"Not as regularly," Danny said. "Probably because he reckons he'd see anyone going down there, and it's usually only me who does that anyway."

"I could do it," Percy said. "Sneak down there one night, take a look-see."

"No," Katy said firmly. "If you got caught, you'd be in real trouble. I couldn't let you do that. If anyone goes, it'll be me."

The men all looked doubtful, but Katy was determined. She'd told Fran she was going to find out what was in the crates and she meant to do it, by hook or by crook.

"Danny," she said. "Leave the keys to the hold in the galley one night, as if you've forgotten them. That way you can't be accused of giving them to me."

Danny looked at Captain Roberts, who shrugged. "Who are we to stop her?"

The cook nodded. "All right, miss. But just you be careful, you hear? I'd not dismiss his threat about setting you adrift in the lifeboat too lightly, if I were you. He's a nasty one."

"Don't worry," Katy said. "They'll never know. I promise."

Another two nights passed before the opportunity arose. The weather was beginning to worsen, storms gathering on the ocean. The *Alerte*, weighed down with her additional cargo of mysterious crates, listed low in the water, swinging this way and that. It made the gentlemen sick, their sea legs not helped by the quantities of wine they were enjoying with each meal. This particular night, they all went to bed early and the worse for wear. When Percy came to tap lightly on Katy's door earlier than usual, she knew the time had come.

They said nothing as they crossed the galley, but Katy could see Danny's silver keys glinting from his tiny worktable. She glanced at Percy, who nodded and went up on deck. Katy brushed her fingers over Shadow's head and then, when the cat looked up at her, she nodded towards the first mate. Shadow understood perfectly and followed

Percy up on deck.

Besides the keys, Danny had also left an oil lamp and matches out for her. Katy crept through the galley, scooping these up as quietly as she could. A loose deck board creaked underfoot, the sound loud in the dark. She froze, listening for any sign that she'd been heard, but there was none. Someone snored loudly, someone else groaned a little as the ship rose and fell with the heavy swell of the sea, but that was all.

Katy dared not light the lamp yet. She moved quietly to the door that led down to the hold and slowly fitted the key in its lock. Thankfully it turned easily, with no more than a tiny *clunk*. Katy pushed the door inwards on its silent hinges and stepped into total darkness.

Chapter Forty-Seven

Beyond the door Katy could see nothing at all. She pushed it shut behind her, listening to the creak of the timbers as the weight of the ocean squeezed against them. She struck a match and lit the lamp, sighing with relief as the greasy yellow light swelled around her.

She needed to be quick. Katy made her way down the stairs, ducking her head as she reached the bottom to avoid the low timber there. The hold was cramped and awkward to move around in – what a nightmare it must have been for Percy and Martim to load everything that had been stacked there! The space had been filled almost to bursting.

A sudden wave rocked at the *Alerte* and Katy almost lost her footing. She put her hand out to steady herself against the ship's bulkhead and the rough wood was cold and clammy beneath her palm. The hold smelled musty and a little damp, and if Katy had been prone to nervousness she definitely would not have chosen to come down here alone. But she had a job to do.

She had to find something that she could get into without her tampering being noticed. Katy made her way around the stack, squeezing between the ship's walls and the various crates and barrels before picking one of the smaller square chests. She set down the oil lamp and reached for it, only to discover that it was not nearly as heavy as she was expecting. Katy lifted it to the floor and set the box down.

There was a sudden loud creak from overhead, followed by the unmistakable *thump-thump-thump* of several footsteps on the deck above her head. Katy froze. The crew were all up on deck, why would any of the gentlemen be moving about? Had one of them heard something as she moved around down here? Katy felt utter panic as she realized she hadn't locked the door behind her. If anyone suspected someone had come down here and tried it…

She held her breath, hoping that whoever it was just needed some air. Then she realized that if whoever it was went up on deck, they would see Shadow, which would be even worse. If Katy got caught down here, nothing really terrible could happen to her, could it? But if Derby or Mazarin saw *Shadow*…

She heard the footsteps again – now they were in the galley. The person *was* coming to the hold door! Panicked, she looked around for somewhere to hide. The hold was full of dark corners and stowed gear, vital ship's clutter and assorted clobber. Katy spied a gap between some of Danny's food stores and blew out the lamp, plunging herself into total darkness. She dropped to her knees and crawled blindly towards the gap, hoping it would conceal her from whoever it was about to appear at the top of the stairs. She squeezed behind the stores and realized that to fit she was going to have to lie flat on her belly and pull herself in, and even then she wouldn't know if her feet were hidden.

Katy hauled herself into her hiding place, heart pounding. She crawled face first into a spider's web, the sticky fibres of silk spreading across her nose and mouth. She disturbed the spider who had spun it too – she felt the large creature scrabbling against her cheek but couldn't lift her hand high enough to bat it away. Katy shut her eyes instead, telling herself not to make a noise.

It's just a spider, she told herself, to calm her pounding heart. *It's just a spider...*

She wondered whether it had come from England, where there were no poisonous eight-legged arachnids, or whether it had come aboard with their supplies from Brazil, where she thought there were probably plenty of spiders that could kill with a venomous bite.

Don't think about it. Don't—

Above the hammering of her heart, Katy heard the striking of a match and then the dimmest of lights washed around the dark edges of her hiding place.

"Who's down here?" said the suspicious voice of Lucas Mazarin.

The spider crawled across her face, big enough that its feet felt like a mouse's pitter-pattering footsteps on her skin.

Please don't go up my nose, Katy begged it silently. *Please don't!*

The spider began to make its way down her neck, tickling with every move it made. Katy held her breath, eyes squeezed shut even though it was so dark she couldn't see anyway. She hoped the creature wouldn't find a way to get beneath her shirt.

More footsteps, the light a little brighter still as Mazarin moved down the stairs and into the hold. He stopped suddenly and Katy wondered what he was doing for a moment. Then she remembered the little crate she'd moved. It was still on the floor!

There was another sudden flurry of footsteps at the top of the stairs. "Mazarin? What are you up to? The hold's off limits to all but the crew, you know that. It's not safe to be down here during the voyage, not when it's as full as it is now."

Captain Roberts!

"Sir Thomas is sick and needs water, Roberts," Mazarin said. "There was none in the galley, so I took it upon myself to fetch some for him from the stores. I was not expecting the door to be unlocked, and yet it is, suggesting there is someone snooping around down here."

The captain's heavy tread came further down the steps. "Don't be ridiculous, man," he said. "Can you see anyone down here?"

"This crate has been disturbed."

At that very moment another wave hit the *Alerte*, tipping her on the swell. Katy was wedged into her hiding place, but she heard the shuffle of Mazarin's footsteps as he tried to keep his balance.

"I believe," the captain said wryly, "that we have discovered the culprit. The crate merely slid from its place, that's all."

"I'm not convinced," Mazarin said coldly. "I wish to be sure that the girl is in her cabin, where she should be."

"Of course she is," said Roberts. "You really think she's down here somewhere, with the rats and the spiders? If so, where? Don't be ridiculous, man. She is fast asleep in her bed, where no gentleman of any standing would disturb her."

There was another moment of silence.

"Very well," said Mazarin. "I will take you at your word. But whoever left the hold unlocked should be punished for their negligence. There is valuable cargo down here, Captain, and you will be held responsible for it."

Chapter Forty-Eight

Katy remained still as they went back up the stairs. The door shut and the hold was plunged into absolute darkness once more. Still she waited, scared to make any noise at all. Their footsteps faded away. Eventually all was silence apart from the *Alerte*'s own creaking movements in the wash. Katy inched her way out of her hiding place. The moment she could, she reached up to brush the spider away and heard it land on the timbers with a little thump before skittering into some crack or other. She scrubbed at her face to rid it of the spider's silk, then scrabbled around for the oil lamp. Her heart refused to settle, pounding, pounding, pounding in her chest.

The crate she had taken down had been stacked back on the pile. Getting to her feet, Katy took a deep breath. She'd come this far, she may as well finish the job. She couldn't go back above decks yet anyway – if Mazarin was still awake he might hear her. Katy lifted the crate down again and set it on the floor. Then she took out the penknife Percy had let her keep and knelt in front of the box. She slipped the blade between the lid and the box to lever it open.

Gradually, the nails began to lift and then, eventually, the lid had opened enough for her to get her fingers under it. Katy pulled at it with both hands. The last nails separated from the box with a faint *pop!*

Katy set the lid down and peered inside. The first thing she saw was a sheet of paper, printed with large words that read *Property of Sir Thomas Derby, the British Museum, London, England.* She took this out and stared at what was beneath. Whatever the object was, it had been wound in sturdy cotton fabric and then packed in sawdust. Katy lifted the object out – it was very light and a strange, uneven shape – and gently freed it from its wrapping.

It was a small bird. Dead, of course, and stuffed, but still beautiful. The iridescent green of its feathers glinted faintly in the light from the oil lamp, as did the shiny black beads that had replaced its eyes. She stared at it with a creeping sense of horror and then looked up at the stack of crates that filled the *Alerte's* hold. Did they all have something similar inside them? A creature once wild and free, now dead and stuffed?

All of them?

Katy set the bird down amid its wrapping and got slowly

to her feet to look at one of the largest crates in the stack. It had been sealed so that its lid was set on the side rather than on its top. Katy stared at it for a moment, her mind buzzing. She'd previously resolved not to open any of the big crates for fear of her tampering being too obvious. But she had to know. If each of these crates held a dead creature, what was in the largest of them?

Her heart burning in her chest, Katy set to opening the crate. It took longer to prise apart than the smaller box, so long in fact that the oil in her lamp began to burn low, casting out flickering shapes. Eventually Katy worked the lid free and it fell open at her feet, sawdust tumbling around her ankles. Whatever was inside had been wrapped in the same fashion as the bird and Katy knew at once that she would not be able to get it out alone. Still, it was in the vague shape of a creature standing on all fours, and so she determined to unwrap the head. She pulled apart the cotton layers until she could see what was beneath, and when she did Katy let out a little sob.

Looking back at her was the beautiful golden and black spotted face of a jaguar. It had green eyes, just like Shadow, and it had been stuffed, just like the bird.

Katy stepped back, staring at the dead animal. She remembered passing through the jungle with Celia and Theo, the rainforest silent apart from the sound of their own footsteps because everything else had been hunted or had fled for its life. How could Derby, as a naturalist, participate in that sort of behaviour? She remembered the hunters who had tried to kill Shadow and—

Katy gasped.

The hunters! Had they been collecting animals for Derby? They had clearly been expecting payment for every specimen they shot, and Derby couldn't have hunted all these animals on his own, could he, not in the short time the *Alerte* had been in port? But Theo had said that the men with the guns were working for the plantation, so that would mean that Derby...

Katy covered her mouth with one dusty hand.

Was *Derby* the owner of that new rubber plantation? The one doing all the damage to Theo and Celia's home? The one forcing the villagers away from their homes, or else taking them as slaves? Could that be the 'secret mission' she had heard Sir Thomas and Mazarin discussing on the outbound journey?

Katy's shocked gaze fell on one of the barrels that Derby had loaded beside the crates of slaughtered animals. They couldn't have creatures in them, surely? And hadn't she seen a barrel that looked exactly like this, waiting on the dock beside that horribly ruined land of the plantation? She reached out both hands and tried to tip the barrel. It was heavy, and she had to use all her weight against it. Whatever was inside shifted as one, as if it were liquid. Katy dared not open the barrel if it was – in this heavy swell it might spill, which would give away for certain that someone had been snooping around down here. As the barrel moved, her dim light caught the words that had been printed on the side of the barrel.

Private property of Sir Thomas Derby. Not to be opened.

Chapter Forty-Nine

When Katy crept back up on deck, it was to find herself in a rising gale and a heavy sea. Wind whipped viciously across her face as Doctor Whitaker caught sight of her.

"The captain has told me of your close call," he said. "I wanted to make sure you were all right."

She smiled grimly, looking past him to the stack of even more crates that stood in the centre of the *Alerte*'s crowded deck. "Oh, *I'm* fine," she said bitterly.

The doctor followed her gaze with a frown as Shadow came trotting towards them. "What is it? Have you discovered what Derby's game is?"

Katy relayed what she'd seen inside the crates. The doctor listened gravely, nodding.

"He'll want them for the museum," he said. "It sounds as if he's aiming to open with a grand collection."

Katy didn't mention the barrels and her suspicions in that regard, thinking it best to keep that secret until she had formulated clearer thoughts about it in her own mind.

A fresh wave hit the ship, rolling the *Alerte* hard. She had to grab Whitaker to stop him tumbling to the deck. A hard, icy rain began to fall, slicing the night air to ribbons.

"You must go below," Percy shouted, appearing beside them. "Both of you."

The storm raged for days. Katy sat at her desk and wrote in her notebook about her discovery of Derby's specimen collection and how he had obtained it, including details about how it had affected the rainforest and the people who lived there. Katy also made notes about her suspicions regarding his connections to that awful rubber plantation, all the time wishing that Fran were there to talk to. She wondered what her friend and Theo were doing at that moment – had they already discovered the truth?

There were nights when the weather was so bad that Katy and Shadow could not leave the safety of the cabin at all. When that happened the cat, so big now that his head was the height of Katy's hip, paced in circles, too restless to settle. It worried Katy, because she could see how awful Shadow found it to be so confined. It made her think of those animals that had been captured for zoos and put in cages not much bigger than their room on the *Alerte*. She couldn't allow that to happen to Shadow, but she didn't know how she was going to stop it, not when they got to England. Still, better that than him end up like one of those poor creatures in the hold because he had run foul of Derby. Neither end was what Katy wanted for him, though. She regretted again not doing more to make sure he stayed in the jungle.

It was on one of these nights that disaster struck. The sun had set, although it was hard to tell, because the day had been so dark and stormy that it had barely got light at all. Katy had been sitting at her desk but the rocking of the boat was so violent she couldn't write. She was trying to distract Shadow as she waited to see if anyone was going to knock on her door. The cat was in desperate need of exercise – they both were. Katy craved fresh air, not least because the cabin was beginning to stink of the fish that the mates had brought each night for Shadow to eat. The big cat was becoming so agitated that he even snapped at her a couple of times, his blade-sharp teeth grazing her skin.

When the knock at the door came, it was Percy on the other side of the captain's door. He held a bucket of still-flapping fish in one hand and a covered plate for her in the other, and Katy's heart sank all the way to her toes.

"We can't stay in here another night!"

Percy shook his head. "It's not safe to come out," he whispered hoarsely. "Can't you feel the swell? The deck is awash!"

"Shadow has cabin fever," she whispered back, even as the boat pitched against another wave. "If he doesn't get exercise he's going to run mad!"

Percy glanced over his shoulder, towards the darkened recesses of the bunk corridor. "I can't promise that everyone's asleep," he said. "How could any landlubber not be awake in this? It's not safe, Katy."

"Just ten minutes," she begged. Shadow was behind her, pushing against her legs, trying to get out. "Just *five*, even!"

"All right," Percy said. "But be quick about getting up those stairs!"

Katy stepped back and Shadow was past her and up the steps so quickly she barely saw him move.

Up on deck the timbers were slick and wet, difficult to cross. The wind wailed and screamed around the masts, tearing at her clothes, throwing rain in cold, knife-like slices against her hands, neck and arms. Still, it was so good to be out of the cabin. Katy held on to the grab rail, shut her eyes and tipped her head back into the storm.

Her relief didn't last long. When she turned around she found herself staring straight at Lucas Mazarin. His hair had been plastered against his head by the rain, but he still had that cruel twist to his lips.

"You," he said. "You're not allowed out of the cabin."

"Leave her be, Mazarin," Percy yelled over the storm. "She needs air. She's doing no harm."

Mazarin turned on the first mate. "Hold your tongue. Derby will hear that you've allowed this. You'll lose your pay. You'll *all* lose your pay."

Katy looked around, trying to find Shadow amid the

pitching chaos of the ship. A glint of clouded moonlight shone against a black shape at the prow.

"Go below," Percy told Katy.

"I can't," Katy said, raising her voice over the noise of the crashing waves.

"Why not?" Mazarin asked. He turned, surveying the rocking deck again. "What are you looking for?"

"Nothing," Katy said, heart thumping at the thought of Mazarin seeing Shadow. But she couldn't leave the cat up here, not alone, not like this!

"Miss Willacott," Percy shouted again. "Go below."

"Do as you're told, girl," Mazarin said. "Or it'll go badly for everyone aboard this ship who expects to get a wage at the end of this journey."

Katy had no choice. She went back into the captain's cabin with Mazarin watching her from the galley, a satisfied smile on his mean face.

She felt sick. What would happen to Shadow? He didn't listen to anyone but her, not really. Mazarin would be waiting for her to creep back out of the captain's cabin, so if any of the crew tried to bring Shadow back down to her, he would see.

It seemed an age before there was another quiet knock on the door. Percy opened it and stepped right inside, pulling the door closed behind him with a swift glance down towards the bunks.

"Where's Shadow?" Katy asked.

Percy held up both hands. "It's all right. I got him into the lifeboat. He'll be safe there."

Katy covered her face with her hands. "If Derby finds him – or Mazarin—"

"They won't," the first mate said. "It's probably better that he's up there anyway, isn't it? That way he can pop out when he needs to. Whereas you…"

"Whereas me – what?"

Percy sighed and shook his head. "You can't come out again, Katy. Not now. Mazarin will be checking on you."

Katy looked around the tiny room in which they stood. There was barely enough space for both of them to stand beside each other and they were still three weeks from port.

"I understand," Katy said. "Just make sure Shadow's safe, won't you?"

"I promise."

Katy shut her eyes as he left, listening to the storm howl around the *Alerte* as if it were a wild animal itself. Weeks stuck inside this poky room and now she didn't even have Shadow for company.

Chapter Fifty

By the time another week had passed, Katy was beginning to think she would go completely insane. The worst of the storms had blown out, giving way to calmer weather. She opened her porthole as wide as she could and spent a lot of time with her face leaning out of the small circle that led into the outside world, just so she could feel the breeze on her face.

The crew did their best to make her feel better. Martim put notes with her meals, little lessons in Portuguese, scrawled in his untidy hand. Doctor Whitaker smuggled new books to her.

There came a time, though, when Katy had exhausted every form of entertainment available to her. She had even run out of paper. That's when the terrible boredom and misery set in. She had no one to talk to, nothing to do.

It was then that Katy was desperate enough to risk getting the meteorite out of its hiding place. Since that first night in the captain's cabin, it had remained wrapped and out of sight at the bottom of her bag, tucked deep in a dark corner beneath the bunk. Katy had been too fearful to remove it, heeding Fran's word to keep it secret until she reached home. Now, though, she furtively retrieved it and began to paint representations of its surfaces into the last free corners and margins of her journal. That way, she could at least hide her work away quickly should she need to.

Katy made observations on the meteorite's character. She used Werner's to help her pick which of her watercolours to use as she painted. It was a blessed new distraction that passed the hours as the *Alerte* sailed on, and Katy devoted herself to it so completely that when the argument outside her door started, at first she didn't even notice it. Two voices, raised in anger as they remonstrated. She listened a moment and realized that the voices belonged to Derby and Doctor Whitaker.

"… this will not be borne!" Doctor Whitaker was shouting. "The cruelty is too immense! You will let me see her, Derby, or the papers will know about it!"

"The papers will know what, Doctor?" Derby demanded. "That I brought the child home safely, despite her wayward nature? That I kept her safe?"

"Safe!" Whitaker repeated, with a snort. "A prisoner, you mean! And I will not countenance it any longer – not as a doctor, nor as a decent man! There's damned all you can do about it, Derby. It's not as if you can dock *my* pay, is it?"

"Fine," Derby shouted back. "But make sure she stays out of my sight!"

The sound of heavy feet stomped away and Katy stepped away from the door. There was a brusque knock, and then the doctor's voice, clipped and clearly still angry.

"Miss Willacott, may I enter?"

Katy blinked. The meteorite was out on the desk!

"Just a moment, please," she called, rushing to secrete the rock back into her pack and shoving it back in its hiding place beneath the bunk. "Come in, Doctor!"

Katy hurriedly closed her field notebook as the cabin door opened. Doctor Whitaker's face was still creased into an angry frown, though he smiled when he saw her.

"Miss Willacott," he said quietly. "I believe that this evening, you will be able to perambulate the deck. Wait just a few more hours, until these awful excuses for gentlemen have gone to bed. Can you bear that?"

Katy smiled, relief flooding through her. "Yes, Doctor, I can."

That night, for the first time in far too long, the knock at Katy's door wasn't just so that one of the crew could give her some food. Captain Roberts himself stood there and gave her a small smile as Katy looked up at him.

The crew and Doctor Whitaker were all waiting for her on deck and gave a small cheer as Katy appeared. The fresh air was delicious and above her the sky was full of stars. Katy felt a hundred times lighter, as if she could float into the clear night air and drift among the starlight. How she had missed just being outside!

"Hang on," Percy said. "We're still one hand short…"

He went to the tiny lifeboat that was moored against the *Alerte*'s side. Martim joined him, helping to untie the canvas sheet that covered the open deck. Together they hauled it back and a lithe black shape jumped out.

"Shadow!" she said, overjoyed to see the animal was safe. Then she blinked as the cat padded towards her. It was astonishing how big he had become. When he reached her Katy actually felt a brief flicker of alarm. Shadow's head was huge and so were his teeth. But he rubbed his ears against Katy's wrist as if he were nothing more than an overgrown housecat.

"He's missed you," said Arthur. "Every night, he goes looking for you, so he does."

Katy smiled at the boy. "Have you been feeding him for me?"

Arthur nodded solemnly. "Aye, and he's a hungry so-and-so, that's for sure! Takes two whole lines of fish now, before he's had his fill!"

Katy laughed. "Maybe I can help you tonight, then. Is there a line to haul in?"

Arthur brightened. "There is! It's a heavy one, an' all!"

"Lead the way," Katy said, Shadow still at her side.

"Well, well, well," said a voice from behind them. "It seems you have yet another secret, Katy Willacott."

Chapter Fifty-One

It was Lucas Mazarin, standing there with his hands on his hips and a cruel little smirk on his face. His gaze was fixed on Shadow. Katy turned ice cold.

"Get below, Mazarin," growled Captain Roberts. "Before I decide that the best place for you is over the side, with the fishes."

"Oh, please, Captain, let's not pretend you have any power here," Mazarin sneered. "One word from me and you'll be begging on the streets. You'll never get another ship."

"You can't tell Derby about Shadow," Katy said. "You *can't*."

"Really?" Mazarin asked. "Why not? This is Sir Thomas's expedition, is it not? He should know that he has managed to gather this rather magnificent specimen for his collection, don't you think?"

Katy's skin crawled. "He's not a specimen! He's a living creature. I won't let you do what you've done to the rest of the animals on this ship, Mazarin."

"Whatever do you mean?" Derby's secretary asked. "This is a scientific expedition, girl, and it has collected scientific specimens. The collection we have amassed will allow thousands of people to see what they otherwise never would." He pointed at Shadow. "Why should only you be the one to see that beautiful black coat? He should be preserved so every museum visitor can appreciate him."

"There is nothing scientific about what you and Derby have done!" Katy cried. "You didn't even go into the rainforest yourself. You didn't see any of these creatures in their own habitats, you didn't study how they live! You don't care about them, or what you've destroyed to get them! You're just interested in being famous and rich."

Mazarin flicked his fingers in dismissive disdain. "Really," he said. "Such a tantrum. What an embarrassment you are to your parents. Now, if you'll excuse me, I believe I have some news for Sir Thomas. As for the rest of you, you'd better start preparing yourselves for being jobless, homeless and without prospects. And say goodbye to your *pet*."

"I'll throw you overboard, so I will!" cried little Arthur, his face red and his fists bunched. "You won't touch 'im! No one will!"

Mazarin eyed the boy. "You'd better watch your lip, rat,

or the first thing you'll see when we reach port is the law. Threats like that are no joke."

"Leave him alone," said Doctor Whitaker. "You're nothing but a bully, Mazarin. Come after the boy and you'll have me to deal with."

Mazarin curled his lip into a cruel smile. "Words, Doctor. Just words."

He turned away again and this time it was Katy who spoke up, her heart sick and pounding.

"Wait," she said. "Just *wait*. What if… What if I could give you something else? Something … something better than a black jaguar?"

Mazarin stopped. For a moment there was silence and then he turned around. "And what, pray, would *that* be?"

Katy hesitated. The rest of the crew – her friends, who had put their livelihoods on the line for her – looked at her. She couldn't let them suffer. She couldn't let *Shadow* suffer. But the only thing she had to offer Mazarin was the reason she had embarked on this journey in the first place.

Mazarin huffed at her silence. "You're wasting my time, little girl. I'm going—"

"A meteorite," Katy said, her voice clear in the cool, calm night. "I can give you a meteorite."

Katy heard Doctor Whitaker suck in a gasp.

Mazarin stared at her. "You're lying."

"I'm not. I found a meteorite. That's why I went into the jungle."

Mazarin narrowed his eyes. "I don't believe you. How would *you* be able to find a meteorite?"

"I found people to help me," Katy said. "I'll give it to you if you promise on your life that you won't tell Derby about Shadow. And you make sure that each of these men get their just pay."

"Let me see it," Mazarin said. "And I'll think about it."

"No," said Katy. "No, you agree here and now in front of these witnesses. *Then* I'll get it for you."

"Why should I?" Mazarin asked. "Why shouldn't I have the meteorite *and* the jaguar? It all belongs to the expedition, anyway."

"It's hidden," Katy bluffed, her heart racing, because now she wished she'd put it in a safer place. "You'll never find it. I'll throw it overboard before I let you take it without agreeing to this."

"Katy," said the doctor. "You shouldn't have to do this."

"No, I shouldn't," Katy said bitterly. "But I will."

Mazarin seemed to be considering his options. "Very well," he said suddenly, stepping forwards and abruptly holding out a hand for Katy to shake. "We have a deal. I will keep your secret if you give me the meteorite. But if it turns out to be a common rock…"

"It isn't," Katy said. "You may be assured of that."

Mazarin gave a sneering laugh. "As if your assurances mean anything at all."

They shook hands, although Katy had to stop herself

from recoiling at the man's touch.

"Get it," he ordered. "And hurry up. I'm tired."

Katy ran back to the captain's cabin and dragged her pack out from beneath the bunk, fumbling open the ties to pull out the wrapped bundle within. Once she had the rock in her hands, though, she stopped. Katy didn't want to hand the meteorite over, not after everything she had been through to get it. Not when she knew that if she did, no one would ever know that she had been the one who found it. Katy knelt on the floor and lifted the heavy bundle between both hands, feeling the tears welling in her eyes. She could imagine Sir Thomas Derby, standing in front of a crowd at the museum, holding it up and declaring his find the most important ever in scientific history. And it wasn't his, it wasn't! This was *her* find. Hers! Not Mazarin's, and certainly not Derby's.

But what could she do?

Then Katy remembered what Grandfather had said. *Perhaps your journey was not about the meteorite after all, but about you, yourself.* What would it say about her, if she valued being known as the finder of this rock over the well-being of her friends? That would make her no better than Derby and that was the last thing Katy wanted. After all, she didn't own the meteorite, did she, because who on earth could own a piece of the universe itself, any more than they could own the great and ancient rainforests of Brazil?

Katy stood and carried the meteorite up on to the deck.

She stood beneath the stars and held it out to Mazarin. She just had to hope that he would not double-cross her and decide to tell Derby about Shadow after all.

Everyone was silent. Mazarin unwrapped the rock and hefted it into the lamplight, turning it around to examine it carefully. He looked up at Katy, who set her jaw so as not to give him the satisfaction of seeing her tears fall.

"As if *you* deserve this," Mazarin said. "You, instead of Sir Thomas Derby. You should be ashamed."

"No," said Doctor Whitaker. "It is you who should be ashamed, Mazarin. And Sir Thomas, if he dares to claim this find as his own, instead of attributing it to the person who actually found it – Katy Willacott."

Mazarin wrapped the meteorite up again and tucked it beneath his arm. "I don't know what you mean. This was an expedition led by Sir Thomas Derby to find a meteorite, and it was successful. What else is there to say?" He looked at Katy. "Except that I believe your father's livelihood is dependent on Sir Thomas's favour and your mother's may soon be too. You should remember that. It wouldn't take much to cast them both out into the street. Would it?"

He turned his back and walked away, taking the meteorite with him. Then there was no sound but the wind tugging at the *Alerte*'s sails.

Chapter Fifty-Two

The atmosphere aboard ship was jubilant as the *Alerte* continued on. Katy heard it in Derby's raised, happy voice through the door of the captain's cabin as he celebrated the unexpected additional success of the trip. There was a lot of singing and drinking going on, she could tell, as they finished off the last of the voyage's stores. She saw them a couple of times, through a crack in the cabin door, carousing around the galley table.

Derby's good mood actually extended to Katy too. She got word that she was to be allowed out of the cabin more, although Sir Thomas continued to act as if she did not exist.

Katy tried not to care about the loss of the meteorite but it was hard. She wondered where Derby thought it had appeared from and what exactly his secretary had told him. At least she still had her field notebook, catalogue sheets and Anahí Monroe's journal. Shadow too, of course. Thus far, Mazarin appeared to have kept his word about the great black cat.

Doctor Whitaker's indignance on Katy's behalf remained undiminished.

"I've tried to talk to Derby, Katy," he told her one night as they stood at the grab rail and watched the dark line of land that denoted the coast of France. "He just ignores any mention of you. What an odious excuse for a man. It won't stand, I tell you. It won't."

Katy was grateful for his care but nervous of what it could mean for her family.

"Please don't say any more," she begged him. "Remember what Mazarin said about my parents. I couldn't bear it if they both lost their positions because of me. Please, Doctor."

Whitaker sighed unhappily but nodded nonetheless.

They sighted the coast of England amid an icy squall that heralded how close the country had moved to winter in their absence. It rose out of a chill morning mist and a dawn that Katy had stayed up to see. Percy was at the mizzen for first watch and sometimes, when no one else was around, he'd let her take the tiller. Shadow still prowled the deck, stalking the seabirds that had begun to appear the closer they'd got to land.

"There we are," Percy said, pointing through the miserable morning. "See it? Home."

Katy peered through the grey morning to the uncertain

line on the horizon. A strange feeling fluttered in her heart. She was going home. It somehow felt as unreal as the idea of this journey had, back before she had run away to make it happen. She had travelled halfway around the world alone, she had been part of a crew on an ocean-going vessel, she had trekked through the jungles of Brazil, and now she was going back to tiny Rose Cottage in Kew Gardens. How could life continue as it had before?

One thing was certain, though – she was looking forward to seeing her family, to being back in their rowdy kitchen. All the time Katy had been busy on this trip she'd been able to hold her homesickness at bay, but on this journey home she had realized just how much her family meant to her. She *missed* them. She missed Edie too, despite her having spilled the beans about where Katy had gone. Katy knew that faced with both her parents, Edie wouldn't have had much choice. Anyway, it would be wonderful to see her familiar face. She hoped they would all be there, waiting for the ship to come in – waiting to see *her*.

The *Alerte* passed the Isle of Wight and headed for Southampton, the waters of the Solent busy with ships, large and small. As the sun rose and they drew closer to the dock, Derby appeared on deck. He glanced at Katy for the first time since she'd come aboard in Salvador, looking her up and down in disgust.

"Don't you have anything decent to wear?" he asked.

Katy looked down at her trousers and shirt, shabby

and threadbare after the weeks of adventure. She couldn't imagine wearing a dress now. Would she have to, once she was back at Rose Cottage?

"This is all I have," she said. "I did have another shirt, but now it's wrapped around my meteorite."

Derby levelled an icy look at her. "Your what?"

Katy raised her chin. "The meteorite I found in Brazil. The one you have in your possession. *My* meteorite."

Derby laughed so dismissively that Katy felt her blood begin to boil. "What an imagination little girls have. *Your* meteorite indeed. What an idea!"

"Are you proud of yourself?" she asked him, her anger making her bold. "That you did no work on this expedition but still you will take all the credit?"

He stopped laughing. "I really don't know what you're talking about, child, but really, what kind of person would even think about ruining the successful return of a scientific expedition for their own glory?"

"But that's not—"

"Sir Thomas," Mazarin called from the prow of the ship. "I do believe the press are here to greet you!"

Derby turned his back on Katy as if she were no longer there. He strode to the front of the ship, waving at the small knot of people gathered at the dock where the *Alerte* was about to berth. Katy thought about leaning over the grab rail and shouting down to the waiting gaggle of men, perhaps something about having a story to tell, one that Sir

Thomas would not reveal – anything that would draw the journalists' attention.

As she went to the grab rail, though, it was another figure that caught her eye and made her breath catch. Below on the dock stood her father. He was alone – there was no sign of Mary Willacott, or Stefan, or Grandma Peg and Grandpa Ned. Josiah Willacott was looking up at the *Alerte*, searching for her. He hadn't spotted her, though, and Katy realized why with a little pulse of misgiving. The last time her father had seen her, she had looked like Katy Willacott. But now, with her shorn hair and grubby boy's clothes, she looked like just another member of the ship's crew. Not even her own father recognized her.

Katy waved. Her father's gaze passed over her for a second, looking away before flashing back to stare at her, wide-eyed.

His expression grew darker. Katy felt a little sick as she realized that her beloved papa didn't look overjoyed to see her.

He looked old and tired. He looked worried and unhappy.

He looked angry.

Chapter Fifty-Three

Once the *Alerte* was anchored it was as if a whirlwind overtook the ship. The journalists all crowded around the gangplank, shouting questions. Derby strutted towards them and then stopped, his attention caught by Josiah Willacott, standing all alone. Derby turned to look at Katy and then shouted at her father.

"You!" he shouted. "Willacott! Come here. Get out of the way," Derby ordered the journalists. "Make room, or I'll not talk to a single one of you."

That was enough to ensure that the gaggle separated and let Josiah Willacott pass. Derby grabbed him by the arm and dragged him up the gangplank, away from the newspaper men. Katy was shocked at how much older her father looked than the last time she'd seen him. She wanted to hug him, but Derby still had hold of his arm.

"Listen to me, Willacott," Derby hissed. "You get her out of here now. She doesn't speak to anyone, ever, about this. I never want to see or hear of her again, is that clear? Or your work for the British Museum will be over. You'll be finished, forever. Do you understand?"

Josiah Willacott nodded, his face turning grey at Derby's awful threat. "I understand."

"Go, this instant."

Derby let go of Josiah's arm with a nasty little push, and then turned back to the journalists. "Gentlemen," he called. "Do come up on deck. You should learn about the triumph of my expedition aboard the ship that carried me all the way to South America, don't you think?"

"Come on," Katy's father said to Katy as the group of men all moved at once, gathering around Derby at the prow. "We must go."

He pulled her towards the gangplank. Katy held back – she couldn't just abandon Shadow! And what about her pack, the notebooks and her catalogue pages? They were all still in the captain's cabin. She needed to say goodbye to the crew too.

"Wait," Katy said. "I can't go yet, I need to—"

"Katy Willacott," her father hissed angrily. "You've caused your family enough worry and trouble to last a lifetime. You will do as you're told, do you understand? How can you be this selfish?"

Katy felt the air leave her lungs as the shock of her

father's words hit home. Josiah Willacott bustled her down to the dock and into a carriage that must have been waiting for them. Her father banged on the ceiling once, hard, and the horses set off, rattling them away.

The journey back to Kew was long and uncomfortable. Her father barely spoke to her, and the carriage travelled at a punishing pace. They changed for horses once after night fell but did not stop to sleep. By the time they had reached Richmond and crossed the river, dawn was breaking and Katy was exhausted, aching and heartsick.

Katy looked out as they approached Rose Cottage. It seemed so much smaller than the last time she had seen it. The hens were pecking around the open front door, and she knew that Grandma Peg would have just thrown them a handful of grain. Now she would be filling the old kettle and getting it on the stove ready for tea, while Grandpa Ned pulled on his uniform for another day of strolling the pathways of Kew Gardens. Her mother would be getting ready for the herbarium and Stefan would probably still be in bed, trying to steal another few minutes' sleep.

Everything was exactly the same as she had left it and yet Katy realized that nothing would ever be the same again.

The door was flung wider as the carriage rattled to a stop. Grandma Peg appeared with a wild shriek.

"They're here!" she cried, rushing down the path with her arms flung wide. "They're back!"

Grandpa Ned appeared behind her, quickly followed by

Katy's mother. Even from where she still sat on the hard carriage bench, Katy could see how pale her mother was. Katy's stomach was tied up in knots as secure as any that she'd fastened as a cabin boy on the *Alerte*. She jumped down from the carriage and found herself enveloped immediately in a storm of hard hugs.

"Oh, my dear," said Peg, crying freely. "You're back, and alive! Look at you, just look at you!"

"Katy," said her mother, her voice cracking as she gathered her daughter to her. "Oh, Katy. I thought I'd never see you again, my darling. I thought you were lost to me forever!"

Katy hugged back. She was shocked at how thin her mother had become. It finally began to dawn on her that the worry she had cast upon her family had been far more terrible than she had imagined or intended.

"I'm sorry, Mama," she said, her voice muffled against her mother's neck. "I did not mean for you to worry so. I am fine. I'm absolutely well."

Mary Willacott sobbed and held on to her, and when she finally pulled away it was only to cup her daughter's face in her hands. "Look how tall you are!" she said, hiccupping over her grief and relief. "*Look* at you!"

There came a sound behind them and Katy saw her brother Stefan coming down the path, still rubbing the sleep from his eyes.

"You're back in one piece then, sis," he said. And then,

looking her up and down, "So *that's* where my shirt went! I've been looking for it for weeks!"

"Sorry," Katy said awkwardly. "I'll wash it for you, Stefan, I promise."

Her brother wrinkled his nose. "No, it's fine. You can keep it."

"Come on, lass," said Grandpa Ned. "Let's get you inside. What an adventure you have to tell us about!"

"No," said a voice from behind them.

They all turned to see Josiah Willacott standing there, having sent the carriage on its way. He had his hands on his hips, and his face was weary and grim.

"We will never speak of this disgrace again," said Katy's father. "It will be as if it never happened."

"Josiah – my dear—" Mary Willacott began, but her husband held up a forbidding hand and she fell silent.

"We will *never* speak of it," he said again. "Katy, from now on you will not leave this house without my permission. You will go nowhere without one of your family with you. I have allowed you too much freedom in the past, I see that now, and it has led nowhere good."

"But Father," Katy protested, horrified. "That's not fair!"

"Not fair?" he repeated, his eyes glinting angrily. "Not fair? Shall I tell you what's not fair? That a child I have raised, cared for and educated did not think twice about scaring us to death! Moreover, that she cares so little for her parents that she thought nothing of destroying the work of

314

both their lives! Do you have any idea just how fragile my position at the museum is now?"

"Yes, but—"

"Yes, but it doesn't matter to you, is that what you were going to say?"

"It does," Katy said, almost in tears now. "It does matter, Papa! But don't you want to know what I did? Where I went? What I saw? What I found? Tomorrow the papers will all say that Sir Thomas Derby found a meteorite in Brazil, but it's a lie, Father. *I* found it. *I* did! And there's more I have to tell you – much more!"

"I. Don't. *Care*," her father said, so bluntly that Katy felt the words like a punch to the stomach.

He strode past them and Katy went to follow, wanting to make him see how he was wrong. But her mother pulled her into another hug and by the time they had gone into Rose Cottage, her father had shut himself in his study.

Chapter Fifty-Four

After Grandma Peg had made breakfast, Katy went up to her room, where everything was the same, but nothing was quite right. Her mother came with her, seeming reluctant to let her daughter out of her sight. They sat together on Katy's bed.

"Don't think badly of your father, Katy," Mary Willacott said softly, squeezing her hand.

"But he thinks badly of me," Katy pointed out.

"Please, Katy," her mother said. "He was so worried about you. That's where his anger is coming from. Try to understand."

"I'm tired," Katy said, not sure she believed her mother and not wanting to talk if the one thing she wanted to tell her about was forbidden.

"All right," said Mary Willacott, with a sigh. "I'll leave

you to rest." Her mother kissed her forehead and left, pulling the bedroom hatch quietly shut to leave Katy alone. Katy sat still for a minute, looking down at herself. Then she laid her head against her pillow without removing William Chandler's outfit. She kept thinking about Shadow. What would happen to him now? She thought about what Derby would have told the journalists too, and how the headlines in the papers would read.

Esteemed British Naturalist Locates Prized Meteorite!

Sir Thomas Derby's Latest Expedition a Resounding Success!

Katy couldn't sleep. She missed the rocking of the *Alerte*. Still, she must have fallen into a doze when, some time that afternoon, she heard a knock at the front door that pulled her fully awake. Katy could hear voices talking but not what they were saying. The door closed and she heard the heavy tread of footsteps as someone was led into the parlour. Then her mother called her from beneath the attic hatch.

"Katy, you have visitors. Come down, please."

Katy sat up. "Is it Edie?"

"No. It's Captain Roberts and Doctor Whitaker."

Katy shot out of bed. Had they somehow brought Shadow to her? What about her pack, with Anahí Monroe's precious journal? She hurried down the stepladder and followed her mother to find the strange sight of Captain Roberts squeezed into one of Rose Cottage's 'good' armchairs. He looked like a grizzly bear at a dolls' picnic. Doctor Whitaker sat opposite, but both men stood as she came in.

"Captain! Doctor!"

"Katy," the doctor said with a smile.

"Miss Willacott." The captain nodded.

"But – what are you doing here?" Katy looked around but could see no sign of Shadow.

Mary Willacott appeared with a tea tray and set it on the table. Then Josiah Willacott stepped into the room. Everyone sat down as Katy's mother poured the tea.

"You left in such a hurry," explained the doctor. "The captain and I didn't feel it right to let you go without saying a proper goodbye. Besides, I thought you would want this."

He bent down into the shadows beside his chair and when he straightened Katy saw that the doctor had something in his hand. She realized it was the carrying basket that Celia had given her to hold the little plant Katy had so carefully carried with her on the *Alerte*'s return journey. He smiled as he held it out to her. "I've kept it watered. It seems to be thriving. It's still small but growing well."

"Oh," Katy breathed. "Thank you, Doctor. Thank you so much!"

"I needed to return this too," added the captain, taking out her pack. "Nothing inside has been touched."

"Thank you," Katy said, truly grateful to them both. "You can't know how much that means to me."

"I believe you have suffered a great injustice, Katy," said the doctor. "It is our hope that your papers will help to set that straight. They do, after all, tell the complete story of your extraordinary journey and what you found during the course of it."

"May I?" asked Josiah Willacott, holding out his hand for her pack. Katy hesitated, but her father's face was set. He didn't look at the bag when she passed it to him, just laid it on the floor beside his feet.

"You have a remarkable daughter, Mr and Mrs Willacott," said Doctor Whitaker. "I want you to know that I will support any stand you make together against Sir Thomas Derby."

"As will I," added Captain Roberts. "Katy Willacott is one of the finest sailors I have ever had the good fortune to travel the seas with. I would take her with me again as crew any time."

Katy stared at the captain, astonished. "Thank you, Captain Roberts," she said.

"We are grateful to you both, gentlemen," said Josiah Willacott, in a quiet, calm voice. "But please understand – for this family, the matter is done with. Whatever you think of my daughter, she is still a child. None of this is appropriate."

"But," said Doctor Whitaker, puzzled. "Do you not feel that she should get the recognition she deserves? She has achieved something great, you know."

Katy looked at her father, who was frowning slightly as he met her eye. "Katy," he said. "Leave us. Go back to your room or help your grandmother."

"But Papa—"

"Now, please," he said.

Katy looked at Captain Roberts and Doctor Whitaker. "What about Shadow?" she asked.

Captain Roberts glanced at Doctor Whitaker. "You don't need to worry about Shadow."

"He can't go to a zoo," Katy said. "He'll die if you put him in a cage!"

"He's not going to a zoo," the captain assured her. "I promise you that. Plenty of ships have a ratter aboard. The *Alerte's* is just … well, a little bigger and more fearsome than most, that's all."

Katy stared at him, open-mouthed. "You're going to keep him?"

Roberts shrugged a little. "It's a funny thing, but the crew have taken a shine to him. Besides, with a cat that size and with those teeth and claws aboard, I've a hunch the *Alerte* will never be robbed while she's in port." His eyes twinkled a little. "Don't you worry about your Shadow, Katy Willacott. We'll take care of him."

Katy felt herself sag a little as a horrible weight was lifted from her shoulders. She trusted Captain Roberts and the crew of the *Alerte* with her whole heart. At least, out of all the things that had gone wrong with her return home, she could be sure that Shadow would be safe.

"Thank you," she whispered.

"Go, Katy," said her father. "Now, if you please…"

Katy pointed to the parcel still at her father's feet. "Can I have my pack?"

"Katy," he said, his voice tight and clipped. "Just go."

Katy took a last look at both Doctor Whitaker and Captain Roberts before she did as she was told. She thought it was unlikely she would ever see either of them again.

Chapter Fifty-Five

Katy ate dinner in the kitchen at Rose Cottage that night, but it wasn't as she remembered. There was no chat about her mother's day in the herbarium, or what Ned had seen during his patrols of Kew. Stefan did not tell her what he'd been learning at school. Josiah Willacott did not even appear – he had gone back to his study once their visitors had left and had remained there with the door shut ever since.

That night, Katy climbed out on to the roof. It was chilly and the sky was clear, a silver moon casting a pale glow over the gardens of Kew. Over her head hung the glinting pinpricks of stars. She lay on the uneven tiles, stared up at the universe and wondered what her life would become now. Katy had chased a falling star and found it, and she had travelled half the world to do so. Would she ever do anything as wonderful again?

The sound of the skylight opening announced her mother's arrival. Katy turned to see her smiling through the open window.

"Oh," said Mary Willacott quietly. "How I have missed finding you up here. Do you know, there were nights while you were away that I would come up here and lie there just as you are now, looking up into the stars and thinking about what you might be doing. It was how I felt close to you."

Katy felt a fresh pang of guilt. "I'm sorry, Mama," she said. "I'm sorry that I worried you all so much."

Mary Willacott climbed out on to the roof, pulling a wool blanket with her. They settled side by side beneath it, and Katy snuggled in close. It had been so long since they had done this. Katy had missed it without even realizing.

"Will you tell me, Katy? Will you tell me everything?"

"But I thought Papa didn't want me to talk about it? Not to you – not to anyone."

Mary Willacott sighed and paused a little as she considered what to say. "I love your father in all things," she began eventually. "But in this, he is wrong. I understand why he feels the way he does. It looks like anger, but that isn't it at all. He is afraid. He is afraid of losing what he has, and he's afraid of you too, my darling."

Katy frowned at this. "Papa? Afraid of me? That can't be true."

Her mother kissed her lightly on the forehead. "He's

afraid of what you will become, Katy – and of where your achievements might take you. Away from here. Away from *us*. I understand that perfectly. I am afraid too – of what could happen to you, and of what people will say about you. But I don't think that's enough of a reason to stop you being yourself. We can't pretend that you didn't do this remarkable thing, or that you won't do more remarkable things in the future, however afraid – for you and for us – they make us. Please, Katy. Tell me everything about your adventure."

Katy thought for a moment about how to start and then she did. It took a long time to tell her mother everything, and the night grew later and colder. But Mary Willacott listened intently, only making a tiny sound when Katy recounted the events of the storm in which the *Alerte* had almost lost her mast and then later, when the hunters had pursued them through the jungle.

When Katy finally finished speaking, the two of them lay there together, looking up at the same stars, and Mary Willacott was quiet for a while longer.

"I am proud of you, Katy," her mother said at last. "Even if I'm not entirely pleased about the way you set out on your adventure. I looked at the catalogue pages of the plant specimens you collected and they are excellent. As for Anahí Monroe's book – well, it is truly extraordinary. I think I will be working through everything she found for many months to come. It is a treasure trove."

"There were some plants in there that I didn't recognize," Katy said. "And neither did Doctor Whitaker."

Her mother smiled. "I think there's a good reason for that. I need to do a lot more research, but I think many of the specimens she collected have never been catalogued before."

"Really?"

"Really," Mary Willacott said. "I think it quite possible that Anahí Monroe is single-handedly responsible for producing the definitive work on the flora and fauna of her region." Then she added, "That little flower you brought back, though... I can't find it in her notebook. I don't think it was something she ever collected."

"I couldn't find it, either," Katy said. "That was one reason I wanted to bring it back as a whole plant. Did you notice that on the voyage it has begun to produce seed pods?"

"I did," said her mother. "I think we should try to propagate some so that we can observe its whole life cycle." She squeezed Katy gently. "I need to do a lot more research, but I think it might be a previously unknown species. And I know that isn't quite what you wanted to bring back with you, but it might mean that you end up with a plant named after you. How about that?"

"No," Katy said. "It should be named after both of us. You'll be the one doing the real work – researching and cataloguing. It's only fair. I didn't even know what I was collecting."

Mary Willacott was quiet for another minute and then hugged her again. "I'll tell you what," she said. "Why don't we work on it together? I know the herbarium isn't really where you want to be, but I could really do with the help, especially when it comes to Anahí's notebook, and—"

"I'd like that," Katy said, realizing that it was the truth. "But … what about *my* notebook?"

Mary Willacott gave a heavy sigh. "I'm sorry, Katy. I don't know what your father has done with it."

They stayed there in silence for a while, watching the night sky above them.

Chapter Fifty-Six

Five months later

Kew Gardens was beginning to reawaken after winter, spring finally pushing the first green shoots up through the chilled earth. The early morning March air was cold, and Katy stamped her feet as she went up the path to the back door of Rose Cottage, carrying the basket full of eggs she had just gathered from Peg's hens.

"They've been busy," Katy said as they went into the kitchen. "I think we'd better do some baking and—"

She stopped talking mid-sentence. The usually noisy kitchen had fallen silent as soon as Katy had entered. Every member of her family was studiously looking away. All except her father, who was looking straight at her.

Things had been difficult between Katy and her father

ever since her return. She wasn't sure she would ever be able to forgive him for confiscating her field journal. She'd never seen it again and could only assume that he had burned it or otherwise disposed of it in some way so it could never cause any trouble.

After that, they hadn't talked much. Katy really had nothing to say. She had dedicated herself to her work with her mother instead. Actually, after her adventures, Katy had begun to see botany in a new light. She was enjoying working with Mary Willacott far more now, especially since they were close to announcing that Katy had, in fact, returned with an example of a species that had not previously been recorded by Western scientists. Together, Katy and her mother had identified that the little red flower she had carried all the way back from Brazil was a miniature passion flower.

It would be called *Passiflora nana scandus coccinea*, 'Willacott's Jewel', and its discovery would be attributed to both Katy and her mother Mary, who had first realized that it could be an unknown species.

It meant that Mary Willacott would finally have a plant named after her.

This was something that Derby could not steal and her father could not forbid, any more than either could take away the many happy hours that Katy had spent with her mother since her return.

Together, they had also been comparing Anahí Monroe's work to the examples already in the herbarium's archives and had found that Theo and Celia's mother had collected and catalogued a vast number of new species. Between them, they had agreed that Mrs Monroe's journal was simply too spectacular an artefact in its own right to break apart and that it (and its author) should be known properly. They were working on a book that reproduced the journal – it would be called *The Flora of Bahia Province, Brazil: A Botanist's Diary by Mrs Anahi Monroe*. Mary Willacott would write the foreword, one respected botanist introducing another. Katy herself would write a short afterword. Both Mary and Katy were determined that in some way or other, the proceeds from sales of the book would reach Theo and Celia.

Katy hoped to be able to let her friends back in Brazil know about this somehow. In fact, she longed to hear what had been happening in the rainforest over the past few months. She wanted to know whether their brother had returned, whether the hunters had gone now that Derby had returned to England, whether Fran had found out any more about the rubber plantation and whether Katy's own suspicions about Derby's involvement were in fact true. But the only way she could think to do that was to write to Fran, and that was one of the things her father would not allow her to do.

"What is it?" Katy asked into the silence of the kitchen, looking at her mother. "Mama? What's going on?"

"Katy," said her father. "There's something you should see."

Her father held out a newspaper. Katy looked at him for a moment, then took it and looked at the headline on the front page.

Sir Thomas Derby to Present Famous Meteorite, it said, and then in only slightly smaller writing, *Early Patrons of the Natural History Museum to See History Being Unveiled.*

Katy stared at the page for a moment. She had known there were articles about Derby's expedition and the meteorite, because none of her family would let her see a newspaper for days after her return. Perhaps they had been afraid of what she would do if she saw Derby crowing over 'his' success. It was true also that as Katy scanned the words and read lines like *intrepid trek into dense jungle* and *considerable personal peril* she felt a spark of indignation, knowing that Derby was getting the credit for things he had not done. But Katy had let go of the fierce rage that had first consumed her following her return. Derby was a fraud. He knew it. The other members of his expedition knew it. Let him live with that, even if the rest of the world still thought him a hero.

It wasn't enough. But it was all Katy had.

She handed back the newspaper. "Well," she said, turning away. "I knew it would happen."

Josiah Willacott cleared his throat. "I've been invited to the unveiling. I would like you to accompany me."

Katy froze for a moment, her back still turned. "What?"

"It is important that we put this behind us, you and I."

She turned back to him slowly. "I have put it behind me," Katy said. "I have not mentioned it for months. I am working alongside Mama, just as you wanted. I didn't answer Fran Brocklehurst's letter when she wrote to tell me she was back home. I have done everything you ordered, Father." At this, her father flinched a little. "I am not sure what else I can do."

Josiah Willacott looked at her with sad, serious eyes. "You can come with me to the gala, Katy. You can show Derby that this matter is closed. It's what he wants. I have had a letter to tell me as much."

"Do I have a choice?" Katy asked.

"I'd like you to choose to come," he said.

"That's a no, then?"

Josiah Willacott sighed and Katy saw that it was hopeless.

"All right," she said. "Since I can't say no, I will have to say yes, won't I?"

Chapter Fifty-Seven

The new Natural History Museum building was huge, made of yellow sandstone that shone in the spring sunshine of a Friday evening. There would be no public visitors here tonight. It wasn't ready for a full opening. This evening was strictly for those connected to the museum in some way, as well as journalists and dignitaries, in the hope that the institution could gather more patrons to finance it prior to opening in a year's time. The road outside the grand main entrance was clogged with carriages that stopped to let out fine people in fine clothes, with fine hats perched upon their heads. To Katy it felt almost as if she were back on the busy Southampton docks, watching the ships and their masts vie for space on the waterways.

Katy had been excited about the Natural History Museum since she was little, ever since her father had told her it was being built. Now she was going to get to see inside it, to explore rooms full of fantastic collections brought back from places so far flung that she might not have even heard of them before. Katy was trying hard to be happy that she was getting to see inside it now, despite knowing what else would be there. All those animals that Derby and Mazarin had paid men to kill, animals that had meant life to the people of her friends' village and others like them. It made Katy see the museum and others like it in a different light. The British Museum, for example – all those artefacts she had spent hours poring over on visits with her family. Who did they all belong to, really? *Where* did they really belong? To people just like Theo and Celia and Grandfather; to monuments like the Old Place, which had been taken apart by visitors who did not know – or did not care – that they should stay where they had been found, out of respect for the people who had built them. Surely, she thought now, there was a better way of learning about the history of the world than stealing it?

The great entrance hall was so crowded with people that, as cavernous as it was, it was hard to move around.

"What do you want to see first?" her father asked as they stood at the bottom of a grand flight of stairs.

"The meteorite," Katy said immediately. "I want to see the meteorite."

They found the rock on a waist-high marble plinth surrounded by golden posts linked together with red silk rope so that no one could get too close. They couldn't actually see the meteorite – it and half the plinth had been draped with a heavy red silk cloth.

"Derby wants to be able to unveil it to the world," Josiah Willacott muttered. "How very like him." Then he sighed. "Well, the presentation isn't for a while. Let's tour some of the other exhibits, shall we? Not every gallery is open, but some are. Where shall we start?"

"I don't mind," Katy said, still staring at the hidden meteorite, her heart heavy. "I'm sure it will all be amazing."

Katy's assessment was right. There was so much to see, so many different rooms full of an extraordinary array of artefacts. Katy lingered over each case of collected specimens, from beautiful gems in various hues to the slices of an immense redwood tree, its trunk as big as the kitchen at Rose Cottage. She wondered how long it had taken to cut down and where the rest of it was. She realized that she would never enter a museum again without thinking about where each item had come from.

She looked up from the tree and stopped dead. From across the room stared a beautiful feline face, golden with a scattered pattern of black markings. The jaguar that she had first seen in a crate in the *Alerte*'s hold. Katy's heart clenched – it made her think of Shadow.

"Katy!" called her father, waving at her from the doorway of the room. "It's almost time."

Back at the meteorite, a crowd had gathered around

the plinth. At the centre of it stood Sir Thomas Derby, his cheeks red with pride. He was flanked by two people – on one side stood the museum's director, and on the other Lucas Mazarin, who scanned the crowd with cold, sharp eyes. A hush descended as the museum director clapped his hands together, calling for quiet.

"Ladies and gentlemen," he called as the hubbub subsided and the crowd stilled. "It is my great pleasure to introduce – although of course, he really needs no introduction – Sir Thomas Derby, the British Museum's most accomplished naturalist. He has been instrumental in assembling a large proportion of the specimens for this museum. Besides that, you will have seen in the papers that Sir Thomas returned triumphant from his mission to locate one of the meteorites that fell over the Brazilian rainforest. Now we will turn to him for his own words on this remarkable feat – and his remarkable find."

Loud applause followed this introduction. Katy stood on tiptoe and managed to glimpse Derby through the throng, holding up his hands to quiet the audience as he began to speak.

"Friends," he said indulgently. "It is so good of you to come to this illustrious building and witness the unveiling of some of our most precious scientific finds. That I have the honour of presenting a piece I myself brought to these hallowed walls – well, such a moment fills me with humble pride."

Katy couldn't help but roll her eyes as another enthusiastic storm of clapping overtook the crowd.

"For sure," Sir Thomas said loudly as the sound died away once again, "the path to such scientific acquisitions was long and fraught, as such things always are, with great difficulty. But perseverance and hard work, my friends, have always been among the very best qualities that our great race has to offer the world."

Katy had to stifle a bitter laugh at that. As if Derby knew what hard work and perseverance were!

"And so," the man said, oblivious to Katy and her thoughts. "Without further ado, I present to you the crowning glory of this great new institution."

Derby reached forwards and whipped away the red cover, revealing the meteorite. The clapping began again, echoing like thunder around the high, vaulted ceiling. Katy stood on tiptoe but couldn't see. She heard the ripple of amazement and appreciation from the crowd, though, and also Derby's voice.

"I will allow a few minutes for everyone to observe this magnificent artefact," he said. "And then I will deliver a short lecture about this rock and the endeavour that went into retrieving it."

Katy felt a hand on her back. It was her father, guiding her through the throng. They reached the red rope and stood looking at the rock that Katy had travelled an ocean to find.

The meteorite had been set on a spike. On the plinth beneath it was a plaque, describing how it was found and who found it. The name inscribed there was not, of course, Katy Willacott.

Seeing the meteorite again like this made Katy feel strange. Had she really gone all that way, had she really been the one to find this remarkable artefact? She knew she had, and yet it also felt unreal. There it was, engraved into brass, right in front of her – *Meteorite recovered by Sir Thomas Derby.* Looking at it now, in this grand building surrounded by grand people, none of whom would even spare her a glance, Katy found even herself doubting the truth.

"But where did you find it?" said a high, nasal voice, from the other side of the plinth. It was a tall, pale woman dressed in a stiff emerald-green dress that reminded Katy of the way the light filtered through the leaves of the rainforest canopy. "I would like to know the specific circumstances. Surely, to locate it amid so dense a rainforest must have been a huge undertaking."

Derby gave an oily smile. "Indeed it was, my dear lady, and as I said, I will shortly be delivering a lecture—"

"It won't answer your question," someone shouted from the back of the crowd. "Not truthfully, at any rate. For the simple reason that he doesn't know the answer. Do you, Sir Thomas?"

Katy's heart stopped beating. She knew that voice.

An astonished rumble passed through the throng, which parted to reveal Francesca Brocklehurst, her hands on her hips and a forbidding look on her face. By her side were Theo and Celia Monroe, and behind them stood a young man Katy did not know. He stood straight and tall, wearing garments made of many layers of dried rushes. On his head and fastened around his upper arms were bands of feathers. His skin reminded Katy of Grandfather's, and his face was just as proud, stern and determined. He had one hand on Theo's shoulder. Her friend was smiling and Katy knew at once who this must be.

It was Ubiratā, Theo and Celia's older brother.

He had returned, just as Theo had always insisted he would. And now he was here, in London.

Chapter Fifty-Eight

"You!" Derby shouted at the newcomers, outraged. "Get out! You have no place here!"

"Actually," Fran said, walking through the parted crowd. "I'm covering the event for my newspaper. They sent me because I was there in Brazil, not long after the meteorite was found. Which was not by Sir Thomas Derby at all."

A shocked noise ricocheted around the hall.

"Is this true?" asked the museum director.

"Of course it's not true," Derby spat. "This girl is nothing but a liar, a pedlar of ridiculous stories! Call the guards!"

"Oh, it's true," said Fran stoutly, over the rising noise of the crowd. "The meteorite was found, not by this man, but by a young woman called Katy Willacott. You can ask her about it, actually, because she's right ... *there*."

Fran pointed straight at Katy.

Derby, who had evidently not noticed either Katy or her father until that moment, bellowed at Josiah Willacott.

"What did I tell you?" he shouted. "What is *she* doing here? I warned you to keep her away, Willacott! I *warned* you!"

Katy looked up at her father, confused. "But … I thought you said—"

Josiah Willacott placed one hand on his daughter's shoulder and smiled. With his other hand he reached into his jacket pocket and pulled out an old, travel-worn journal. Katy's jaw dropped open as she realized what it was.

It was her field notebook. The one her father had confiscated. The one she thought he had destroyed.

"What Miss Brocklehurst says is absolutely true," said Josiah Willacott loudly. "All the details of my daughter's trip and how she located the meteorite are recorded here, along with some particularly damning information about Sir Thomas's conduct on that trip. Which is what Miss Brocklehurst and her companions are here to set right."

"Lies!" Derby bellowed, his face scarlet with rage. "All lies!"

The crowd erupted into raucous conversation. Katy and her father fought their way through the mass of people to reach Fran, Theo and Celia. Katy pulled her friends into a fierce hug, overjoyed to see them. She looked at the tall young man standing with them and offered a smile, which he returned.

"What are you doing here?" Katy shouted to them, over the noise. "Is this your brother? Is this Ubiratā?"

"Yes!" Celia said, happily. "He's alive! He came home!"

Ubiratā stepped forward and held out a hand.

"I'm so happy to meet you," she told him as they shook. "But I don't understand—"

"You're going to get your meteorite back," Fran told her. "And Sir Thomas Derby is about to get his comeuppance for all manner of far worse transgressions."

"We're all here as witnesses," Theo added over the hubbub. "Ubiratā and Fran know *everything*!"

"Ladies, gentlemen," the museum director begged, trying to make himself heard over the storm of shouted questions. "Please, some decorum—"

"This is nonsense!" Derby was shouting. "Look at them! Who would believe such rubbish spouted by women and … and … *natives*?"

Lucas Mazarin suddenly appeared at Josiah Willacott's side. He tried to grab at the notebook, but Katy's father pushed him away.

"You have no proof of anything!" Mazarin yelled.

"Please, please," yelled the museum director. "Let us be *calm*!"

The noise hushed a little and Derby took the opportunity to speak into it.

"As I was saying, this is all completely—" He stopped as someone appeared at Katy's side.

"I can corroborate that Sir Thomas had nothing to do with finding the meteorite," said Doctor John Whitaker. "I was there with him in Brazil. He didn't even attempt to find what he said he was going to locate."

"And I," said another, booming voice, "can tell of the exact circumstances when Sir Thomas Derby's secretary took the meteorite from Miss Katy Willacott for his employer. I can do this because I was there too. As were others."

It was Captain Roberts. Derby's face turned scarlet and then went as pale as milk.

"It's Katy who should answer your questions, on this matter at least," Fran said loudly, before the crowd could erupt again. "You, Lady Dunwoody," she called, to the woman in emerald green. "You wanted to know where in the rainforest the meteorite was found. Try asking Katy Willacott."

The woman pushed forwards, her nose still in the air as she glared at Katy. "Well. I must say this is most irregular. But *can* you answer me, girl?"

Katy looked at Theo and Celia, then at Ubiratã and finally at Fran.

"I can," she said. "It's true, I was the one who found the meteorite, with the help of my friends here. It's all detailed in my journal and I can answer any questions you want me to. But…" She broke off as the rumble of the crowd rose again and had to raise her voice to continue. "*BUT…* I think there's another more important story to tell first.

About why Sir Thomas Derby really wanted to go to Brazil. And that's not for me to tell."

Fran raised her eyebrows as the crowd murmured again. Then she smiled.

"Ah," she said. "I believe that Katy is talking about the rubber refinery that you've built outside the city of Salvador, Sir Thomas. Shall we tell these ladies and gentlemen all about *that*?"

Derby looked as if he'd been slapped. He opened and shut his mouth several times but no sound was forthcoming. His eyes bulged.

"No?" Fran asked. "Very well. Now this is a long story, and I can only tell part of it. But here is how it begins." The journalist turned in a slow circle as she addressed the crowd. "The fortunes of the Derby family were waning right up until they found a way to refine rubber at the source. It makes the process quicker, the rubber better quality – as long as one doesn't care about the horrible consequences it has for the environment, which Sir Thomas doesn't. It will no doubt revolutionize the industry. Derby knew that if he could perfect the process and begin to ship his rubber quickly enough, his new product would trounce his competitors. His family's fortunes would be restored. He would have to keep this new method under wraps, of course. If others knew about it they could copy the process and get the jump on his business before he had a chance to establish it. That was why he moved his base of operations to somewhere entirely new – to the other side of Brazil, to Salvador, Bahia province, far away from his family's previous plantation, and he swore his new plantation managers to absolute secrecy."

Derby finally pulled himself out of his shock, squaring his shoulders, his face like thunder. "This is preposterous!" he snarled at Fran. "I will destroy you, you stupid girl. Giving away my trade secrets to all and sundry like this!"

"If I were you, Sir Thomas," Fran said smoothly. "Trade secrets would be the last thing I was worried about right now. Because this is where someone else needs to take up the tale." She held out a hand to Theo and Celia's brother. "Ubiratã, Theo and Celia are here to explain what this meant for the people whose lands Sir Thomas decided he wanted to take. Theo will translate for us."

Theo and Ubiratã spoke quietly between themselves for a moment, and then Theo's brother began to speak in Tupí, pausing frequently so that Theo could translate for everyone assembled. Ubiratã spoke of the destruction of the rainforest, of how men had come to clear the land and then, finding the work too hard for them, had made people of the local tribes do the work for them, in terrible conditions. He described how the refinery poisoned the air, the water, the earth, how the men hunted too many animals with their guns, how they burned and cut the trees without caring what a scar it left on the land. Ubiratã explained how this violated their way of life, how there was no respect shown for any of the animals or people who lived there.

"Nonsense!" Sir Thomas shouted. "Poppycock! I *own* that land! I have the deeds to prove it! It's mine, to do with as I please, as any honest businessman might!"

"Honest?" Fran asked, turning on him. "If you think any of what we've just heard makes you honest, I will surely despair, Sir Thomas. But even by your own rules, how can it be honest? You launched an expedition under false pretences in order to cover up the real reason you were going to Brazil, didn't you? You never cared about bringing back a meteorite for the museum. Even the animals you hunted while you were there were just a side venture. All you wanted was to find a way to visit and check on your new secret plantation without anyone knowing what you were doing. You used the good name of the museum and the good money of men like Doctor Whitaker here to do that – *didn't you?*"

Derby snorted. "I returned with more than enough scientific material to justify the trip. Don't you have eyes?"

"I see a meteorite that your lackey had to steal to get," Fran said coldly. "I see animals shot by their hundreds by men you paid to also hunt for slaves."

"Lies!" Mazarin finally shouted. "Foul, foul lies!"

"It's true," Theo shouted back, his fists clenched at his sides. "His refinery pollutes the rainforest and kills the trees. His hunters kill or take everything else!"

"Our village is empty because of *you!*" Celia cried. "And

it's not the only one!"

"These people from the affected region," Fran added in the last calm before the breaking of an almighty storm, "have come to England for the express purpose of giving legal testimony to support the irrefutable evidence we have gathered about what is happening under the orders of Sir Thomas Derby."

The room erupted. Everyone was shouting. The place was in chaos.

"Police!" the museum director called, over the ruckus. "Someone fetch the constables!"

Chapter Fifty-Nine

It took hours before the pandemonium abated and the museum emptied. Derby and Mazarin were both taken away by policemen that the museum director had called. Sir Thomas was still protesting his innocence as he went. He really seemed to believe he had done nothing wrong.

"He won't get away with it, will he?" Katy asked doubtfully as she stood with her father and friends in the empty atrium of the museum. "He seems so sure of himself."

Fran patted her arm. "I will do everything in my power to make sure he doesn't," she said. "Tomorrow morning every newspaper from here to New York City is going to be full of what happened here this evening. Ubiratã spent months hiding in the jungle, writing down everything he saw Derby's men do, and that's just the tip of the iceberg.

Your journal will help, Katy. You kept such good notes of everything you heard and saw. Derby will have the full weight of the law coming for him – I'm certain he'll end up in jail."

Katy looked at the notebook her father had handed back to her, and then up at Josiah.

"I never thought I'd see this again," she told him. "I thought you had destroyed it,"

"I'm sorry," he said. "I truly am, Katy. I was wrong to say you couldn't talk about your experiences. I was wrong to be more worried about my own position."

Katy shook her head. "But what about what Derby said? What about your work?"

Doctor Whitaker spoke up at that. "If the British Museum were to punish your father for Derby's transgressions now, you can be sure there'd be hell to pay."

"Besides, none of that is important," said Josiah Willacott. "What's really important is what you did, Katy. What you experienced. What you learned. No one should take that away from you, especially not me. I realized that as soon as I read your journal – which I did at your mother's insistence. I'm ashamed to say that at first I refused. But she persisted, and when I did finally delve in, it was clear to me immediately that I had made a mistake. I have spent the past few months finding a way to set that right, with Fran's help and the amazing friends you made on your journey.

I should never have reacted the way I did. Your voyage was extraordinary. As are you. I am just sorry," he added, looking regretfully at the meteorite, still on its plinth and still with Sir Thomas's name emblazoned beneath it, "that you did not get to tell everyone here tonight your story of how you found the meteorite."

Katy looked past him and then went to stand in front of the rock that had set her adventure in motion. She looked at Sir Thomas Derby's name and frowned to herself. Did it matter that the name written there wasn't the right one? That the story that went with it was incorrect? Perhaps, after all, it *did* matter. Not because Katy wanted glory in the same way as Derby had wanted it. But because the truth of where a thing came from, and how it got to be where it was, mattered.

"Well," said Captain Roberts eventually. "I think it's time I made way. Come and visit the *Alerte* before we set sail again, Miss Willacott. I am sure that Shadow still misses you."

"Where are you going this time?" Katy asked.

"They're going to take us home," Theo said. "Ubiratã wanted to come here to make sure Derby was arrested, but we don't want to stay. We want to go home as soon as we can."

"Grandfather will be missing us," Celia added. "Fran's going to come back with us. Aren't you, Fran?"

Fran smiled at Celia, and then at Katy. "I am."

"Please come and visit Kew first," Katy said to all of them. "I must give you your mother's journal back, and show you the book that we are making out of it! Mama will want to meet you too, and Peg and Ned and Stefan. Please say you will. Will you ask your brother if he will come too?"

Theo looked up at Ubiratã and then translated Katy's words. His brother smiled and replied in Tupí.

"He says yes," Theo said, looking pleased. "We will all come tomorrow."

Doctor Whitaker bid them goodbye too, shaking Katy's hand, and then her father's.

"Thank you," Katy said. "For coming. For everything."

"It was the least I could do," said the doctor.

"Mr Willacott, Miss Willacott, Miss Brocklehurst," the museum director interrupted, appearing behind them flustered and exhausted. "It seems there are a few adjustments we must make to the meteorite exhibit before we can open. Proper attribution to the person who found it, for one."

Katy looked at Fran, Theo and Celia, who all beamed back at her with extra large smiles.

Chapter Sixty

"What's that one, there?" Fran pointed to one of the constellations glinting brightly overhead.

"That's Ursa Major," Katy said.

"And that one?"

"Ursa Minor."

Katy heard Fran sigh a little, shifting on the tiles of Rose Cottage's roof. "There's such a lot to remember."

"You'll get them eventually," Edie told her, from the other side of Katy. "I've been practising ever since Katy embarked on her voyage. It took me *ages*. I know them all now, though."

Katy smiled at her friend. Edie had been convinced that Katy would never want to talk to her again after she had broken her promise not to let on where Katy had gone. Katy, though, had realized Fran had been right when she'd said Edie had done the right thing, really. After all, if Fran hadn't found her in Brazil, Katy would have been in real danger of missing the *Alerte's* voyage back to England. Derby might never have been exposed for what he really was.

"Are you girls not cold?" asked Mary Willacott, who was lying on the other side of Fran. "Perhaps I should go down and make some hot chocolate for us all."

"What's hot chocolate?" Celia asked, from where she lay next to Mrs Willacott.

"Something else we got from your part of the world, if I'm not mistaken," said Josiah Willacott. "Although we mix the melted chocolate into milk."

"It sounds delicious," said Theo, who was not lying on the roof, but sitting on the sill of the skylight, next to Stefan. The pair had quickly become very great friends indeed.

"I don't need anything," Katy said, not taking her eyes from the sky, which was clearer than it had been for days.

"Me neither," said Fran. "Although I suppose I should make the most of such luxuries. I'm not sure there'll be any hot chocolate aboard the *Alerte* when we weigh anchor."

"Danny always used to have some," Katy said. "He kept it for the crew. He didn't tell Derby about it."

"Good man," Fran said. "And if that's the case, I don't need any now, either."

"I want some," piped up Stefan.

"Then why don't you go downstairs and make some for

all of us?" suggested his father. "And ask Ubiratã if he wants any while you're at it – he's still in my study, looking at some more of my books." The two of them had been in there all afternoon already, with Theo acting as interpreter. Katy had been pleased to see how much they'd all had to talk about.

"It's so amazing that you're going back to Brazil," Katy said to Fran as Stefan huffed.

"Well," said Fran. "Ubiratã's determined to make sure the world knows what's happening to the rainforest and the animals and the people who live in it. I feel that my skills will be useful there."

"Do you think it'll help?"

"It has to," Theo says. "Or in the future we'll have nowhere to live and there might not be a rainforest at all."

"The rainforest is home," Celia agreed. "It can't disappear, it can't."

"It's such a terrible thing to contemplate," said Mary Willacott. "I keep imagining how many plants may have already been destroyed by such recklessness. It's why we are so very lucky to have your mother's collection of specimens. I am so happy that Lady Dunwoody has decided to pay for the full-colour publication of Anahí's book. It will help so many more people to see how much we have to learn from local knowledge and expertise such as hers. I admit, I do envy all of you that have actually seen what she wrote about. I do wish I could go there myself."

"Well…" said Josiah Willacott, with a deep breath, "Why don't we? Go to Brazil, I mean."

There was a moment of shocked silence as everyone looked at Katy's father.

"There's no need to look so astonished," he laughed. "It's Ubiratā's idea. He wants people here to understand the rainforest and its history, not from our perspective, but from the perspective of the people who know it best. He's suggested that we go back with them and use our skills to do just that while we learn about the rainforest properly, from his people. And I think… I think that's a wonderful idea. Don't you?"

Katy was so stunned she couldn't speak. Go back to Brazil? With Theo and Celia? With her *family*?

"What do you think, Mary?" Josiah prompted his wife.

Mary Willacott blinked. "Well," she said thoughtfully. "I know Kew is looking for a new expedition to sponsor… Perhaps I could put myself forward for that and suggest this venture as the project?"

"Oh!" cried Celia, hugging Mary with both arms. "Oh, *please* do come with us! It would be so wonderful to have you there! I can show you all the places our mother wrote about, Mrs Willacott! We can continue her work together!"

"It sounds exciting," Edie said. "But you'll have to count me out. Celia keeps telling me about all the snakes she's seen." She shuddered. "And I'm still having nightmares about that spider!"

Fran nudged Katy. "Well?" she asked. "What do you think? It'd mean you'd be reunited with Shadow. We'd have to move quickly, mind. The *Alerte*'s due to set sail in a week. Luckily, I know Captain Roberts is looking for a new mate for the journey…"

Above them, a bright pinprick of light shot across the sky.

"Shh," Katy said, following it with her eyes and crossing all her fingers and toes. "I'm making a wish, and I really want it to come true…"

Her father reached across and squeezed her shoulder. "You don't have to wish, Katy," he said. "You've already made it happen."

AUTHOR'S NOTE

When I was young, I used to spend a lot of time planning imaginary trips to Brazil. A jungle seemed like the most exciting place I could possibly visit. I wanted to see exotic plants and animals. I wanted to paddle down the Amazon River in a canoe. I wanted to discover long-lost civilizations that no one else knew about.

The thing is, though, that plenty of people who look like me had already done that, ignoring the fact that Brazil was not theirs (or mine) to explore. The great rainforests of South America were never empty and never needed to be discovered. They had people living in them – and looking after them – long before colonists from Europe arrived and decided there were things in the rainforest that they wanted to take, whether or not the people who lived there wanted to give them up. These colonists behaved as if they owned not only the jungle and the land, but the people in them too. Very dark things happened to the people of South America and other places around the world when Europeans 'discovered' them.

When I came to write the story of Katy Willacott, I realized that I couldn't send her on this adventure without touching on some of this history. I have tried to do so with as much awareness as I can as a white woman writing in the twenty-first century. The language that Theo and Celia's family speak, Tupí, is a real language, but the classical version they would have spoken at this time, once widely used in the area of Brazil where the book is set, is now extinct. Like other languages in countries that were colonized, the colonisers suppressed the local language in favour of their own until it eventually stopped being used. The Tupinambá people are a real tribe that live in this area of Brazil to this day. The clothes that I describe Ubiratã wearing when he arrives at the museum are based on traditional Tupinambá ceremonial dress.

Trying to find period-appropriate given names for the inhabitants of this area was difficult, especially when it came to Theo and Celia's mother, Anahí. Women are often left out of historical records entirely and this is doubly true when it comes to women from indigenous backgrounds. On the rare occasions that they do appear, their names have often been changed to colonial ones. Instead I took names from a website that encourages users to submit names from their own cultures. Both Anahí and Ubiratã have been listed there as Tupi names. Although these may be in modern usage rather than from Old Tupí, I have tried to make sure they are from the correct area of Brazil. In Tupi-Guarani legend 'Anahí' was the name of a tribal woman killed by Spanish conquistadors and turned into a flower, which I thought was fitting for Theo and Celia's botanist mother. 'Ubiratã', meanwhile, means 'strong spear'.

The Old Place is not a real ruin. Instead, it represents the many tribes that were destroyed as a result of colonial expansion, not just in South America, but all over the world. Often entire peoples died of diseases brought to the shores of their country on the colonialists' ships before the conquistadors even reached their cities. Many of their artefacts were taken by Westerners for display in museums, usually without permission. They were then displayed, often without accurate information about the culture from which these items originated. Many museums around the world are now trying to correct these thefts and mistakes in attribution, but in some cases it is simply too late.

The horror of slavery permeated this period of South American history just as it did other parts of the world where white people assumed control through a racist attitude of superiority and violence. The early rubber industry thrived through unforgivable methods of forced labour that saw whole tribes wiped out. I have given both Katy and others – most notably the crowd at the museum – the appalled attitude that we hold for these practices now, though they may not be entirely accurate for the time. They are horrified because they *should* have been horrified – as we should be horrified in remembering. After all, the long-lost civilizations I wanted to discover as a child were lost because of people who look like me.

There is, of course, nothing wrong with wanting to see the world and learn about the wonders created by other cultures. In fact, that's what we should want to do! The absolute best way to do that is to learn directly from the people of these cultures – and it is just as important to understand, as Katy comes to, that wanting a thing does not mean we automatically have the right to take it.

Sharon Gosling, March 2022

ACKNOWLEDGEMENTS

Writing this book has been something of a voyage in its own right and as always with such a book, I have a lot of people to thank for it finally getting to the page.

Firstly, I'd like to give a very large thank you to Suzanne Cubey, the Deputy Herbarium Curator at the Royal Botanic Garden in Edinburgh. Visitors to the herbarium are usually from other herbariums or scientific institutions, but Suzanne very kindly invited me along to talk to her about her work and to look at specimens from their collection, despite the herbarium itself being out of action because of a disastrous roof leak that had compounded the miseries of Covid for the dedicated staff. Suzanne had pulled out various examples of flora from Bahia province, Brazil, which were fascinating to look at. She then completely blindsided me by opening a folder to show me a type specimen – meaning it was the first time that the plant had been recorded by a Western scientist – that had been collected and recorded by Charles Darwin during the voyage of the *Beagle*. That experience will stay with me for a long time! Suzanne's generosity with both her time and expertise were hugely helpful, and the Royal Botanic Garden of Edinburgh is a beautiful place to visit – I thoroughly recommend a trip.

No book would get anywhere without a talented editor, and Katy and I were lucky enough to have more than one working with us on this story. Ella Whiddett and Lauren Ace championed Katy's adventure from very early on and worked with me through the first two drafts. We were then joined by Melissa Gitari, who, despite having to come aboard during the weird limbo of Covid times, expertly shepherded the book through final crucial edits and publication. Thanks to everyone for all your efforts; it's been a pleasure to work with you.

The wonderful cover was designed by Pip Johnson and illustrated by Kristina Kister, and I can't imagine how it could possibly have been better – thank you both so much for your expertise and efforts. Thanks, too, to all the many other people at Little Tiger who had a hand in getting Katy Willacott to the shelves, especially Dannie Price and Summer Lanchester in Marketing, Nicola O'Connell in Rights, Demet Hoffmeyer in Production and George Hanratty in Sales.

Thank you to Manu Shadow Velasco for providing an excellently insightful sensitivity read that helped inform the text in its latter stages.

As always, I couldn't have produced this book at all without my wonderful agent Ella Kahn, who continues to go above and beyond for her clients. I am so lucky to be in your stable, thank you for everything.

Lastly, thank you to my husband, Adam Newell, for pep-talks, patience and generally continuing to be the best partner a person could possibly wish for. Sine qua non.

Sharon Gosling is an award-winning writer who
lives in a small village in the far north of Cumbria. Her first
middle-grade book, *The Diamond Thief*, won the Redbridge
Children's Book Award in 2014. Her young-adult horror title,
Fir, was shortlisted for Lancashire Book of the Year 2017.
The Golden Butterfly was nominated for the 2020 CILIP
Carnegie Medal. *The House of Hidden Wonders* was published in
2020. She has also written audio dramas and books about film
and television, including *The Art and Making of Wonder Woman*
and *The Art and Making of Tomb Raider*.

When she's not writing children's fiction, she writes stories for
adults and chases baby rabbits out of her allotment.

@SharonGosling